Heavy Du

Iain Parke / Ma

bad-press.co.uk

Also by Iain Parke

Heavy Duty Attitude

The Liquidator

To my parents for what they put up with and their support,
P for the same,
and to NM for first inspiring me to write.

The only reason for doing this is to tell people what I've learnt over the years. So keep it simple, don't exaggerate it with the sort of crap that people always write about us.

I want it told straight, just the way I've told you.

People can either take it for what it is and like it, or they won't, in which case they can fuck off.

Damage 2008

PART 1
Monday 25 April 1994

It's like old Nick says right at the start, all clubs that have ever existed are either dictatorships; run by a top guy until someone comes along and knocks them off their perch, or democracies; run on the basis of consensus.

They always have been, and always will be.

Damage 2008

1   THE OFFER

I killed the engine and instinctively let the big machine sink underneath me, the long side stand sliding across the cobbles of the courtyard until it found its stable resting place. Still sitting I pushed my goggles up onto the brow of my lid, pulled off my leather riding gloves and reached under my chin to release the strap of my helmet and pull my faded chequered scarf from across my nose and mouth. Then I swung the handlebars hard to the left, feeling the bike settle again in a sort of aftershock as its centre of gravity shifted, and turned the key in the ignition to lock the steering.

Only then dismounting, I turned to face the club house, squinting against the harsh light of the security lamp above the door which threw the bikes filling the yard into a jumbled network of black shadows.

Gloves stuffed into my lid, I pulled my scarf loose around my neck as I walked across the yard towards the warmer yellow light spilling out from where the steel security door was ajar, semi- silhouetting in a cloud of cigarette smoke Spud the striker[1], who was on yard duty tonight. He stood aside as I walked up and nodded a greeting as I reached him that I didn't bother to return. He was wrapped in a thick fleece jacket under his cut off. He would need it, he would be there all night until the meeting broke up, keeping an eye on the bikes outside and acting as security.

Strikers always had to work their passage, demonstrate their commitment to the club by taking on all the crap jobs that came their way until after a year or sometimes two, they had a chance to be voted up to full patch status, if they ever made it.

As I pushed the door shut again behind me I nodded to Wibble, one of the other current strikers who was relaxed, feet up on the desk

---

[1] *Across all 1%er clubs there are distinct classes of association that can lead ultimately to full membership. Potential recruits go through a period of association with the club (usually known as being a 'hang around' or something similar) before, if they seem suitable, a member may put them forward for consideration. They will then go through a period of trial or apprenticeship which lasts for at least one and sometimes more years before their membership is voted on. The Legion used the description striker for guys at this stage (a term also used in Australia and some US clubs) as the equivalent of a Hells Angels' 'Prospect', or a 'Probationary Outlaw'. NB: All foonotes by Iain Parke.*

inside the door beside the CCTV monitor, and headed on into the warmth and noise of the bar.

The third striker, Fat Mick, was nowhere to be seen. I guess he was out on patrol as part of the security detail.

You never normally saw a striker sitting at all. It was all fetch and carry. Some of the guys just used them like personal slaves. They were deliberately treated like shit but they all knew what was coming, what they'd signed up for in taking a bottom rocker. As a tagalong they'd have seen how it worked.

It was also fun to watch. You could tell the smarter ones, they quickly developed a skill of just melting into the background when a particularly crap job was in prospect, being around and doing what they needed to, to serve their time and prove themselves, while leaving the dumber ones to catch the dumber shit. You could respect that, the nous to work the system. It was all part of the game, although it wasn't just a game. This was deadly serious. It was a test.

We wanted to make sure they had what it took, the total commitment needed to join the club.

So we would run them ragged, work 'em from pillar to post, fetching beer, cleaning the clubhouse, stomping round outside in the cold, night after night on guard duty, doing whatever the shit a member told them to do. It was a time of working like a dog and just sucking it up to show what they'd got, what they were made of. That they had the self-discipline and dedication we were looking for.

Would they pass the test?

To do so the club came in front of family, work, friends, everything. A striker had no friends outside the club any more.

But once they'd got patched, then they'd got that knowledge, that self-assurance that they had made it, that they had won their way through to a place in the elite; that from then on they weren't going to take any shit, any more, from anyone, ever again. Then that was what made it all worthwhile.

So seeing Wibble sitting with his boots up on the desk was a rarity. But then Wibble was nearly there, he'd done almost a year, he'd shown what he could do, what he could put up with, what dedication he could put in to making the grade. It was almost time to vote on him and I guessed Tiny, his sponsor, would be putting him up soon.

3

But he'd also shown he'd got the smarts. After all, he was the one sitting down. I liked that.

I wasn't sorry to see that Spud had drawn the short straw tonight again. He was an arsey little wanker, too cocky for a striker I thought, and that Butcher was his sponsor was the final straw as far as I was concerned. I'd be voting against him when the time came. It wasn't just that I disliked him. It was more than that. When you were deciding on whether a guy could become a full patch you were making a judgement call. You had to be sure that he would be there for you, to get your back whenever and whatever the circumstances. And if you weren't sure you shouldn't be saying yes.

Even though I was a well respected member, that on its own wouldn't be enough to keep him out, I'd have to explain my objections. But one more dissenter, one more black ball and that would be it. Two votes against and he would be out automatically and it would be another six months as a striker before he could reapply.

The club house was out in the wilds, right on top of the Pennines about five miles up into the hills above Enderdale, and as everyone said, it was a fucking good club house. We had bought it out of club subs as a half derelict ruin about five years ago just after the merger, and then we had all worked on it to get it right. Set back in a dip in the ground high up a track across a field from the road and screened by a thick belt of trees, the old farm house offered privacy, with the space in the fields below and above for partying when we hosted other clubs. The club house itself faced onto a cobbled yard that offered secure parking for the bikes, flanked along either side with barns that gave room to take them inside and work on them if needs be, together with the kennel for Wolf the guard dog.

Buying our own club house and the land around it had been a great move.

Whenever we were out in a bar or somewhere there always some tension. Not that we went looking for trouble when we were out. But not that we backed down from it either. If you acted with respect, you got treated with respect. But there would always be some wariness, someone with a potential attitude in the crowd, some dickhead, somebody who fancied themselves, someone who made a comment, someone who provoked and who had to be answered.

4

Because if you acted like an arsehole, you would get treated like an arsehole.

In our own club house, there was none of that. In the club house we could relax, josh, play fight with each other with no one calling the plod. In our out of the way old farmhouse with its bit of land in the hills we knew we could go and get wasted, party, and host other clubs without getting any hassle.

We got on OK with the locals normally. We were about two or three miles from the nearest village so there were only a few isolated farms around about us. We kept ourselves to ourselves and they didn't interfere so there wasn't any issue really. After all, a lot of us were brought up round here, Billy Whizz and I used to play in the woods below the road when we were kids for example, we'd been to school with the other local kids so he and I knew most of the local farmers and sorted out any problems that might crop up. They were used to the fact that on a couple of weekend evenings over the summer we would be hosting a bash and there'd be music and noise but otherwise we didn't cause any problems locally.

It had been a traditional uplands farm, with a small square two storey farmhouse and adjoining byre. Inside on the ground floor of the house there was a bar and a kitchen-cum-canteen while the byre had become a pool room with its visitors' wall decorated with plaques and badges presented by clubs we had hosted. Upstairs the bedrooms offered space for any member who needed to crash, while we had made the first floor of the byre into a meeting room big enough for club business. Which was why tonight we were all going to be here.

Beer in hand, I settled in to chat to some of the guys and wait.

Over the next twenty minutes the occasional roar of bikes pulling up outside in the courtyard announced the arrival of other members as the clubhouse filled up with patches. But tonight there were no tagalongs. This was billed as a serious meeting about club business so tonight it would be insiders only. Other than full patches the only people who would be here would be the three strikers, and they wouldn't be in the meeting, they would stay out of it, handling security.

By half past seven the bar was pretty full and I guessed we would need to get started soon. Billy Whizz said he thought Tiny was through in the pool room, so together we threaded our way across the crush around the bar and, bottles in hand, pushed our way through the adjoining door into the stairwell and then through the second door into the old byre.

Standing just inside the door, we could see that on the far side of the room Tiny, the President, and Butcher, Sergeant at Arms, were deep in conversation; with the one outsider who I had seen would be here tonight.

Most of the bikes outside were in variations on the Imperial colours of purple and gold, but I had seen the one parked up by the door suggesting that its owner had arrived early, its red and black paintwork harsh in the glare of the halogen. I knew the bike and its owner. It belonged to Dazza, President of The Brethren MC's north east charter[2] for the last six or seven years although thanks to Gyppo I'd known him on and off for more like ten or twelve.

'What's Dazza doing here?' Billy asked quietly as we looked across.

'Beats me,' I shrugged. 'Not a clue. Thought you would know if anyone did?'

'Not me mate. Way above my level. In fact the whisper I hear is that he's moving up in the world. About to transfer over to The Freemen.'

The Brethren, otherwise known from their black and red colours as the 'Menaces', were one of the big six international clubs, up there with the Angels, Bandidos, Outlaws, Pagans and Rebels. Each country where there was a Brethren club had a national charter from the mother club in the US and so here their members wore a national bottom rocker saying Great Britain. Within the country they then had a dozen or so regional charters, but most were spread across London, the South, and the West Midlands, with Dazza's charter as a northern outpost.

Over and above these local charters were The Freemen, an independent charter in each country, not tied to any single locality. Each country was broadly left to run its own affairs but generally The Freemen charter's members were the national management of the

---

[2] *The more correct term for what is usually referred to in the press as a 'chapter'.*

6

club, they were The Brethren's elite, a club within the club and very much the top of the tree. They were also generally a self-selecting group, membership by invitation only and rumoured in many countries tending to be those within each national club who were into serious business.

Somebody had obviously said something or noticed that we were there as, looking up, Tiny raised his beer bottle and beckoned me over.

'See ya later,' I nodded to Billy, as I acknowledged the invitation and headed round the table.

'Yeah, watch yourself,' he answered, turning back towards the bar.

'And you know our Road Captain, Damage here,' Tiny said, as I joined them.

'Sure!' said Dazza, smiling and sticking out his huge hand for a surprisingly formal handshake that then opened up into a proffered hug that gave full sight of the leering blood red dyed ʃʃ style *Totenkopf* badge on the left breast of his cut off just underneath his President title, 'Yeah, I know Mr Clean and Organised here.'

I smiled at the familiar jibe. It was a long standing joke between us. As I say, I had history with Dazza, we went way back. We embraced, slapping backs.

He was right though. You have to be organised to be the club's road captain, sorting out the runs and all the hassle. The job also went to me because I had a relatively clean record since the road captain usually ended up dealing with any plod issues on a run.

'Not seen you since our last party back in the summer.'

'Hey I'm good. Busy planning next weekend.' The May Day bank holiday weekend would be our first full club run of the year.

'Good to know, always good to have tight people around you.'

Patches and rockers of course were club property and the back of your cut off had always been strictly regimented as the club's uniform, proclaiming your membership and your charter. But in the early days there was a lot of individualism otherwise. Club officers would have their President or Sergeant at Arms tabs, and members might have some other club specific badges, but guys across all the clubs wore all sorts of other stuff on the front of their cut offs; bike logos, weed, swastikas, whatever they wanted.

7

But as clubs gradually became more disciplined these slowly disappeared so that the front of your cut off became more club focused while the club became ever more all involving and defining.

Flash nowadays was almost always just club business; you would only wear tabs awarded to you by the club. And since tabs were club business, no outsider to a club should ever ask a club member what a particular badge meant. After all, if it was club business, it was club business. But guys within affiliated or friendly clubs were always expected to just know as though by a process of osmosis. The *Totenkopf* tab on the front of Dazza's cut off declared, without saying anything, his membership of the feared Bonesmen.

And then it was time and the bar emptied as the crowd of guys filed dutifully and noisily upstairs to the meeting room, leaving Wibble in the lobby on the cameras and Spud outside in the cold.

As one of the club's officers, by tradition I was always one of the last in. Standing at the bottom of the stairs waiting for him, I heard Tiny say something to Dazza about roll call.

'No problem mate. We in The Brethren of all people respect other clubs' traditions. Just give me a shout when you're ready.'

*

Upstairs a few moments later the guys were packed around the edges of the room. There were about three dozen of us all told. As the biggest of the founding clubs, we ex-Reivers made up the largest contingent with about a dozen of us as the Borders cohort from the valley and the dales. There were ten of Gut's Westmorland cohort from over the border into Cumbria, another eight or so from Popeye's Northumberland cohort from up along the North Sea coast, and finally the half dozen of Butcher's feared Wearside cohort, universally known as the cleaver crew from Sunderland. Some were perched on a selection of battered chairs, some were standing. Billy Whizz was sprawled on the floor rolling a smoke. We could be raided at any time by the plod so the general rule was you could bring anything you wanted to the club, but only if you could swallow it if needed.

Butcher as Sergeant at Arms pulled the doors shut and the hubbub of voices died to a hush as he strode to join me, Gut the VP, and Popeye the secretary-treasurer, in flanking Tiny, standing behind two

8

tables facing the assembled brothers.

Prayers, our weekly club meetings, were compulsory and unless you were down or incapacitated, if you missed more than one in a row, you could be fined. Miss more than two and you had better have a bloody good explanation or you could be looking at your patch. But since the empire covered such a wide area, each of the cohorts had their own weekly prayers. We only got together for High Church at the beginning, middle and end of the riding season, or on special occasions.

This was a special occasion, High Church, a full dress club meeting. Attendance was compulsory for all patches. That meant everyone had to be there, unless you physically couldn't make it like Prof laid up in hospital with a broken leg and Little Matt and Scottie, both on remand charged with GBH after a run in with The Hangmen last week.

Whether weekly prayers or High Church, every meeting started the same way, with the roll call as Tiny as President read the register in alphabetical order and we answered.

'Andy?'

'Here,' came a voice from the back.

'Damage?'

'Here,' I said.

Tiny continued to ask as he worked his way slowly and regularly through the list with replies returned from around the room until at last he got to, 'Gyppo?'

'On the road,' I intoned.

As Road Captain it was my responsibility to answer for each of the fallen brothers whose pictures adorned the far wall of the club room, in the same way that Butcher as Sergeant at Arms answered 'Down but not broken' for the guys that were inside, who were also always with us in spirit.

It was just strange that Gyppo was the first, in both ways.

With the register finished and the roll call taken, we waited in silence as Tiny closed the book on the desk. I and the other officers pulled out our chairs from under the tables and sat down.

Tiny remained standing, and seemed to take a moment to gather his thoughts before leaning forwards, knuckles planted on the table he announced, 'I've got something to say.'

This was it at last. The reason for the urgently called High Church meeting. You could feel the expectation in the air.

'You've all seen that Dazza from The Brethren is downstairs so you'll have guessed why we're here tonight as a club. Dazza called me last week and asked if he could speak to us. So according to our rules I need to ask you for your permission to invite a stranger to address a club meeting.'

*

A few moments later, Butcher escorted Dazza up. In silence, Gut ushered him to a space that had been made for him to stand beside Tiny who nodded in greeting, while Butcher closed and locked the doors from the inside.

Tiny waited for Gut and Butcher to resume their seats before speaking again.

'You all know Dazza here. So I guess I'll just let him say what he has to say.' He turned to Dazza and with a gesture gave him the floor as he pulled out his own chair to sit down.

Dazza nodded to him and looked out across the room, calmly meeting the guys' eyes as they stared at him.

Dazza had a presence. You could never deny that. And it was a very calmly delivered speech, very businesslike, almost a formal diplomatic address delivered to a hushed hall.

'Well firstly I'd like to start by thanking you guys for the opportunity to talk to you here tonight at your club meeting. I know you like to keep club meetings private, so do we in The Brethren, so I appreciate being invited in.'

Very polite. Very correct. We waited.

'We in The Brethren have known you guys now for many years, we know that you are stand up guys that we can respect and we've always had good relations.'

It was like hearing the ambassador from a powerful country address the parliament of a smaller, but fiercely proud, friendly power. He obviously had a message to deliver and would do so courteously but firmly, and despite being alone in this room, he was calm, protected by the knowledge of what an assault on him would mean.

I was still thinking about that *Totenkopf* skull and crossbones on his cut off and what Billy had said. Being a Bonesman didn't automatically entitle him to membership of The Freemen, otherwise he'd have been in what, six or seven years ago? But it was widely understood as being a necessary qualifier.

'Obviously some of us have long standing business relations with some of you, and we don't do that lightly.'

'Some of us' was a bit of a generalisation on his side of the house. I knew full well that Dazza was the main guy in the north-east charter who dealt. Since Gyppo, I wasn't involved in any of that any more but I knew he did deal with many of our guys as a way of moving his product into our club's territory. Billy for one, but Sprog and a number of others who either dabbled for a bit of extra bread, or dealt more seriously, mainly in whizz or blow as their main lines, together with acid and E for the dance crowds, although rumour had it that supplies of snow were starting to become much more available as well.

So what was coming here I wondered?

'I'm here to offer you guys a choice. The world is changing, you've seen that. The Duckies are organising in Scotland and now we hear that they have been talking to The Hangmen.'

There was a stirring amongst the guys. The Duckies were The Rebels MC, The Brethren's main rivals over here. In addition to Scotland, this side of the border they had charters that ran in a band across Liverpool, Salford and over the Pennines to Leeds where they ran into The Dead Men Riding, as well as down across most of Wales. Their patch featured a screaming eagles' head that The Brethren insultingly dismissed as looking like a duck.

The Hangmen however were very much our regional rivals and *bête noirs*. They had charters in Lancashire and South Cumbria so we regularly ran up against them in a border war that had been simmering and flaring up at odd intervals for the best part of ten years or so now. A link-up between The Hangmen and The Rebels could make us the meat in the sandwich and potentially lead to a serious escalation in hostilities.

But over and above our local beef with them, might it also mean that a wider war was in the offing? The Brethren were currently the top dogs nationally and they would refuse to let that change. If The Rebels absorbed The Hangmen that would strengthen their presence significantly and might even make them numerically the largest club in the country. The Brethren want to prevent that happening which meant that they might either be looking to recruit extra troops to fight, or just to ensure they retained numerical superiority.

'The regional independents are being rolled up – you've all seen it happening. So guys like you sooner or later are going to have to choose whose side you want to be on.'

So I could see what was coming. We and The Hangmen had in effect provided buffer states between Rebel and Brethren territory. If The Rebels made moves to absorb their buffer, then The Brethren would have no option but to respond in kind.

'You might say why do we need to choose? Why can't we just stay out of it, stay independent? Well that's a mistake. You can't.'

He certainly had balls coming in here and saying that to the guys' faces. If he wasn't who he was, he would probably have been stomped. And it wasn't that we were scared of The Brethren that was stopping anyone. It's difficult to describe to an outsider, but it was like I say, a respect thing. Almost as though he was here to parley under a white flag. He was an envoy. So it was like a tradition, his person was inviolable as he came here to speak. If we fought them later over this we would stomp him without question if we caught him. But here and now, we would hear him out and he would unquestionably walk out unharmed.

'If you try to stay neutral in a war, you will end up the losers. And the losing side in the war won't be able to help you, while the winner won't have needed you to win or have any reason to value you.

'But don't get the wrong idea here. I'm not here to threaten you guys.

'We don't recruit, we recognise.

'And I'm here to tell you, as guys we respect, we want you on our side.

'So as I say, I'm here to offer you all a choice.

'It's time to step up to the big time. Time to join the international Brethren world.'

Oh fuck, I thought, so that was what was coming.

'We want you to patch over. We want you to join us to expand the North-east charter across the region.'

Oh fuck. The what happens if you don't was unsaid. Once The Brethren had made an offer like this we were either in or against them. It was not a choice being offered but an ultimatum, however quietly and smilingly delivered. It was join us or disband.

And it was always a one time offer.

Once Dazza had finished, Tiny stood up to formally respond. He thanked Dazza for coming out to see us and for setting out what he had to say so clearly. Obviously there was a lot to take in and we as a club would need to consider what he had said; to consult; we would need to ask the brothers inside who weren't here tonight what they thought; we would need to come to a view.

'Of course,' said Dazza. 'That's only natural. Now I could hang around but I know that this is something you guys will want to discuss amongst yourselves so I suggest I leave you to it. Obviously you guys know where I am if there's anything you want to talk to us about.'

Butcher stood up to escort him from the room.

'But before I go, there is one thing I would like to say in conclusion.'

The room waited in silence.

'Just don't take too long.'

The storm of noise and voices broke after he left the room.

It was a heated discussion, freewheeling was always the way in the club. But immediately, it was difficult to put a finger on it exactly, there was already a bit of a change in atmosphere. The discussion was perhaps just a shade less open than it would have been normally. I just got the feeling that some people were being more careful about what they said than they would normally be. That this was serious, that the wrong words here could have serious consequences later on, of interests being assessed, of positions being considered.

Irrespective of what we thought of him or the message, as a representative he had clearly given a good impression for his club. As the evening wore on I heard a number of people say more or less the same thing:

'He has balls coming in here like that.'

13

'He was pretty cool about it.'

'You've got to admire his balls, walking into our clubhouse to deliver a message like that.'

We broke up that night without any formal decision being taken. I hadn't expected it would be. We were a strangely democratic group in many ways; we were brothers and we tended to naturally seek to reach a consensus. With most things Tiny would take soundings, discuss the offer with small groups, and gradually we would come to a view as to what we, as a club, would decide to do.

*

It was a crisp cold night under an inky black sky filled with millions of brilliant white stars and the ride home from the clubhouse took twenty minutes or so.

I loved riding on my own at night.

There was something about the blackness, the cold wind biting my face, the streaming smear of light on the road ahead, the howling solitude, the unthinking way that I followed the road, long grooved with memories, testing each familiar curve just one more time, that made me feel as though I was riding towards the end of the world; by myself in my own private bubble of time and space.

Alone in a dream I roared up and across the high empty moors. Then the dry stone walls started to close in on either side of the road's curves as I left the high ground behind and descended through the curves into the rolling foothills with their fields and occasional yellow-windowed dales farms.

Down here, the road home was along a mix of straight old Roman roads that just begged me to gun the motor, the wind whipping past my ears singing the strange music, and sudden twisting curves familiar through years of instinctive riding, requiring fierce braking at the last possible moment, the bike drifting, using all of the available road to get the right positioning to hustle through them, the bike heeled over to maintain the speed and set me up for the acceleration that pulled me upright again as I set up for the next bend. Before the glow of the first streetlight ahead signalled the start of the final drop down the long straight into the valley, the lights of the town opening up before me as the machine and I roared out of the dark.

It was the type of riding I always enjoyed. It was very Zen

somehow. The speeding solitude, with just the sound of the wind, and the mix of unthinking instinct, and fierce full mind and body concentration required on the here and now of the riding freed my mind to wander, it gave me time to think.

But tonight was different.

It had been fascinating, sitting back to hear and see Tiny our pres, and Dazza theirs, in operation, and to mull over the difference.

All clubs are either dictatorships, run by a single dominant individual until such time as someone successfully usurped their rule, or democracies, run on the basis of consensus. They always have been and always will be.

We in The Legion were a democracy, certainly the ex-Reivers' part was, some other cohorts less so. That was why Tiny had called the meeting tonight. If there was something important to be said, we all needed to hear about it if we were to decide what we as a club were to do.

Dazza by contrast ruled his charter with a rod of iron. A bit like Butcher did with his boys down in Maccamland. I'd never been surprised that those two got on so well.

It was gone eleven when, bike locked up around the side, I walked in through the back door and parked my lid on the table.

'How did it go? What's up? Can you tell me?'

Sharon was an old school old lady. She knew that club business was club business and that sometimes I couldn't tell her everything.

I hadn't yet decided how much I would tell her. But I had to say something.

'In a word? Trouble. With a capital F!'

PART 2
1983 – 1994

Some clubs are old, with long established rules, some clubs are new.

Damage 2008

2   THE KID

I was just a pretty much fucked up kid of twenty when I first got involved that night back at the Golden Lion.

I'd dropped out after my first year at uni, doing history. It was a pity in some ways. I really liked history, I still do, and I'd cruised through A levels just doing enough to get by, but I just couldn't hack student life, which was pretty much the final straw as far as my folks were concerned. Looking back I can't really blame them, what with the booze and the dope that had got me my nickname of Brain Damage, usually shortened to Damage by my mates, although I did at the time.

I think I was probably about as low as you get at that stage at that age. I say I'd dropped out, the reality was that I just couldn't cope.

As I say, pretty much a fucked up kid, living in a fucked up shared flat with Billy, one of the guys I'd known from school who was also into bikes and heavy metal, riding a fucked up GS250T rat, a strange bodge of a mini custom with a 2 into 1 Neta exhaust and a pair of ace bars in place of the touring ones Mr Suzuki had intended. They say your bike reflects who you are which I guess is true. I sort of think I was inspired by the black café racer Harley sportster that they had out, but really it was a bit of a mess.

Billy was away that evening, out somewhere on his flash RD250LC, can't remember where now, and none of the other guys were around or wanted to go out. So as I sat there smoking in my room I had a choice. I had a bit of cash so I could get some beers at the offie and stay in staring at the walls while I got tanked up until I passed out. Or I could go out and at least have the blast there and back.

A suicidally reckless death ride into town suddenly felt a hell of a lot less self-destructive than sitting in my room so with a 'Fuck it,' I stubbed out my Silk Cut and reached for my lid.

Whenever I was on the bike, I just always had to ride as fast as I could. That was all there was to it. I just had to do it. Had to fly. Every ride was, and still is to a degree, a potential street race where I need to push it, to prove myself against the odds just one more time.

Riding fast was a way of continually testing myself. When I was

18

on the bike there was the exhilaration of being free, being solely in control of my own life, and yet and yet, at some level I actually lived for those moments when things went out of control, those terrifying seconds of extreme calm, when my heart leapt into my mouth, and when everything hung in the balance.

The moment when the tyre chirps and starts to drift on a slew of gravel across a corner and you think in that instant – Is this it? Is this the one?

And when it does.

The peaceful inevitableness of the feeling of the bike sliding away from underneath you.

The way time slows so that you can watch and admire all the details at a quiet distance.

There's no pain on hitting the deck.

It always happens in complete silence.

And the images stay with you in your mind forever.

The sparks of the steel scraping along the road.

The petrol spilling out from the filler cap as you slide towards it.

The first wondering realisation aren't bus wheels big from down here?

But not tonight.

Tonight the instinctive life force was too strong. As I felt the bike start to slip on a slew of gravel across the apex of a bend, with an instinctive reaction I kicked down hard onto the road with my left leg, brutally wrenching the throttle open at the same time, the engine snarling as I booted the bike back upright just enough to make it back onto the clear tarmac and then engine roaring as with a wave of adrenaline I screwed it open, feeling the bike wrenching beneath me as the tyre grabbed traction and the bike picked up its head, clawing its way up and out of the corner, the acceleration pushing me back down and into the seat.

As it said in a joke I'd read in one of the bike mags, 'Slide, don't roll – and don't do it in front of steamrollers.'

The Golden Lion was a bit of a dive. It was a small pub set back from the town's main drag, with a function room behind that was a heavy metal disco every Friday night. As I pulled into the car park it was filled with bikes and I found a space in the far corner to chain mine up.

The back of my hand stamped, I walked on into the pounding gloom lightning lit by the flashing orange and green lights of the DJ's sound system. As my eyes adjusted to the dark I could see it was the usual black tour T-shirt, denim and leather clad crowd. Dinosaur Heavy Metal never really dies, but back then the NWOBHM[3] was having a brief moment of fashionable success and so a lot of the crowd my age were really just pimply heavy metal kids, into the music and the image before jumping into their Mum's borrowed Mini to drive home again after an evening of headbanging and posing to Whitesnake.

Then there were those like me, the ones who were seriously into bikes.

I resented the heavy metal kids in their black leather jackets who never rode, seeing them as poseurs trading off our image and the risks we took. We bikers were the ones who took the danger. We were the ones who gave black leather jackets the edge of glamour. Testing made us different, what did they ever do?

Of course resentment of heavy metal kids was nothing to the degree to which I despised the disco kids with their smart clothes and happy songs. What were they doing that was dangerous?

And then there was a mix of older rockers and hardcore bikers.

My mates hadn't come and I'd never got to know anyone else there to go and sit with, so grabbing a pint of lager above the wailing guitars of Boston's *More Than a Feeling,* I found an empty table in the black shadows of the back at which to hide, watching the groups of people talking together, the knots of friends, the gangs of mates, the friendly scrum at the bar; and knowing that I wasn't part of it.

The local bike gang had their spot in the far corner, everyone knew where they sat and you left their tables to them if you didn't want any trouble.

They were older guys, mostly in their late twenties or early thirties, some possibly more. Back then they weren't a patch club as such, but they clearly already had the BTL/FTW[4] mentality. I came in from out

---

[3] *The New Wave of British Heavy Metal typified by bands such as Iron Maiden which emerged after punk.*

at Enderdale then, about 10 miles up into the hills outside town, so I'd been to secondary school down in town and knew some of the heavy metal kids from there. But these guys were strangers to me. Other than that I'd seen a couple of them working in the bike shops in town, and that the same faces were always there every Friday, apart from Gyppo, I didn't really know any of them.

Every club is made up of two kinds of guys; those who are open to talking with outsiders, and those who aren't. Gyppo had got his nickname from his Zorro like appearance which of course he then played up to. A slim swarthy guy, about 25, with straight dark medium length hair, thick gold hoop band earrings, a drooping moustache and usually a bandana, he dealt a little dope and was always happy to say hi and let us score.

You've got to remember that this was back in the 80s, not like now when skunk's all around. For us kids out in the sticks getting hold of a bit of blow, usually some Lebanese black, was a bit of a big deal.

Gyppo was OK. He was approachable, he had a sense of humour and you could make a joke with him, like when he asked us to sponsor a parachute jump and we offered him 2p a mile, without worrying that he was going to drag you outside and fill your face in. He wasn't like some of the really heavy hostile guys, the ones that gave off an aura of being unexploded bombs just looking for an excuse to go off at any second. While you had to respect him, you instinctively felt that Gyppo drew a distinction between some friendly banter and a deliberate insult that called to be dealt with.

I sat there alone in the darkness, nursing my beer, not speaking to anyone.

The temporary high of the ride had worn off and the downer of reality had sunk in again. Why had I bothered, I wondered to myself? Why am I here? What had I thought I would achieve by coming out tonight?

I had always been alone, been different from others, been conscious of being an outsider, wanting to belong but somehow never knowing how, unable to make friends.

And it was something that fed on itself. I pretended to myself that I

---

[4] *Biker slogan Born To Lose/Fuck The World (or occasionally, Fight To Win, depending on who's talking).*

didn't care, that I didn't need people. That people would have to like me for myself.

So that to then test people to make the effort I made myself as obnoxious as I could.

I dressed like shit. My jeans were filthy, ripped and oil stained. I wore a donkey jacket over my leather just because it looked more scuzzy and my mum hated it. And over that I wore my own colours, my denim cut off, the arms hacked roughly from a proper denim jacket, not some posey waistcoat.

I was a lanky beanpole with hair that I grew straight, long and greasy, and a scrappy beard.

I got stoned on dope and anything else I could get hold of. I dropped the tranqs the doctor prescribed me into pints of lager and drank myself to oblivion.

As I said. A bit of a fucked up kid.

My mates were all into either the music or the bikes or mostly both. But somehow it was different for most of them. It was a lifestyle. They would give it up as they got jobs, moved on.

With me, it was my life. It was what gave it meaning and made it bearable. And the only time I lived was when I was on my bike and could forget it all in the here and now of taking risks.

Truly it was better to travel than to arrive.

The only place for me was on my bike. It was a place where being on my own was right; and not a reminder of what I wasn't.

Overwhelmed with a sudden feeling of despair I got up and slipped out of the exit and into the night air.

*

And so I was outside in the car park, kneeling a few yards from the back door, invisible in the dark with my back to the pub, undoing the padlock on the heavy chain securing my bike, when it happened.

I didn't pay any attention as the door swung open while I was putting on my lid and a flicker of blue strobe flashed across the bikes the other side of the entrance. With the strap done up and my gloves pulled on I fished out my keys and was ducking down beside the back wheel when the door banged again and two guys came out, I could hear voices but with my lid on I didn't hear what they were saying.

And then there was a shout and the noise of a struggle.

22

'You cunt!'

I recognised Gyppo's voice.

Starting up and looking round, the clatter of my heavy chain as I pulled it free of the bike's back wheel was masked by the grunting of the fight.

I could see immediately what was happening. It was an ambush. Gyppo had come outside with one of the guys, obviously to do a deal, only to be jumped by the guy's mate who'd slipped out just before to lie in wait.

Now the two of them had him slammed up against the wall, each one holding him with one hand and pummelling him with punches to the body with the other.

I didn't really stop to think. I just acted.

The chain was of case hardened steel. The idea was that it would stand up to a set of bolt cutters with a big ugly guy jumping up and down on the handle. The padlock was the sort of thing that dark ages' dungeon locks were shut with. Swinging with all my might from behind him, I hit the guy closest to me straight across the side of his head with the chain, the padlock lashing round to smash him full in the face. The surprise impact knocked him sprawling away against the wall, as I just stood there, my chain hanging in my hand.

Gyppo with both hands free now grabbed the other attacker by his jacket and head butted him as they fell struggling to the ground.

The guy that I had hit turned towards me, his hands reaching up to his face to where the blood was streaming from his mouth. Then with a shake of his head as if to clear his sight and grabbing something out of his pocket, he suddenly lunged at me at the same instant as I realised what I had done.

It was now a matter of survival, so I swung the heavy chain back again catching him across the other side of his head as he lurched towards me. The blow knocked him to his knees and as he put his hands out to break his fall, something metallic clattered to the ground.

As he reached forwards to grab what he had dropped, I realised that there was only one thing that it could be, a knife. In desperation I stamped down on his hand, feeling the crunch as my heavy biker boots stomped on his fingers. Then grabbing hold of the chain in both hands, I swung it high up over my head and brought in crashing down in a club like blow across the back of his head, almost feeling rather than seeing him slump to the ground, while behind me I heard the sound of Gyppo overpowering his attacker.

It must all have been over in a few seconds.

Then suddenly there was the noise of heavy boots on the gravel all around me as the others came pouring out of the club door and piled into the attackers, boots swinging to kick the bodies on the ground.

For a second it felt unreal, I felt strangely peaceful. Then the shock hit me, as breathing heavily, my body flooded with adrenaline. Almost shuddering, as with trembling fingers I slipped the strap of my lid and pulled my scarf from across my mouth, I saw the world through different eyes.

'Who's this?' said a voice as the guys left off the kicking and turned to look at Gyppo and me.

I'm six foot two but I don't think of myself as tall. My whole family is big and the guys that I hung out with at school were as well, so I think of myself as 'normal'. The speaker was a giant guy, six foot six or so and built with it. The gang were surrounding me now and suddenly I was very conscious of my cut off. The hand-painted lone wolf on the back, copied from the cover of a Steppenwolf album, framed by the words 'Family Disgrace' above and the defiant 'No club' below.

Gyppo was spitting blood.

'You cunts!' he swung a final vicious kick at one of the prone bodies groaning on the ground. Then turning and still breathing heavily, 'Tried to jump me. The kid's alright. He can handle himself. The big bastard had a knife and he took him out. Saved my fucking arse.'

'Did he now?' The giant turned back to me with a grin on his face. 'Nice one kid. Good work.'

The giant was obviously in charge. Someone was delegated to fetch their gear from inside.

'You OK to go?' He asked Gyppo who just nodded.

The guys were already dispersing to their bikes, knowing that they had better split before the cops arrived.

'You too kid,' he said, looking at me as I stood there. 'Better make yourself scarce.'

The next week they spotted me as I walked into the disco.

'Oi. Kid, over here,' the giant waved me over to their corner. 'Grab a seat!'

I wasn't sure if it was an invitation or an order, but it sounded friendly enough, I didn't feel any sense of threat.

'Er thanks...' I started but he wasn't even listening as he had turned to shout over to where Gyppo was standing talking at the other end of their bit.

'Gyppo! Get the lad a drink.'

But just as some of the gang were squeezing up to make space for me on the end of a bench the cops arrived.

One of the guys that I'd noticed hanging about in the hallway suddenly appeared with a whispered 'Busies'. Out of the corner of my eye I saw Gyppo sliding quickly towards the gents as the DJ turned down the volume and the house put up the lights.

There were two of them, an older sergeant and a younger PC and they headed straight for our table, to be met with silent stares.

'Evening lads,' said the sergeant with a menacing cheerfulness. 'Now then, I think you know what I'm here about?'

'No officer,' said the giant standing and moving to face him so close that the cop had to look up at him, 'I don't think we do; do we lads?' he added over his shoulder.

There was a muttering of Nos and shaking of heads behind him.

'There was a serious assault in the car park outside here last week. Two men are in hospital. So we were hoping that you lads could help us.'

The giant shook his head slowly and regretfully over the gang's complete lack of knowledge about how such an unfortunate event could have happened out in the car park and their sorrow that since the whole group had all been inside, all the time, they didn't know anything about it that could help.

The sergeant wasn't buying any of it. Everybody knew it. But as his gaze travelled across the guys sitting facing him, everybody including the cops knew that there wasn't anything he could do about it, not unless someone was talking.

His eyes stopped on me. He obviously knew the others and knew that I wasn't one of their gang. He could see I was younger than them. I might be willing to talk, more easily intimidated. He obviously decided to try his luck.

'What do you know son? What did you see?'

I could feel the tension around me. Other than that I'd pitched in last week out of the blue and had bought from Gyppo in the past, they didn't know me at all. They would have no idea what I would or would not be prepared to say. And worse the cops had walked in just after I did.

'Sorry mate,' I shrugged. 'I didn't see anything. Left early.' And washed the chain afterwards, I didn't add.

'Left early? Really? Is that right?'

I looked at him straight.

'Yes,' I said.

'Anyone see you?'

'No, I was on my own.'

'Are you sure about that son? You might want to think about it for a moment.'

There was a few seconds of silence.

I looked him in the eyes and said in what I hoped was as firm a voice as I could muster.

'I'm sure.'

He grimaced in frustration.

'I think you've just made a serious mistake son, that you might live to regret.' Then as he turned to leave, gathering the younger constable with a gesture he added in an undertone, 'I'll remember you son. And I'll be looking out for you.'

*

The giant who introduced himself to me, obviously enough as Tiny, sat opposite me while Gyppo elbowed his way to the bar and back to squeeze in beside me with pints for all three of us.

'Cheers.'

'Cheers.'

'Cheers. No problem mate. You've earned it.'

'Can keep your mouth shut as well,' said Tiny. 'That's good. Can't have guys about who go blabbing to the cops. What's your name kid?'

26

I didn't have much choice I thought. I was the one who actually smacked the guy on the head with a steel chain putting him in hospital.

'My mates call me Damage.'

'Damage eh?' Tiny laughed. 'You really are OK kid, aren't you? Good, cause we don't want no wimps around, we need people who can handle themselves.'

I shrugged. 'It's just what you do.' What did he mean by 'around', I wondered.

Tiny seemed interested in having a talk. I'd obviously seen him here before and because of his size, appearance and evident leadership in the gang he was someone that I would always have avoided. But now over a beer he was quite different from what I'd imagined. He wanted to know who I was, where I came from, what I was doing, who I knew. It was quite a friendly chat, but one where he was asking all the questions.

I obviously didn't drop any bollocks as Tiny seemed quite relaxed with what I was saying.

Around me the gang were chatting. There seemed to be general surprise that the boys from the gang down the valley had jumped Gyppo, and general agreement that they were due a good kicking to keep them in line as well as some perfunctory discussion about how and when that would be arranged.

But they were also talking about other stuff and my intense but avuncular interrogation was brought to a close as one of them interrupted to ask Tiny about the next day's run.

'What do you reckon, about tennish?'

'Yeah, seems about right.'

'Blast up to Edgeside for a brew and then see who's about, where we feel like going.'

*

Tiny and Gyppo nodded a greeting as I rolled into the car park at ten to ten.

To my relief they didn't look at all surprised to see me, almost as if they had been expecting me.

I almost hadn't come. I had lain in bed the night before agonising. I hadn't actually been asked if I wanted to join them. I didn't know if they would want me along or not? But then I decided, what did I have to lose by trying?

Dismounted, I joined them for a smoke. Gyppo seemed to have taken some kind of responsibility for me and introduced me to the others as they arrived over the next half hour or so.

It was a sunny morning. The mood was peaceful. Blokes stood around in knots, talking, or checking out their bikes, waiting for the signal. Eventually at about quarter to eleven, Tiny and the others around him decided that it was time to go, and the squadron dispersed.

Cigarettes were stubbed out. Helmets were pulled on. Last words before the off were exchanged. Keys turned. Kickstands clattered up. The whirr of electric starters being cut off by the roar of motors catching. Owners of the older Brits jumped down hard on their kick-starts. Engines snarled as throttles were blipped to ensure the bikes had properly caught.

The group bunched at the entrance to the car park. Tiny at the front on a Zed one. I pulled up to the rear of the pack on my much smaller two fifty, although I noticed that Gyppo was hanging back to take up the Tail End Charlie slot.

We were ready to go.

And then at a gap in the traffic we were off, pulling out onto the road, a cacophony of exhaust blast echoing between the shop fronts as we headed up the main drag through town and the Saturday shopping crowds on either pavement.

As we rode slowly along the road behind the traffic it was my first experience of riding with a group this big.

There was a sense of the power waiting to be unleashed, the over-revving of the engines just to get more noise bouncing between the walls on either side, the ratcheting up of our own adrenaline. I could feel a wild exuberant excitement welling up within me, a feeling of invincibility.

There was a sense of power. When you see a group of bikes, you know they are together. You know they are a pack of guys who know each other. You know that they are heading somewhere together deliberately, as a group. You wonder where, you wonder why, you wonder who they are and what will happen on the way. And now I was part of that.

Heads turned to see us go past. You didn't look, just like you didn't look at your reflections in the plate glass windows of the shops. But out of the corner of your eye you could see the heads turn. The small children point.

We crested the top of the rise and headed towards the crossroads and the drag up the hill out of town that allowed us to pull past the cars in front.

If you've ridden bikes then I don't have to tell you what it's like.

If you haven't then it's difficult to describe.

You drive a car. You turn a wheel, you press a pedal and it goes. A car is an object that you control.

You ride a bike. You dance with it, it goes where your body tells it. Your bike is your partner, it sways and shimmies with you as you move your hips and twist your body to shift your weight.

In a car you are inside, insulated from the world, surrounded by a cocooning wall of steel.

On a bike you are outside, exposed to the world, feeling the wind, the rain, the warmth, the cold, and with only your skill, your luck and a leather jacket between you and the ripping tarmac tearing past you below.

As we headed into the open countryside, the line of bikes began to string out. The gang were all on bigger bikes. Seven fifties and upwards, mostly a mix of UJMs[5] and some older Brit twins and back in the car park there had been the usual good natured joshing about Brit shit and Jap crap.

On the more open roads we came swarming up from nowhere in seconds behind cars that we caught, and barrelling past them, rocketing by in a wail of powerful noise without even slowing down.

But then in more twisty bits we might get caught up without the clear overtake, bunching up behind a car, all bright lights, chrome, noise and thunder just behind the driver's back bumper, feeling the tension, the eyes in the rear view mirror, the kids in the back seat turning round to look open-mouthed, before the road straightened out

---

[5] *Disparaging term for Usual Jap Multi – a reference to the ubiquitous layout at the time of larger Japanese bikes of an in-line four cylinder mounted across the frame – on the grounds they were therefore all the same.*

again as we crunched down a gear and with a bawling scream of pure exhaust noise we launched ourselves past the outside of the car, tearing up the road again to the next bend.

Riding in a pack was completely different from riding on your own. As a rider on your own machine, you are still singularly alone, testing yourself, totally responsible for your own actions and how far you are able to push yourself. You against the road.

Yet at the same time there was both that feeling of invulnerability, of being part of something bigger, us against them, and that feeling of competitiveness with the other guys, As a pack you are always egging each other on.

At the back on my two fifty with Gyppo on my tail, I was having to scratch hard to keep up with the charging pack. And failing. So the times when we got caught behind something, bunching up into a jostling knot of bikes and power and noise, just waiting to be fired past the car's windows at the first hint of a gap were great for me as they gave me a chance to catch up before the more powerful machines howled away again into the distance, stringing out into a line of glinting swerving disappearing spots as the road opened out. Finally on the last stretch, Gyppo pulled out and twisting the throttle, zoomed past me at probably ninety or so into the final bends leading up to the summit.

As I pulled into the Edgeside car park I must have had a grin a mile wide.

Most of the gang had dismounted and were already filing into the café. Gyppo and Tiny were standing by the row of bikes as I kicked down my side stand at the end of the line.

'Not bad considering it's a two fifty.'

'You're going to need to get yourself a bigger bike kid.'

I got the feeling that I had just passed another test.

*

And then we were off again, down the falling hairpin curves of the Edgeside pass and out towards the flat valley below.

Riding at the tail of the pack, for the first time in my life, I truly felt accepted in the company of men. I belonged.

I had become a tagalong.

3   THE PATCH

I sold the two fifty and just about anything else I could lay my hands on, lied through my teeth to get a loan, and two weeks later bought myself a second-hand silver Honda CB750F, the double overhead cam job. Gyppo gave me a lift over to the west coast to collect it. Heading out onto the road on it for the first time to follow him back, feeling the neck snapping surge of acceleration that could send the world around me into reverse, was like falling in love with biking all over again.

Over the next few months I gradually just drifted in, becoming absorbed into the gang. We weren't a club back then so the process wasn't as formal or structured as it is now, so in some ways I never went through the whole striker thing.

Instead I just hung around with Gyppo a lot, sat with them at the Golden Lion, tagged along on runs, joined them on parties.

Gyppo began dropping in at the flat for a smoke and a brew when he was out our way, or for when we fancied a session in the pubs around the village square where he could crash out overnight at our place.

Billy followed me in really. He sort of became my tagalong's tagalong.

Billy was thin and lanky, scruffy with a pony tail and sheepish grin while his bones sort of looked too long for his body. He limped from a bad shunt he'd had, flying down a country lane on his first LC[6] when a tractor with a trailer pulled right into a field in front of him. At close on a ton he hadn't stood a chance. The bike smacked straight into the side of the trailer and Billy went over the bars, right across the top, and slammed onto the dirt on the other side. He spent nearly six months on his back with a smashed up pelvis, and another six months or so afterwards dealing with clips and catheters or some such shit every time he wanted a piss. He hadn't bothered to take his test when the 250 ban came in, so rather than trade down to a 125 he just went out and bought an XS1100, the big shaft job. He reckoned the

---

[6] At 250cc, the liquid cooled two stroke Yamaha RD250LC was the fastest bike a learner could legally ride and in one jump took the speed at which you could ride, aged 17 on L plates, to over 100mph.

cops wouldn't be bothering to check anyone on a bigger bike, they'd just assume he had a licence.

He started to ride at the back with me in a sort of threesome with Gyppo as our leader.

We were all brothers of course. But it was just a bit like Billy was my younger bro.

It was dumb really, we were the same age and all. It was just that he had always tended to follow me. I never really knew why and I don't think he did really either. In many ways as a kid it ought to have been the other way round. He was the more fun of us, I was always the more serious. He was the one with the cheeky grin, the one who would have the balls to chat up the girls, I was the one who sat silent. He was the popular one, never valuing or putting any effort into friendships as they came so easily to him that he never thought about them, there was always another one coming along when one fell away, whereas I never put any effort into friendships as they never touched me. We were always a strange pair. I have no idea why it worked, why it started even, or why it endured so long. But it did.

To this day I still don't know what I did for him, why I was the one friendship that lasted for year after year after year. I'm not sure he knew either, in fact I'm damn sure he didn't. He wouldn't have stopped to think about it for a minute. That's not what Billy did. It was almost as if he felt that he could leave the being serious and silent and thinking to me while he had fun and just followed where I went. And so despite his success with the girls, his happy go lucky lifestyle, the fact that he so obviously didn't need me, that you could drop him into any situation and he would just turn on those blue eyes and that smile and everybody would be falling over themselves to help him, I felt responsible for him. I worried about him.

Like I said, he was my brother. But he was like my younger brother who I felt I had to look after. Like he fucking needed it!

As we became more and more involved with our new lives within the gang, inevitably we drifted away from the other guys we had known before, and they started to drift away into jobs and careers and couples and kids and straight lives.

Sometimes we went back to Gyppo's place.

And that was when I met Sharon again, when she opened the door that first time.

She was petite, slim and pretty, with medium length straightish chestnut hair framing her elfin features as it fell in a great curve to just above her shoulders, and soft hazel eyes that caught and held your gaze. Her delicate, almost boyish figure very feminine in a dark blue chiffon blouse embroidered hippy style with a mass of small white flowers, the material so thin that I could see right through it to the white top she had on underneath, a clatter of bangles at her wrist, tight faded blue jeans and leather moccasins. She was twenty-two, but with a shock I recognised her as she stretched up to kiss Gyppo as he came through the door.

Christ how couldn't I have done? She had been in the year ahead of me at school and one of the girls that we had all fancied like mad without ever having a hope in hell of asking any of them out. I had an abiding memory of having seen her at a party I crashed once, one of those when I was doing my level best to get as blind drunk as possible, as quickly as possible. It was a sort of slow motion, bottom of the bottle image of her as she brushed a strand of hair away from in front of her face, as she turned away from talking to some hunk from the school football team.

She was training to be an artist, their flat was decorated with her pictures, beautifully intricate compositions of light, colour and joy.

Gyppo introduced me and her smile was like the sun coming out. She had obviously heard the story.

'Thanks for helping Gyppo out.'

And then, my God, she reached up and kissed me on the cheek.

*

Gyppo dealt. It was his main thing. He was a relatively small scale dealer but it made him a living and he always seemed to have access to a ready supply of dope or speed.

Billy and I were both doing odd jobs just to get money for petrol, beer and to buy blow from Gyppo, as well as to pay the rent; mainly a bit of despatch work for cash in hand. We were both signing on for some dosh, as was Gyppo of course.

We were scratching a living but he always seemed to have cash for smokes and drinks. So it wasn't long before we were starting to deal in a small way for him, buying a few ounces and divvying it out in

33

eighths at a time. After all, we were known to the guys out in the valley and to our contemporaries from school, we had the links into the club to get the stuff from Gyppo, so it wasn't long before we had a reasonable network of customers to supply. But it was all still minor stuff; blow, a bit of whizz, the occasional experimental blotter acid that just made me rant continuously for twelve hours straight while drinking every drop of alcohol in the flat, from the beer through to the dregs of every bottle of spirits I could get hold of, apparently without any effect whatsoever.

Gyppo had really taken us under his wing. So when, after about three months of this, he pulled up outside one day, rang the bell and asked if we fancied coming for a ride to meet someone, we didn't ask questions. We just grabbed our gear and mounted up.

He led us out across the countryside and down into town. But then instead of stopping, we headed out again, across the bridge and up the hill to turn right at the roundabout and down onto the fast sweeping dual carriageway heading east towards the city. Wondering where we were headed, Billy and I settled into the usual staggered formation to give ourselves some roadway behind him as we cruised at a steady eighty-five to ninety along the outside lane.

We parked up behind a rough looking pub in the terraced backstreets down where the shipyards used to be. We took off our lids and gloves and Billy as the most junior was delegated to stand watch over the bikes while I followed Gyppo inside.

It was one of those old fashioned working men's pubs. All dark wood, scuffed lino, yellow stained ceilings, Guinness mirrors, frosted glass windows, cardboard hangings of KP nuts and pork scratchings and ripped vinyl upholstery.

It was also quiet as we walked in, our eyes adjusting to the relative gloom of the interior against the glare of the day outside.

Gyppo hadn't said anything to warn me, so the sight of The Brethren patches bent over the pool table and sat on stools at the bar gave me a start. I just hoped that I hadn't shown it as the door swung shut behind us.

But Gyppo was advancing into the room with a friendly 'Hey Doggie!' to the guy with the shaved tattooed head and spade beard just standing up from his shot at the pool table and looking round.

A smile spread across the guy's face, 'Hey, Gyppo, how's it going?' he said, sticking out a hand for Gyppo to shake.

'OK mate, thanks,' as the handshake transmuted into a short backslapping bear hug at The Brethren guy's lead.

'And you?'

'Good, good. You here to see Dazza?'

'Yeah. Is he about?'

'Yeah. I think he's next door.' The outlaw nodded his head, indicating the door through to the lounge bar as his eyes wandered back to the table.

'Cheers. See yah soon.'

'No problem,' he said bending back down to look for his next shot.

It was as though I didn't really exist. I tagged along invisibly behind Gyppo as he headed across the bar. I guess I would speak when I was spoken to.

The lounge bar boasted dark and intricately patterned carpets and a series of banquet type booths, although I noticed that despite the upholstery fabric, the phantom seat slasher had been at work here as well.

Spreading his arms out wide in greeting Gyppo approached a figure at one of the tables who had looked up to check us out as we had opened the door, and was getting up to greet us, both arms outstretched.

Even without his name tag on his cut off and his VP title I had realised immediately that this had to be Dazza.

He was about six foot tall, aged thirty or so I guessed, with a dark stubbled broad face and high forehead. His hair was black, swept back long at the back down to his shoulders, but cut short and spiky on top. He had a barrel chest and thick, tattooed, and well-muscled dark-haired arms showed beneath his cut off and the tartan lumberjack shirt rolled up to his elbows.

His voice in growling a welcome to Gyppo was deep and measured. He had presence.

As they disengaged from their hug and we stood before him, Gyppo introduced me. 'Dazza, this is Damage. He's working for me now.'

I stuck out my hand silently and without a word he took it in a firm

35

dry handshake.

Then with a gesture he indicated that we should take a seat.

So then I found out where Gyppo sourced his stuff.

*

I was his right-hand man. So I spent more and more time with him. And that inevitably meant I spent more and more time with Sharon as well.

We spent any number of evenings together, the three or sometimes four of us if Billy was there. Smoking joints, listening to music, drinking beer, getting quietly peacefully wasted together until one evening merged pretty much into the next.

There were other girls hanging around the gang of course, and Billy went after them like mad, but I never did. I had chances of course, some of them made that pretty clear. And you would have thought that would have been something I would have jumped to take advantage of. But somehow I was never interested.

And the reason was Sharon.

I didn't understand our relationship, or wasn't even certain that we actually had one at that stage. She was Gyppo's girl. They were together. Any idiot could see that. There was a depth of feeling and intimacy there between them that I could only ever stand outside of, I could not hope to break it, or break into it, even if I had wanted to, which I didn't.

They were Gyppo and Sharon, my friends. They were happy together and I was happy for them.

But still I ached for her.

I wished that she would look at me in the same way that she looked at him.

*

With more of us in the club dealing in a small way, we all started to need to have some space for business that we would have to be able to defend from anyone who wanted to muscle in on our turf. It was this as much as anything that led us to patch up. With patches that identified us as a club we could mark out our area, we could let people know who they were messing with if they started to deal in our territory.

And so within about a year and a half of my first starting to ride

36

with the gang, we became The Reivers MC, named for the cattle rustling robber clans that had made Northumberland and the borders such a badland of fortified houses and pillaging raids for centuries.

Tiny and Gyppo went to see Dazza first to check out with The Brethren. After all, as the existing senior club in the region we had to respect their position in setting up a new patch club. But this wasn't a problem. Dazza as both VP and acting P, while the P was on remand, was an enthusiastic supporter. And after all, why shouldn't he be? It wasn't as if a local stand alone patch club out in the sticks were ever going to be any kind of a threat to The Brethren.

Quite the reverse in fact, particularly for Dazza. He was already dealing with Gyppo, me and Billy, as well as a few others. The better we were able to move stuff, the more stuff of his we moved. And the more of us that were dealing, the more of us he would come to supply. After all, The Brethren in the city with whom we had good relations were the obvious place for any of our guys to get stuff to sell. And if you were getting stuff from The Brethren, really you were getting it from Dazza.

All in all I guess that Dazza saw this as a great opportunity to build himself a support club out our way to expand his business.

Looking back I wonder if he had even then been playing the longer game. How far ahead had he been thinking?

Patching up gave us an increased feeling of solidarity. Before as a relatively loose riding gang, particularly one spread over such a wide area, people drifted in and out, you were never quite sure who was fully in, and who was out. Now it was clear. If you were in you belonged, you had the colours and the club tattoo. If you weren't, you didn't.

I was in.

And with pride in the colours came an addiction to respect. It was all about belonging.

As a group we had always generated a reaction when people saw us together. But now with the patch it stepped up to a whole new level of response. Of fear. Of wariness. Of respect.

We were a mix of ordinary guys; some of us worked out on farms, a lot were self-employed as mechanics, drivers or in the building trade, and a few like me and Billy and Gyppo basically made a living from dealing. But I could feel it when I was out in my colours. The different way people treated you. Wearing the colours we weren't just some scumbag bikers. We were part of The Reivers, to be treated as such.

We all came to just accept it as our due, for the dues we had paid.

So then we came to expect it as a matter of right. And if you didn't show it we wanted to know why and what you were trying to prove. We weren't just individuals now that we had our patches, we were representatives of the club. We had to protect the club's honour, and to be seen to do so, otherwise any punk might try it on.

Any so any trouble now called for an all out response, on behalf of the colours.

And for Gyppo, me, Billy, and any of the others who were dealing it had another advantage too. As we went on we built up a network of other small time dealers we supplied to. And very few people were stupid enough to try and rip off or burn a patched club member over a drugs deal. If you were dealing with a Reiver, you paid your bills. In cash. In good notes. Or you paid the price.

We offered our customers security too in a way. The more stuff they sold, the more dosh we made. So as and when anyone tried to muscle in on their pitches or tried to tax them, they knew they could turn to us for help in sorting these problems for them. It just made good business sense both in keeping the market clear for moving gear and in increasing the dealers' reliance on us.

So we staked out our territory and defended it against anyone who came onto it. We had to show that we had to be treated with respect as otherwise some other club might think they were tougher than we were and try to take it over. So whenever anyone tried anything, whenever another club pushed, we pushed back hard to show we meant business until eventually things settled down as our reputation spread.

Because of course we weren't alone. Others were patching up at the same time.

Luckily we didn't have too much hassle. Other than a few beefs in the early days, we were broadly friendly with most of the other clubs around us, partly because of our geography in that our respective turfs were easy to define, and had little overlap when it came to places for dealing, a case of good fences making for good neighbours. For example, we had always got on well with Gut's gang over in Cumbria so when they patched up as The Fellmen MC, we partied long into the night with them. But there was a natural border, we went across the moors and up as far as the Edgeside café overlooking the steep drop down onto the floor of the valley below. They had the rolling countryside beneath, west into the lakes. The café was sort of neutral, sort of shared, ground as, set high up on the edge of the hills at the end of some of the most magnificent twisty roads in the country, it was the natural meeting place for riders across the north and packed every Saturday and Sunday with rows of bikes parked outside.

Gut ran a breaker's called the Boneyard, that also sold chrome custom accessories for your bike and exotic chopper parts imported from the states that you would otherwise only see in occasional copies of *Easyrider*. The first time I visited there was a chopped Harley in the window; all springer forks, ape-hangers, twisted chrome sissy bar, coffin tank and an iron cross tail light. I thought it looked impossibly cool. Gyppo just scoffed at its impracticality for scratching round bends.

'Ride a hard-tail like that and you'll be bleeding from your arse after a few hundred miles.'

Inside, beside the racks of engines and rows of wheels there were black T-shirts emblazoned with skulls and the slogan 'Live to ride, ride to live'. Gut was a complete mountain of a man, sat behind the counter of his shop, and when he sold you something the top half of his body rotated to the till next to him, while his enormous beer gut remained still, resting slumped on the counter.

Putting on a bike show seemed a natural way to party together and so that August the first Roof of England Bike show, our joint event at some rough ground on the moor just behind Edgeside, was born.

It was a bakingly hot summer's day of brilliant strong sunshine and blue skies where the beer in the August heat doesn't seem to have the usual effect. But then a sudden thunderstorm broke at about half past four, sending everyone screaming to the beer tent as the heavens opened and for an hour the tent roof drummed as a torrent fell; before the skies cleared again and the ground began to steam in the renewed sunshine.

Sharon didn't always come on club runs. Sometimes she preferred to stay at home and paint. But she was here for this one, a vision in a long floating hippy cotton dress that she had matched with a set of jeans underneath for the ride up.

By six or seven I was already very drunk. I didn't know where Gyppo had got to. Out of it somewhere I guessed.

Then I spotted Sharon. She was on her own, sat on a groundsheet to keep dry. She looked pensive, curled over, her knees clutched in her arms and drawn up to her chest, her head resting on her knees as her dress tented around her as she watched the crowd circulating around the gleaming chrome and glinting paintwork of the bikes on display.

She smiled as, ever the clown, I collapsed onto the ground next to her, beer bottle in hand. And then she made the mistake of asking me how I was.

I don't know why I did it. Even now, I don't know why after all that time I actually said something.

Was it just the drink talking? Or was it just that I was drunk enough for it to be able to sound like a joke if needs be? I don't know.

I told her I loved her.

She told me that of course she knew that.

'You're very sweet.' She smiled at me, shaking her head. 'You know I like you a lot. But you know I have to look after Gyppo.'

And so she stood up, turned and walked away across the field to find Gyppo, imprinting another image of her in my mind, as she delicately stepped across the sodden ground, her skirt lifted slightly to keep it clear of the glutinous mud, her hair outlined in flaming gold by the long rays of the setting sun.

I crashed out dead drunk and stoned in the field that night where I fell beside the bonfire. I'd pitched a tent somewhere but was too wrecked to find it. I have a vague memory of someone spreading a blanket over me in the dark. I assumed it was Sharon. It seemed the sort of thing she would do.

*

I never mentioned it again.

And neither did she.

Looking back, the next five years were a whirl of drugs, drink and

40

dealing.

We worked for Dazza. He was our wholesaler, the senior partner, and we, our little team of me and Billy, led by Gyppo, dealt into the town and the valley as the juniors.

The amount of stuff we were supplying grew. There was more whizz now, acid started to become more popular with the rave kids and we were into E as well that came across from Holland on the ferry.

But we were also suffering the drug dealers curse. With so much stuff around that's available to use, there's so much that you just can get used to using. Billy, Gyppo and I had increasingly large personal habits, alternating whizz to get up and downers and blow to get down again. And as time went by our using got increasingly wild.

Sharon smoked, but she never did whizz. I think she tried it once and scared herself.

But increasingly as the years went by and the money rolled in, Gyppo was using everything he could get hold of that didn't mean sticking a needle in his arm. The club was very tight on that. If we caught a member at it we'd break the spike off in his arm and kick him out. We didn't want any junkies in the club. And so far, Gyppo had managed to hold off from scag although given the highs of his whizz habit and the lows it would produce I was starting to wonder whether he was smoking it to kill the pain.

I knew Sharon was becoming more and more worried about him. She and I stayed close, even after that evening. She told me a number of times that she was worried he was getting out of control. That he was using as much as he was dealing. That she was afraid he was going to hurt himself. Or someone else.

Crank makes you paranoid. Him and me both, I guess.

I don't think Sharon ever said anything to him about what I had said. And for the next three or four years after that night there was no change in our relationship. We rode, dealt, drank, smoked and fought together.

Through all of it Sharon watched Gyppo. She worried about him, we both did, but she was always there for him, except for that one last time.

She never nagged or whined, or tried to hold him back from doing

41

anything that he wanted to do, however crazy or wild, not once. She rode pillion, never complaining as the speed madness took hold, or how stoned he was when riding. Her life was his. But occasionally, just occasionally, when he pushed it too far, when he came to the edge of going over the line, whether it was on the bike or drink or drugs, you could see the silent pain in her eyes and the clench of her fists curling into tight white balls.

We just couldn't stop you see. Gyppo and I shared the urge to roll the dice one more time, to double the stakes again each time we lost to see if we could win it all back, to ratchet up the odds just one more notch.

We always had to keep going. Until we went too far.

Meanwhile in the outside world, bike gangs were getting more serious. You only had to look at Canada, Australia or the Nordic bike wars to see that. The cops started to talk about all of us as some kind of Mafia, all into organised crime, international drug smuggling, all kinds of bullshit. At the same time, the big six were building internationally, extending their existing networks around the world by taking over local clubs. But even while this consolidation was going on there was still room for the independents, there was still a mix of local clubs like us and The Fellmen, as well as the international brands with their national charters like The Rebels and The Brethren.

But we could never stand still. There was always some pressure somewhere and as the clubs to the south of us started to merge into The Hangmen covering all of Lancashire and South Cumbria and Dead Men Riding down in Yorkshire it became clear that we northern independent clubs had a choice to make. We would either combine into a regional club, or risk being picked off one by one by the expanding clubs eager for territory.

So in 1989, five years after first patching up, Tiny and Gyppo went for another ride to see Dazza. And this time I went along too.

*

We in The Reivers took the lead, but the merger message we brought to the other clubs made sense. There was survival in amalgamation into a regional club that would have the muscle to stand up to The Hangmen or Dead Men Riding if they looked to move North, in a way that we as individual clubs wouldn't.

42

We had known the other clubs for years, other really than Butcher's boys who by and large had kept themselves to themselves, so talks went quickly.

At the time I remember wondering if it wasn't it a mistake on Dazza's part, letting The Legion amalgamate, allowing a weaker group of clubs to come together to become stronger, to become numerically superior to The Brethren locally?

After all, the rules for staying top club locally seemed simple and self-evident enough. All Dazza had to do was to keep all the other clubs in the region weaker than The Brethren and preferably dependent on them in some way which was one way in which Dazza's control of the local whizz supply came in handy. Other than that, all he needed to do was to prevent any small club linking up with one of the rival big six clubs, thereby letting another big club that could become a champion or rallying point or alternative protector of the smaller clubs get a foothold in the region.

But then I supposed that if it ever came to a war, Dazza had the rest of the world-wide Brethren's resources to call on if he ever needed to and even a strong regional club like The Legion would think awfully long and hard before mounting a challenge like that.

But in hindsight, even then Dazza was thinking ahead.

He was just brilliant throughout it all. He worked hard for us, smoothing the way. He was the P of the north-east charter now for real, ever since the old P had gone down; and having him on side meant having The Brethren onside. He even hosted the first meeting we had with Butcher's boys, The Iron Horsemen MC, out of Sunderland.

It was strange that he and Butcher did so much together. Normally Geordies and Maccams hated each other but Dazza seemed to have a strong relationship with Butcher, although at the time, again being a Maccam, Dazza wouldn't have had a hope in hell of bringing him into the north-east charter. It was almost as though Dazza had been already using Butcher's boys as one of his private support clubs. My guess at the time was that they handled his distribution on Wearside.

Now with The Iron Horsemen to the south in Wearside, we had a complete band across the region and around The Brethren's city stamping ground.

43

Gut's Fellmen covered northern Cumbria across the lakes and up to the Scottish border, while to the south they rubbed up against The Hangmen in disputes over territory in the south lakes.

We Reivers centred around the valley and up into the hills and dales of the North Pennines.

The Devil's Henchmen MC under Popeye, a wiry, crop-haired ex-marine who ran a fishing boat out of Craister covered northern Northumberland, but were mainly based along the North Sea coast.

Hadrian's Wall was the spine that ran through our territory, and so we became The Legion MC. Our territory became the Empire. Our colours became the imperial colours of purple and gold. Our patch was a grinning skull facing out, and wearing a purple plumed centurion's helmet, with the crenellated wall running behind him. And instead of charters, we had cohorts, based on the amalgamated clubs Westmorland, Borders, Northumberland and Wearside.

We chose our Roof of England bike show that August to unveil our new colours.

The Legion patching party at the end of the bike show was an even wilder rerun of that first Reivers one.

Dazza and the guys from The Brethren were there of course, it was almost as if they were our sponsors in a way. As the only one of the big six clubs with a presence in the region we could hardly amalgamate patch clubs in the area without clearing it with them. We didn't exactly need their permission but it was a show of respect as before. If we had patched up without consulting them, it would be seen as an unacceptable affront to their authority, a deliberate insult if you like, and they would have to act to keep face. At the same time they knew that we would not want to lose face by having to ask for their permission like some little kid at school. So, it was a little game that we all played to observe the niceties and keep the peace. Like I say, good fences, and good manners, keep good neighbours. So as before, we asked their blessing.

And Dazza of course was happy to give it.

We took a group photo of the new club, standing and kneeling proudly in two smiling rows in our new colours. I've still got a copy at home although I don't put it up, it upsets Sharon too much. But there's a framed one in the clubhouse bar that I look at every so often.

Gyppo looks particularly wild eyed and out of it with a manic grin. He was already speeding crazily by the time the photo was taken. Tiny had to threaten to clobber him to get him to crouch down long enough in the front for the camera.

As he loaded on the crank still further that evening, he became dangerously unstable, not knowing where he was, what he was doing or what he was saying half the time; prone to flying into fits of uncontrollable rage.

And worse still, earlier that day of all days, after months of getting to the end of her tether with him, Sharon had finally snapped. She had walked out, leaving him a note in the flat.

'*Fuck it Gyppo, sort yourself out. Gone to my mum's to think it over. Love Sharon.*'

Gyppo's response naturally had been to get completely loaded on uppers and come charging out to the party to hit the vodka hard. By the late evening he was in a mean funk, a human time bomb just waiting to go off.

Things had obviously been getting to a head with Sharon over the past few weeks, I had noticed a sudden change in him, he seemed more distant, wary, withdrawn. As I say, the crank makes you paranoid, and this was when I really started to wonder if he was chasing the dragon.

That night he exploded.

I had been standing with Gut and Sprog by the bonfire when it happened. Gyppo just launched himself at me from the darkness. The first I knew was when I felt a crashing blow from behind that knocked me flying to the floor, my head cracking down on one of the stones around the fire.

As I went down Gyppo was all over me with his boots and fists, screaming wildly that it was all my fault, that I was a scumbag who had stolen Sharon, that he was going to kill me. I heard shouts from the others around me as Gut grabbed him by the arms to pull him off as he tried to stomp my head with his boots, and I managed to roll away from the intense heat of the fire and just out of range of his flailing kicks before Sprog, who was our club's punch out artist, knocked the raving Gyppo to the ground where the pair fell on him, pinning him down.

45

Tiny, Billy, Dazza and Butcher had arrived by the time I was scrambling to my feet.

'What the fuck was that about?' asked Tiny, looking at me darkly.

'Fucked if I know. He's just gone nuts,' I said, running my hands over my head to check the damage, feeling warm blood and smelling singed hair.

Gyppo was bucking and writhing, held down on the ground by four or five guys now, but still raging and ranting about me.

'Are you shagging his bird?'

'No of course I'm not. We're mates. I wouldn't do that to Gyppo and neither would she.'

'He seems to think you are.'

'He's just fucking lost it,' I said, irritated now, my head was starting to bloody well hurt. 'The only fucking problem between him and Sharon is that he's behaving like an arsehole.'

I washed the blood off in the café's toilets.

When I got back, Gyppo was gone.

The Brethren had brought their crew bus to carry their gear and so he had been bundled into the back, trussed and gagged, as Dazza and Butcher volunteered to take him home to sleep it off.

And that was the last time we ever saw him alive.

*

Sharon found him two days later when she went back to the flat.

He'd died of an overdose; downers, and he'd shot some smack, the coroner said, so I reckoned I had been right after all.[7]

And so our first full dress run as a new club was for Gyppo's funeral.

We assembled in the Golden Lion car park again.

There is always a strong turnout for funerals. Not just from our club, we were all there of course, a slow cortège, riding two abreast

---

[7] Adrian 'Gyppo' Leverton, born 26 November 1959, believed to have died of an overdose sometime during the night of Saturday 21 May 1994.

His body was found on Tuesday 24 May 1994 by his girlfriend Sharon Wright at the flat they shared. The cause of death was a cocktail of alcohol, barbiturates and intravenously injected heroin although the pathologist noted that there was little evidence of any previous intravenous drug use.

An inquest was held and the coroner recorded an open verdict.

behind the hearse, silent, solemn and grim as we rolled through the town, a police escort ahead and behind. People on the pavement stopped to watch as we passed but it was a very different feeling from that first time, some seven or so years before.

But also from other friendly, and even not so friendly clubs. The Brethren were there in force, Dazza leading them with their wreath strapped to the pillion pad of his Harley. Down the pecking order there were members of local sidepatch clubs and MCCs, some of them customers, some of them just friends or acquaintances. Gyppo had been a popular and well known guy.

There were even wreaths from clubs like The Hangmen and Dead Men Riding. We might be enemies but we were still bikers who could respect each other.

His family hadn't wanted a church service so there was a memorial event in a hall just at the cemetery gates. He had an open casket so we could all see he was being buried in his colours, colours that he had worn for less than a day.

Sharon had chosen the music. So the coffin left the hall for his final trip to the graveside to *Bat out of Hell*.

I gave her a lift back afterwards.

*

It was Gyppo's death that shocked me out of what had become a downward spiral.

Gyppo. My friend, my brother. Was gone.

Sharon and I held each other and cried for I don't know how long.

We never actually really said anything, but we stayed together.

She moved out of their flat. It had too many memories, so she moved her art and herself into mine, temporary at first but then it became permanent.

We married.

I met up with Dazza again a few weeks after the funeral. I told him that I had decided to get out of dealing. That I didn't want to end up the way Gyppo had. I thought it was going to be a problem, telling Dazza that I wanted to quit, that it would mean trouble. But much to my surprise, he seemed quite relaxed about it.

I collected in the last of the dosh that was due to me, sold Billy the last of my stash and he took over the connection to become Dazza's

47

distributor in the region. By this time I suppose it didn't matter to Dazza if I wanted to lay off as he had plenty of other customers in the club to cover the region, Sprog for one.

I got a job. I had good A levels that had got me into Uni and so I got work in an estate agents as a mortgage advisor of all things. I had to take out my earrings when I went to work and long sleeved shirts covered my tattoos, but then after a few years I qualified as an IFA and went self-employed. It suited me; I had a range of clients who I organised mortgages for along with insurance and some investment advice; I could work when I wanted so I could take time off for runs and club business. My job meant that I had to keep myself clean but then I got voted to Road Captain which helped.

Sharon and I used the last of my and Gyppo's dealing profits as the deposit to buy a little terraced house in the west end of town. I had the money from my business to buy bikes.

I still saw Dazza regularly enough as we met and partied with The Brethren. In fact I noticed he'd got his Bonesman badge the next time I met him.

So by this time, into my late twenties and then past thirty and turned thirty-one I was drifting again, only this time I was drifting out of the life, into being a part time outlaw.

The only problem with that now, five years after the merger, ten years after we had first patched up, was that there was no such thing as a part time member of The Brethren.

The Brethren wasn't a lifestyle. The Brethren was a one hundred percent, twenty-four seven life.

The other guys and I were going to have to make a serious choice.

PART 3
26 April 1994 to 8 August 1994

New clubs are either completely new, or they're an extension of an existing club.

Damage 2008

4   THE CHOICE

A split in a club, pitching brother against brother, is the worst thing in the world.

The following night, we, Tiny, Gut, Butcher, Popeye and me, as the officers, gathered at the club house for a council of war.

As President, Tiny led the discussion.

'I know everyone will have their own views on this, both here in this room and across the club.' There were nods around the table. 'So we need to find out what these are and how we are going to deal with them, as a club,' he said with emphasis, looking around the table at us, 'so that, as a club, we can decide what we are going to do.'

Like most clubs we were very democratic in our own way. We voted on new members. For anything else, in the normal course of things, Tiny would consult, take the temperature, see how the guys felt, until after a time some form of consensus emerged as to what we would do.

The trouble was that this time, we didn't have time. Dazza had made that clear. But still we were a club and we would need to work out how we were going to take a decision.

Next week was the May Day bank holiday, our first big run of the year and the one I'd been planning for the last few weeks which would mean there were no prayers next week. That evening we all agreed the run should go ahead as planned but we arranged that each cohort's prayers over the following couple of weeks would be full patch meetings on their own turf. As the Presidents of their local cohorts; Tiny for the Borders, Gut for Westmoreland, Butcher for Wearside and Popeye for Northumberland, would ensure that every member who wanted to could have their say at these sessions. Then by the end of the month we could reassemble for High Church and a formal secret ballot before the Whitsun bank holiday run at the end of May.

'What about the strikers?'

'What about 'em?'

'Don't they get a say?'

'No.'

'What if they get made up?'

'Yes then.'

'Any of 'em ready?'

'I'd put Wibble to a vote, but not the others.'

Tiny looked around the room. 'OK then, Wibble gets voted on but otherwise that's it?'

No one seemed to object.

'Agreed?'

'Agreed,' we said.

'OK, so let's do it. Meanwhile we need to let The Brethren know what we are doing and when they can expect to hear our decision.'

'We also need to know exactly what they're offering.'

'Yeah, so we need to keep talking to 'em. Damage?'

'OK, no problem, I'll handle keeping Dazza in the loop.'

As the only officer without a cohort to look after and lead over the next few weeks, I was the obvious choice. As secretary-treasurer Popeye would normally be responsible for handling the vote as well but we decided that since he would have the Northumberland cohort to look after, I would take this on as well.

Meeting up with Dazza at a café on the outskirts of town a couple of days later I was surprised to run into Billy at his table already but then Billy was obviously still working for him.

Dazza seemed to be expecting what I had to report. 'OK, it sounds sensible. You need to make sure that you bring all the guys with you. Like I say, we respect other clubs' ways of doing things and I guess it's the way we would do it ourselves.'

'I still don't understand why you need us.' I said, 'Why d'you need The Legion patched over? You know which side we'd be on if it ever came to it anyway so why take in more members in such a big hit? And it's not like the territory'd be worth a lot to you. You'll be getting most of the business out of it as it is through muggins here and the like,' I said, gesturing at Billy who was lounging against the bar next to me.

'Hey don't go looking on the bad side, and don't go putting 'em off making the offer!' objected Billy, 'I for one can't wait.'

'Ah but he's got me,' said Dazza, joking. Looking round for effect he leant forwards and whispered conspiratorially, 'Want to know the real reason?'

'Go on then. Like you'd tell me of course!'

'Holes,' he said in mock seriousness.

'Holes?'

'Yeah, it's simple,' he leant back against the bar, a broad smile on his face, 'haven't you ever seen Casino? You want to watch it mate, it's good stuff. Very educational. Joe Pesci, he says "there's a lot of holes in the desert." Holes are useful, there's a lot of holes in those hills of yours.'

'Yeah right, you want us 'cos you need a body dump. What's the matter, your crew got too fat and lazy to dig their own? Well that explains it all then.'

'Well we have got loads've holes,' chipped in Billy.

'Really?' I was surprised to see that Dazza looked genuinely interested.

'Yeah, there's one just down the hill from the clubhouse in the wood the other side of the road, an old drift mine. They're great places, go in straight for miles some of them, they're really something.'

'Aren't they all blocked off?'

'Some of them are, the ones by the road that anyone can see and some of the ones on private land, but there's still a lot that are open if you know where to find them. There's so many of them around here that nobody bothers to block them all off, they were all over the place. We used to explore them as kids.'

I nodded in agreement. I knew the one he meant, it had been one of our favourites, hidden away amongst the scree and tailings, the entrance almost impossible to see from the road, surrounded as it was by trees. Funny, I'd never taken Dazza for someone who would have an interest in that sort of thing but you never knew with people. I suppose he was a serious guy as well and had some serious interests outside of the club and business.

'So you can still go down the open ones?'

'Yeah, generally.'

'Wow,' Dazza looked impressed. 'Well, I was joking but maybe you boys really do have something here. Must get you to show me sometime.'

'Yeah, no problem. They're full of shit but it's quite interesting.'

54

'You have to watch what you're doing down there though,' I cautioned, 'they can cave in if they get disturbed too much. Still he's right though, they're worth having a look at. Just shows what a fucker it must have been to have to work for a living in the old days.'

Dazza laughed and picked up another bottle of beer. 'I'll drink to that.'

So would I. But I still couldn't work out what he was after.

*

Over the next few weeks the club was a mess of politics and politicking.

Some guys clearly had strong objections. 'They're all about money these days!' was something that a lot of the anti guys said. Which was code for those who were worried about the degree of 'serious business' that might be involved.

But there was an equally strong attraction for others, like Billy.

We were all aware of The Brethren's reputation for involvement in crime, particularly drugs. But as a patch club ourselves, we had a bit of insight into how it worked, we knew that sort of activity was self-selecting, the degree to which any member might want involvement was largely voluntary.

The Brethren was always very clear that the club didn't deal drugs. That was true enough, the club as an organisation didn't.

They always admitted that individual members might deal drugs, they could hardly do otherwise really as again, that was true enough. But they always maintained the distinction for public consumption, that individual members dealing drugs wasn't club business.

But what was really left unsaid was that, just the way it had been for us when we'd first patched up all those years ago, it was the club's reputation, the club's patch, which enabled those people to deal drugs. The Brethren patch was a brand that members could use to make money. As Gyppo had explained to me all those years ago when he first took me to meet Dazza, for anyone who wanted to buy stuff it was safe to approach a member with a Brethren patch because you knew their reputation, that no plod had ever infiltrated them, so you knew they were safe to deal with.

So for the guys at the top of the tree, or anyone entrepreneurial who wanted to try, membership of the club could be a route to making serious money, with a willing pool of bodies amongst the lower ranking patches and support club members after some easy money, together with prospects and even hangarounds looking to prove themselves, to do the work on the ground.

As a patch club with members who dealt, we had the same issues.

Sometimes people would ask us why we didn't disassociate ourselves from one of our guys who got had up for doing something, or condemn what they had done. Anyone asking that sort of question just showed they didn't understand what membership of a club like ours meant.

Within the club we had quite a challenging regime. Like anywhere else you would have your core group of buddies within the club, the guys you hung around with, rode with, partied with. Every group was different, things changed over time, but even within this core group there would tend to be a continual process of mutual testing, winding each other up, checking to see commitment. This went further the less well you knew another member.

But whatever we might say to each other inside the club; whatever we might say in coming to club view; we never, never, never disagreed outside the club in front of, or to, non-members. As a patch, you never betrayed your brothers, whether they were part of your close local circle or someone from another cohort that you hardly knew, by word or deed to anyone outside the club, whatever you might say or do privately. The absolute rule was always absolute solidarity with anyone inside the club against anyone outside; a non-member. Whatever they said, whatever they had done, a brother was always right.

In a club like ours, or like The Brethren, you could rely on your brothers, and their silence.

For them, it was also a world of Brethren. As they said, 'The sun never sets on a Brethren patch,' and so with their worldwide network of charters, members of The Brethren had access to an international set of connections if they wanted them.

So those of our guys who were already well in with The Brethren, dealing with them on drugs or whatever, were generally very pro. Like Billy, they saw this as their big opportunity to move up the ladder from membership of a friendly but separate club to a Brethren patch themselves. Besides, if we fell out with The Brethren and their connections, where else could they get their stuff?

But it wasn't just a simple question of business. There were a whole range of both personal and club reasons why people were pro, anti or undecided.

But one thing was clear. There was now no *status quo ante*. It was join, disband, or fight.

North-east president or not, Dazza wouldn't have the authority to make this offer on his own. This was not a local decision. This affected The Brethren nationally in bringing in a whole club as new members, as well as the impact it would have on the balance of power in their rivalry with The Rebels in the UK. It would have to be something that had been agreed and approved by The Freemen leadership. Making an offer like that without proper authorisation would have been a fatal decision on Dazza's part.

And what an offer. It was almost unheard of. Normally, if a club like The Brethren wanted us to patch over it would mean the entire club, or those guys that were wanted anyway, going back to being strikers for a Brethren patch. We'd put on their bottom rocker, get our heads down and do our time. OK so you'd expect that if they wanted us, we'd be put up fairly soon, fast tracked to a patch vote after say three or six months, no one would be expecting us to stay striking for a year or more the way a straight tagalong, some potential wannabe would. After all, the reason the offer would be made would be because they could see we were stand up guys, good material with what it took.

But the point was, whatever you'd worn before, to wear a Brethren patch, you would still have to strike for it, either individually or as a club.

A straight patch swap, a guy transferring full membership straight from club to club, with no screwing about as a striker? Well sure we knew that occasionally, very, very occasionally it happened, in really special circumstances, but it was the rare, the extraordinary exception.

But this, this was something else. What Dazza was proposing was absolutely unheard of. The Legion weren't just being offered the chance to patch over. The Brethren were offering a full patch swap for the whole club. Just like that.

One day The Legion, the next day Menaces.

It was such a fantastic offer it was scary in itself.

Coming to our club house that evening, Dazza hadn't been speaking for himself, or for the north-east charter, or even for the Great Britain charter. He was by implication speaking for the worldwide Brethren. And to say no was to say no to them all.

It was also a decision that could not take too long. The Brethren would want an answer.

So it was a period of uncertainty.

Me, to be honest I wasn't sure how I felt about it.

I was attracted certainly by the chance to share in their reputation. But at the same time I was cautious. There was no denying it, joining The Brethren was a serious step up in commitment. I knew that if we went in we would have to live by The Brethren's rules, and that meant the club would come absolutely first, the way we had tested strikers, but more so; before family, before friends, before work, before anything, for the rest of my life as a patch. And was I ready for that level of commitment? I had as I'd realised been drifting away from the life for a while now. I was still fiercely proud of my colours, of my club, of my loyalty to my brothers and their loyalty to me. But these were shared now with other things. I had Sharon, we had a home, we had a life at home outside the club, things that I'd not had for many years. I had my business. I could feel myself settling down. We had even talked about having kids.

And it was also a commitment for life, when they said 'BFFB', Brethren Forever, Forever Brethren, they meant it.

*

We jacked Wibble the next week.

Prayers were over and as the guys headed down to the bar Butcher went in search of Wibble who was boots up again on the desk with one eye on the screens and one eye on the porno mag he was flicking through. From up where we were, I could hear Butcher bawling him out, a tower of tattooed rage as Butcher ran him through the bar and up the stairs to where we, the other officers, had hung around in the meeting room.

We'd all picked up baseball bats from where we'd stacked them earlier. Tiny had his on the table in front of him while Gut was swinging his back and forth, just getting the feel of it.

'Fucking piece of shit,' stormed Butcher as he pushed through the doors with Wibble, 'goofing off on the job.'

Wibble looked around the room and then back at us, taking in the bats, the air of pervading menace. He'd never been in the meeting room before. It was strictly for full members and like Dazza, invited guests only with the membership's permission, and by tradition, strikers were never invited. This was the members' holy of holies, this was where we had prayers, so only the faithful were allowed in.

'What's up?' asked Tiny in a dangerously low and controlled voice.

'Like I said, he's jerking off with a mag when he's supposed to be watching the screens.'

'Is that what you are now Wibble?' joined in Gut, 'Just a little wanker?'

'Hey fuck off,' he pushed back, 'screens are clear, everything's secure.'

'There's serious shit going on here Wibble, you know that don'cha?' Tiny continued quietly, 'So you know we can't have any weak links in the chain.'

Watching him, he was loosening himself up for a fight. It was subtle but you could just see it in his body language, they way he was moving so as to give himself some space. Here we were, four guys with baseball bats with the rest of the club downstairs, giving him a bollocking serious enough to have him drag his sorry arse up into the meeting room, and he was starting to square up for a fight? Mind you he might just be thinking that it's what was coming anyway.

'What are you saying?'

Butcher pushed a chair behind him and barked, 'Sit!'

He didn't like that. I could understand that, if I was facing a potential rat fucking I'd want to be standing too.

'I'll stand.'

'Did you hear what I just said?' demanded Butcher menacingly.

'Yeah, what d'ya think I am, deaf? And I said I'll stand. Now say what you've got to say to me.'

'Striker, just shut the fuck up and listen to me,' said Tiny, 'We've got serious shit to do now, a serious decision to make and we can't afford to have anyone around who's not serious…

That was as far as Wibble let him get before erupting in anger, 'Hey fuck, if you don't think I'm serious then you're out of your fucking minds.'

'When you're wearing our flash you know you're repping the club right?' Tiny overrode him in turn, 'From the moment you first tagalong, to being a striker or even god help us if you ever make it to real member, it don't matter. If you've got a Legion tab you've gotta hold the rep up.'

'Hell yeah! You don't think I know that? You don't think I carry the rep for you? I'm the best fucking striker you've had for years, and you fucking well know it!'

Tiny and Gut just exchanged looks.

'You want me gone? Is that what this is?' Wibble was really rising to it now, 'Well I ain't walking out for this crap! If you want me out, you're just going to have to fucking throw me out. So come on then, who's going to try it?'

'Well then,' Tiny said slowly, rising to his feet and picking up his baseball bat. I pulled mine up beside me as I rose too and walked round the table. 'Guys, it looks like we don't really have a choice then do we?'

'Guess not,' Gut said, as we closed in towards where Wibble was standing his ground by the door, our eyes never leaving his face. With a few steps the four of us stood round him in a semicircle, about a bat swing's wide.

There was a moment's silence.

And then Tiny said, 'We're gonna have to get you a tattoo organised pretty pronto kiddo aren't we?' as, reaching into the inside pocket of his cut off, he produced a fresh Legion top rocker and rolled up centre patch and letting his bat slip to the floor, he grabbed the astonished Wibble in a huge bone crushing bear hug that just about lifted the smaller guy off the floor, before pressing them into his hands.

'Congratulations mate,' he roared, 'welcome to The Legion.'

'You complete and absolute bunch of fuckers!' Wibble was almost crying with joy and disbelief as we all joined in the celebration.

'Love you too mate!' I said laughing like I was fit to bust, 'Christ mate, you should have seen your face!'

That was one of the great things about The Legion, we knew how to have a bit of a laugh.

Of course he was in. There was never any real doubt. It had been a unanimous vote. He would be the last of The Legion. And he could hold his mud.

There was an enormous cheer from everybody as the grinning Wibble emerged into the bar downstairs a few moments later with us following him, and a path opened towards it for him.

His piss-up went on until about three or so. I crashed in the bunkroom I got so hammered. Cost him a fortune.

Tiny took him to our inkman the next day.

*

The following week's High Church was it. Tiny, flanked by us officers standing beside him, addressed the room.

'We are a club. We decide things as a club and we do things as a club. That's what we've always done, and that's what we're going to continue to do.'

'And if anyone has a problem with that, then they'd better say so now.'

No one in the room moved a muscle.

'Right then,' he continued, looking slowly around the room, 'Tonight we've got a very difficult decision to make. But we're going to make it the way we do everything as a club, and that's as a club, together.'

He turned to me.

'OK then, so I guess we had better get on and do it. Damage?'

I sat the bucket I was holding on the table in front of me.

With the freshly tattooed and still grinning Wibble who was possibly facing the shortest ever career as a full patch member of a club, we had thirty-nine members now. So I had printed out forty ballots and destroyed one. Just so that there was no mistake I had typed the question twice across the top and middle of an A4 sheet and then guillotined these down into two A5 ballot papers, 'Should the club accept The Brethren's offer of membership – Yes or No?'

Queuing in an orderly and quietly serious line, each member filed past the table and picked up a single ballot paper out of the bucket.

61

Tiny picked out four, one for himself and one each for the guys who were down or inside, whom he had consulted and for whom he would be casting votes.

'OK, has everybody got one?'

There was a mumble.

'Anyone not got one?'

Another mumble but no objections.

'Right then, you all know the drill. The bucket stays here under guard and we count at ten.'

Some guys voted immediately, swapping pens to write out their answers before folding them and dropping them in the bucket. Either they were very certain or they didn't want the hassle of being lobbied any more. Others wandered off to the bar for a beer and a think. They had time, there was an hour left.

Butcher ran a tight ship down on Wearside, almost, some had always said, like a club within the club. There was no question about which way he would go given his longstanding relationship with Dazza and he would be making sure that his boys followed him.

Popeye by contrast was clearly very anti. He'd no business dealings with The Brethren, he worked full time on his fishing business and valued our independence. But he ran his cohort much more consensually and openly than Butcher, so while he would argue and try and persuade, and while many of his guys would undoubtedly follow his lead, Northumberland would not vote in a block the way Wearside was likely to.

I, like everyone else, had a lot to think about as I sat with my ballot paper in front of me.

From a club perspective, we all had a strong pride in our independence, the way we ran our own show. In subsuming ourselves into The Brethren not only would we be losing some of that autonomy, we would also be the new kids on the block. And however big we were in our own little pond, in The Brethren world we would be small fry in the bigger sea.

But the reward for making the change would be the worldwide respect of a Brethren patch and a move up into the outlaw elite with membership of one of the six senior clubs in the world. As The Brethren always used to say, 'There's two types of biker in the world,

Brethren and people who wish they were Brethren,' and there was something to that.

Being the other side of the Pennines, Gut's guys in Westmorland tended to have much less to do with The Brethren than the rest of us and so generally less business interests and relationships to be concerned about, so some were strongly swayed towards the independence option. But as a group they were split, since the guys in the south who were running up against The Hangmen regularly could see what would happen if The Rebels took them over and were keen to patch over to The Brethren in order to maintain parity. Meanwhile the guys in the north, with much less exposure to border problems, tended to have much more of a 'Why should we get involved in The Brethren's beef with The Rebels?' attitude.

Here in our borders cohort I knew guys who held any number of opinions.

I could see that for personal reasons Tiny was obviously conflicted. At the moment he was president of the club, but there wouldn't be room for two presidents in the new order and Dazza clearly had that spot. So in voting for a merger he was in fact voting himself out of office. But I knew Tiny as well as anyone by now, I knew that whatever his personal feelings, he would do the right thing by the club.

As far as I could tell I think that while he valued our independence, had no pressing business reasons to want to make the tie up and would obviously lose out personally in terms of his position, he had decided in the end it was the right move for the club. Dazza had been right, the independents were being absorbed as the senior clubs made it clear to the junior ones that it was a case of with us or against us. So it was only a matter of time before we would have had to choose between The Brethren and The Rebels anyway, and between those two there was no doubt which way we would jump in the end.

And I think it was following that line of thought that in the end led me to write 'Yes' on my piece of paper, before folding it and slipping it into the bucket.

Popeye and Gut brought us up beers as Tiny, Butcher and I as returning officer, stood guard on the bucket, while over the next hour

63

guys appeared in dribs and drabs to put in their papers. A small flurry of half a dozen or so announced that the ten o'clock deadline was on us and Gut and Popeye headed downstairs to round up the troops.

When everybody was back Butcher shut the door again, and then under the watchful eyes of the whole club the count began.

I stirred the papers in the bucket so that they were well mixed and then pushed it along the table to directly in front of Tiny. As he stood there, ready to start, the tension in the air was palpable.

Reaching into the bucket, Tiny pulled out the first sheet, which had been doubled over into quarters. He unfolded it and in a strong measured voice he read out a 'Yes,' and then held it out to show the crowd, before putting it down on the table to the right of the bucket.

The next dip produced a 'No,' which went onto the table on the left of the bucket.

And so we waited and worked through to a result.

It was tight right up to the last moment.

At twenty-one for and eighteen against we had as a club decided to accept Dazza's offer and patch over to join The Brethren.

The only question was, were we still a club?

*

The answer, it soon turned out, was no.

As I'd suspected, Gut and Popeye were the ring leaders. They took their members out that night.

*

It was a still warm evening as Tiny and I pulled off the road and onto the worn out tarmac of the car park. We allowed our bikes to roll to beside Gut and Popeye's machines which were already sat by the low wall at the edge. It was late May and the evenings were growing ever lighter, and we could see miles across the peaceful rolling patchwork of fields in the valley below, with the blue grey masses of the Lake District's mountains rising like jagged teeth in the background.

Edgeside was our traditional neutral ground, so that was where Tiny and I had arranged to meet up with them the following evening. We had come cautiously but alone, it hadn't got to the stage of war yet. Given how everyone knew how Butcher felt, we had decided it would be counterproductive to have him along. As far as possible, we needed to keep channels of communication open with the dissenters if we were to try to influence them. And having Butcher in the room wasn't going to help that process.

We were still hoping that we could persuade them. Tempers had been running high last night. People had said things in the heat of the moment that perhaps on reflection they might have wished they had left unsaid. So we thought it was worth meeting up once things had cooled down a little. We knew that some of the guys in our Borders cohort had voted against but as far as we knew, everyone in our lot would go with the majority view now we had decided. So it was worth seeing if we could talk them round.

They were already waiting when we arrived. We embraced and sat facing each other over a table and three coffees. Popeye had his usual NATO standard tea.

'Shall I kick off?' said Tiny.

'Might as well,' shrugged Gut. Popeye by contrast looked grim, his hard eyed stare glowering out from a face sea-hardened by wind and rain below a fierce buzzcut.

Of the two, Popeye was the more dangerous, I decided. Bike clubs have a lot of ex-forces guys, people who find it difficult to settle back into civvie life, who miss the comradeship of being tight with their mates. A club like ours gave that same identification, the same sense of a home. Popeye was one of these with firstly The Devil's Henchmen and now The Legion. He'd been a sniper in the marines and fought in the Falklands. He'd found it hard to adjust to coming back to peacetime soldiering after the heat of battle and had ended up in trouble for fighting in the barracks. Instinctively unwilling to be told what to do by anyone, it was inevitable that he was eventually demoted and then discharged.

Merging his club into The Legion had been a big step for him away from the feeling of being part of a tight knit group of guys who all knew and would die for each other. He had come into The Legion cautiously at first, a hard ass, one of those determined to make other guys prove themselves as worthy of trust, but blindly loyal in return.

And now you could see he felt betrayed. The prospect of merging again into The Brethren was a step too far, a worldwide network of people who by and large would never meet each other wasn't the blood brother relationship that Popeye believed we stood for. And for others in the club to decide it was, was as good as treason to the club's ideals as far as he was concerned, majority or no majority. Popeye was a visceral ultra anti, driven by very deep personal demons in what made him a biker in the first place. He had rebelled against the Marines. He wasn't going to be marched by anyone into taking orders in any other organisation, ever. There was going to be no persuading Popeye.

Gut was calmer, less angry, but in his own way, equally determined. He had the same feelings about being absorbed into something bigger, but it was more about what it meant for him in terms of loss of freedom. He didn't feel betrayed that others might want to join the bigger league, it was just that he didn't want to and just like Popeye, no one was going to make him, and his boys who were with him, do so against their will.

'Hell, we don't want you to do anything you don't want to,' I protested, 'You guys must know that. We've been brothers now for five years and we've known each other for a whole lot longer than that. But at the same time we want to keep the club together, and the fact remains the club has voted.'

'Well, you can't have both,' said Gut.

'What about loyalty?' Tiny butted in.

'Loyalty to what?' Popeye snapped back.

'To us, your brothers, the club.'

'We are the ones who are being loyal, to the club and what it stands for.'

I could see that had made Tiny angry. Making a choice last night had been difficult for me, it had been difficult for all of us, but I knew it had been an almost impossible choice for Tiny. And part of what we had all had in mind in choosing wasn't just what was best for us as individuals, but what was best for the club. Whichever way the vote would have gone, to go in or stay out, I would have gone with it because that's what we did. And now I could see Tiny thinking these fuckers are saying they were going to go against the vote that the club had had? That their interests were above the club's?

'By refusing to abide by the club's decisions?' he growled, 'Like I said last night, what the club stands for is the guys in it, and what we decide to do as a club.'

'Whoa Tiny,' I cautioned, trying to break this up before it went too far, 'now calm down you two. We're not here to get into that again. We had enough of that sort of talk last night. It didn't do any good then and it won't do any good now.'

'But what good do you think talk is going to do now?' asked Gut.

'Well we decided to join The Brethren,' Tiny insisted.

'Some guys decided to,' Gut said, 'Me, I'm staying put.'

'Does that mean what I think it means?' I asked wearily.

'It means what it says.'

'Has it come to that?'

'Guess it has.'

'Are you sure?'

We sat in silence for a moment and then Gut and Popeye both pushed back their chairs and stood up.

'You join The Brethren if you want,' spat Popeye, 'The Legion's real members are staying out.'

'You fucking...' Tiny started to get to his feet but I put a restraining hand on his shoulder.

'Hold it,' I urged, 'Let it go.'

'The Legion's real members are doing what The Legion has decided to do...' Tiny sneered, as I physically pulled him back down onto his chair.

'Tiny! Let it go I said!'

He slumped back onto his chair as they turned their backs on us.

We waited while they walked out, their patches disappearing through the door. From inside a minute or so later I heard the unmistakable Harley roar of two bikes bursting into life, followed shortly thereafter by the sounds of them accelerating away in different directions. We sat and listened as the noise disappeared into the distance, Gut west, down into the valley, Popeye east and away across the moors.

I shook my head. Tiny was obviously seething with anger. I just had overwhelming feelings of doom and sadness that it had come to this.

'So what happens now?' I asked.

Tiny just shook his head. 'I don't know.'

*

It didn't take long before we found out.

I suppose we should have expected it, by way of a test if nothing else. Normally clubs that wanted to patch over had to apply and then waited years to get into any of the big six clubs. The Brethren would keep them dangling, make them show some class to justify their application, perhaps have them do some time as a support club first with their colours adapted to show their new allegiance. And even when they went ahead and admitted a new club, the whole club would come in as strikers for a year or so before getting the full patch.

This was different, The Brethren had invited us in as a full club, as full members from the get go. Dazza had been very clear that was the deal. But there was always going to have to be a catch.

So when Tiny and I met with Dazza and Butcher the next day to report back, the message was very clear. The Brethren were upping the stakes.

'It's simple,' Dazza announced, 'You guys want in and we won't stand for a club of refusniks on our territory. Either they disband or you guys take their patches.'

'OK,' I said, 'but let me have one last chance of talking them round.'

'Popeye's never going to come over,' said Tiny shaking his head.

'No, I know he won't, but I think I can persuade Gut, and if I do that it brings the whole of Westmorland over.'

Dazza sat back in his booth and thought it over for a while.

'Well I don't need Northumberland, if they want to stay out, fuck 'em. We can deal with them later if we want to. But I do need Westmorland.'

I nodded. As a small club with half a dozen guys or so, Northumberland on its own wasn't of interest to The Brethren or any of the big six. It was only by having merged together into a larger regional club that The Legion had become a piece, albeit a small one, in the game. We had made ourselves into a takeover target.

It was the needing Westmorland bit that puzzled me. What did he mean he needed Westmorland? What for? Most of their patch was just small towns, villages and open countryside. When you thought about it there wasn't a whole hell of a lot in the territory for a club like The Brethren, so what would Dazza think he needed it for? It just didn't seem to make any sense.

'OK then,' he said leaning forward, 'But this is the last chance they get. Just make them understand one thing.'

'What's that?'

He smiled, 'No one says no to us twice.'

With a heavy heart I rode down the twists and turns of the escarpment road to the valley floor below and dismounted outside the Boneyard.

I had come on my own to make my last ditch attempt to appeal to Gut to reconsider. I found out that was a mistake the hard way. There were five of the guys in the yard when I went through who decided that they wanted to send The Brethren and the guys that were going over a message. I went down when the crowbar hit me across the back of the head, after that it was a boot stomping.

They dumped me outside A&E bleeding and unconscious. At least I should be grateful for that.

The cops came round once I was awake. More for the sake of form than anything else they asked me what had happened and did I know who had done it. They got nothing out of me.

So I missed the war, I sat it out in hospital.

My *Flying Tigers* bike was missing and I never saw it again.

I guess Gut scrapped it.

*

Sharon sat by the side of my bed. She had drawn the chair up close and had grasped my hand tightly, asked how I was, doubted what I was telling her. She seemed upset, she had screwed herself up to say something, I could see that, but what I couldn't tell until she started.

'I've never asked you anything like this before.'

'Like what?'

'Well I'm not even really asking as such,' she corrected herself, 'I'm just saying.'

'Saying what?'

'You know I never tell you what to do.' Now I was wondering what was coming. 'Well it's just this, all of this, it seems to me that you've got a choice...'

She tailed off, as if uncertain now she had started as to how to go on.

'A choice?' I said quite gently.

'Yes, to stay in or get out. And I just wanted to say, that if you wanted to quit, if you wanted to leave, then it would be alright by me.'

I looked at her blankly as she stumbled on.

'Look, you've always been a biker, you always will be. I know what it means to you and I'll love you whatever you do, but all I'm saying is there's a change going on here. The Brethren, that'll be something utterly different from what it was before, you know that and I know that. You're not patched up with them yet. You have a moment to choose. To patch or not?'

'Like you mean retire?'

But I wasn't really there for a moment. I was miles and years away, back in my memories of those first days when I'd become involved, the thrills of buying my first seven-fifty, the unfolding and enveloping sense of power in riding with the pack, it had been like finding myself for the first time.

I belonged. That had been the reality of my life for the last ten or twelve years or whatever it was. The club was my home, my other family. Could I ever leave it? My brothers?

'But this is all I have!'

'No it isn't, you've got me, and what we could have together outside of the club. Listen to me. Just this once…'

'Leave the guys now?'

'But it's not your guys any more is it? It's all going to be different from now on. You know that. You just need to have decided that it's really what you've decided that you want to do, that's all I'm saying.'

'Listen love, I made my choices a long time ago.'

'So did I, and I don't mean to change it whatever you decide, but you, yes, you had made a choice, you made it years and years ago when you were a different guy, just a kid really. But you were starting to make a different one over the last couple of years, weren't you? You know you were.'

She was right of course, or partially right in any case. I lay back in bed and stared up at the ceiling. Sharon sat there by my bedside holding my hand and waited. Could I leave? I asked myself. Could I really make that change? Is that where I had been heading the last few years?

Retire? I'd never thought about it before as such. Never had to face the question. The idea had never really crossed my mind.

And if I ended up not being a patched guy, what would life be like? On the outside I mean.

Blokes who left clubs had usually been kicked out in bad standing, stripped of their colours and made to have their club tattoos inked out if they were lucky, removed if they weren't.

Guys did retire from clubs as well of course, older members who decided that they couldn't keep up the lifestyle any longer could apply to hang up the colours. And if they were of good standing then they might get the club's permission, have a retired date added to their club tattoo and off they went. Of course if you ever did retire then you were never really free of the club. You inhabited a sort of twilight world, not a member, so not part of the club or any longer enjoying the respect a patch holder would expect as a right. But you were still always tied to the club and expected to support, never knowing when some of the guys might decide to descend on you in need of a bed for the night or a meal or a drink. Your position was always a bit uncertain, depending on how well respected you had been within the club before you left, and how powerful your remaining mates within the club were and how far they could or would go to protect you.

Unless you broke away completely that was. Started again somewhere far away where you were free from the influence. And to do that either took dosh, serious dosh that we just didn't have and I could see no way in hell of getting, or meant turning grass and getting the plod to look after you and I was fucked if that was a way I was going to go.

The door opened.

'Hi Dazza!' I said looking up. He was a surprise visitor. Sharon's eyes fell.

And then it was too late

She had been right. I had had a choice. But I think it had just walked out the door.

'Not interrupting am I?' he asked, pushing open the door and

71

walking in.

'Dazza mate, no, course not, good to see ya.'

'Hello Dazza,' Sharon said turning to him.

She made her excuses and left us together, 'I guess you guys'll have loads to talk about so I'll get off now then. See ya later.'

'OK love, see ya then,' I said as she leant over and kissed me.

'See ya Dazza.'

'See ya,' he grunted. 'Good looking bird that of yours,' he said to me approvingly as the door closed behind her, 'you're a lucky bastard really aren't ya mate?'

'Thanks, if you say so.'

He pulled up the chair that she had just vacated, sat down next to my bed, asked me how I was, and gave me the news of how it had panned out. The antis had lost of course, outnumbered there had been little doubt about how that would end. Gut and the rest had eventually all been hunted down and had the patches stripped off their backs. They had been forced to agree to disband their remnants of the club.

'But I'm not just here for that.'

I raised an eyebrow inquisitively. It was about the only bit of me that could move without hurting.

'Yeah. I need to clear some shit up with you. Stuff from way back when. It's stuff that we can't have in the way between us or hanging around going forwards.'

I tensed. I didn't know what was coming here. He could only be talking about when I'd gone clean five years ago. He sat calmly in his chair, as self-possessed and quietly menacing as ever with his dark charisma. I looked straight at him.

'Well I can guess what this is about.'

'Can you?' he smiled. 'It might not be what you think.'

'Look,' he leaned forwards, his voice dropping in tone, his eyes boring into me. 'You think I'm fucked off about you walking out on me back then after Gyppo snuffed it. Am I right?'

I met and held his gaze without flinching. Whatever was coming was coming and I would have to deal with it, whatever state I was in, hospital bed or no hospital bed. I shrugged. 'Yeah, I always wondered why you didn't give me more grief about it then. So what's up with it now?'

Was this payback time after all these years I wondered? Had he just used me to help achieve the deal, but now he wanted me out of the club as I wasn't into his stuff?

'Well, I've got news for you,' he said, 'Your going straight. I guess normally you'd be right. Normally no one walks out on me. But that one time it wasn't a problem. I had Billy and Sprog to take up your end, I knew you would keep your mouth shut. And hey, you'd decided what you wanted to do and you came right in to me at the pub and said it to my face with all my guys just next door. That took balls, you could have got well fucked over that day and you knew it, but you didn't give a fuck. You just came right in and did it and you didn't take any shit from anyone. Tell the truth, I wasn't keen on it at the time, but I can respect your decision and I respected the way you did it.'

'In fact now, it's not an issue at all. Now it's useful.'

'In a club like ours, we've got a lot of guys that are good with their fists. But not enough that are good with their heads the way you are. To really make it work we need both.'

'Because,' he said, relaxing back comfortably in his chair, 'once you're back on your feet I want you to do something for me.'

That had been a long speech for Dazza.

'What sort of something?' I asked. He must know that I didn't want to go back into the business again I thought. Not after all these years.

He settled even further back into his chair with a grin and folded his arms. What came next was an even greater surprise.

'I want you to be my financial advisor.'

'Your what?'

'My banker. It's what you do right isn't it? Look after peoples' investments for 'em?'

I just nodded.

'Well then mate, you've just got yerself a new client. I want you to look after my dosh for me.'

Why did the expression 'Oh Fuck' keep coming to me whenever Dazza appeared on the scene, I asked myself once he'd gone.

5   THE TAKEOVER

The guys had some group photos done with their new patches. I wasn't in it of course, I was still laid up in hospital, but I've still got my copies.

It was a happy, sunny day by the look of it and they are all drawn up in the clubhouse courtyard arms across each others' shoulders. From the upstairs windows someone had hung a huge Brethren club flag to act as a backdrop, a blood red rectangle with a white circle in the centre emblazoned with a stylised version of the club logo in stark black. There's two versions of the pictures, one from the front showing the grinning faces of the scurviest gang of thugs you wouldn't ever want to meet, and a back view, with so many guys that to get them all in there are two ranks of colours proudly showing, one standing, one kneeling.

So many faces, with, in the centre, flanked by Tiny and Butcher, Dazza and Polly, current president of The Freemen and so de facto head of The Brethren in the country. Polly was short and stocky, his face all straight lines, planes and angles, with not a curve to be seen, and wiry short silver-grey hair like a fresh brillo pad. He was there to welcome the new guys to the firm, and to take a good look over what The Brethren had just acquired.

So many faces, and so many that wouldn't make it.

It was like any other takeover I guess. Even while we were getting our new club tattoos, The Brethren, but in reality Dazza, were clearly both talent spotting and cleaning house right from the start.

By the time I got out of hospital Butcher's boys, the hatchet crew from Wearside, had been appointed Dazza's unofficial hit squad and personal bodyguard. There had been a couple of objections from some of the older fashioned die-hard Geordies in Newcastle but Dazza had soon used his new crew to silence dissent within the existing Brethren members. There had always been a difference between Dazza and the others. They were all Brethren of course, but Dazza always seemed part of an inner circle, almost a club within the club, I guess that was partly because he was coming close to joining The Freemen, but partly it was his air of self-control, his self-assurance, his watchfulness. Even at a party he was always serious,

74

maintaining a distance.

Then it had been the ex Legion's turn.

Dazza had been happy to take in the club and thereby to obtain the territory, but he clearly didn't have any personal loyalty to the club's individual members. We may have all come into The Brethren, but we certainly weren't all going to stay. If your face didn't fit, or if Dazza as judge and jury decided that you weren't going to make The Brethren grade, then you were soon going to be out. And you'd have one chance to remove your club tattoos before Butcher and his crew did it for you with a hatchet if you left in good standing. If you left in poor standing you didn't get the option.

I didn't like Butcher. I respected him, but I didn't like him, or his crew. He had the dangerous brittle intensity that seemed to mark the coke head and Christ he was a miserable fucking hardnosed prickly bastard. I remember we were riding once and there were some kids coming the other way. Bikers wave to each other, or nod or do something to acknowledge each other, it's us against the car drivers after all.

So I remember the first of these kids on their 250s or whatever they were, he lifted his arm in greeting as we approached.

And Butcher just looked straight ahead, blanked them completely from behind his wrap round shades. Apart, of course, for the one finger salute. It was so fucking funny to watch. What a complete and utter arsehole he was.

But I just thought, why the fuck did you have to do that? It had been a respectful enough greeting. If it hadn't been I'd have been with Butcher like a shot in pulling round, catching them up and giving the little wankers a good kicking. But it hadn't been. It hadn't been presumptuous, it had been civil, so what was the problem?

Don't get me wrong. I didn't think they had to like us, it wasn't anything like that. When you're in a club like ours you know you ain't going to be winning any popularity contests.

But so long as they feared us, that would suit me fine.

You never knew who might be useful at some point in the future. You can't control whether people like you and even if they do, you can't rely on them doing what you want them to because of it. People forget friendship and gratitude and all that shit really quickly when the chips are down.

But you sure as hell can control whether people fear you. And you can rely a lot more on people doing what you want them to if they're scared of you and the swift and sure retribution that will come their way if they fuck-up or wimp out.

But you can be feared without being hated, all you have to do is avoid unnecessarily disrespecting people or stealing their gear, and being hated can be dangerous. Someone who hates you will actively work against you.

So avoid being hated and you will stay feared but respected; and successful was my rule. Waste that respect by behaving like an arsehole the way Butcher did and all you do is breed resentment and hatred that can work against you.

And that was something Butcher never really got. That's why he was a tool. A good one and very useful to Dazza no doubt for some things, but one I recognised as ultimately disposable that could and would be sacrificed with impunity when it suited Dazza.

Mind you he had his funny side as well. Fat Mick had been moaning one evening in the bar about not having been made up before the vote the way Wibble had been. We've a strict rule about no fighting in the club house, you get fined. So Butcher just calmly reached into his pocket, took out his wallet and plonked his fifty quid on the bar. Then he turned round and just coldly smashed one straight into Fat Mick's face that took him completely by surprise and dropped him straight down to the ground where Butcher then launched in with a good kicking, stomping him good and proper for a few minutes, shouting all the time about how he was fed up with all Fat Mick's whining and moaning until Fat Mick was a bloody foetal ball that managed to roll out of reach under a table, while we all stood around with our beers in our hands and had a laugh or shouted encouragement.

A lot of the guys didn't get what was going on and why Dazza was doing this. Why go to so much trouble to bring in new members through the merger, only to then devastate the club he had taken over. And why push someone unpopular like Butcher to the top of the pile?

But to me it made perfect sense.

All the way back to the early days of The Reivers and then on through The Legion, we as a club had always been used to being free to run our own affairs, but life within The Brethren was going to be very different, at least to start with, and that could easily lead to serious problems.

So Dazza had to decide how he was going to hold onto the territory he'd just acquired for The Brethren.

The best thing he could do would probably be to get involved personally, to base himself at the clubhouse where he could be at the centre of what was going on, to be very visibly in charge. The problem was that this wasn't practical for him for a variety of reasons, not least that he needed to stay visible back in town.

So he had a choice, he could leave the club as it was, operating under Tiny as its local leader. But Dazza just couldn't take the risk. It wouldn't be taking control; it would leave the club and its ethos intact, under its old leader and so still a separate unit with the threat that it could, as a unit, go against him at some point in the future. You could see it happening; if there was ever a challenge coming out of the ex-Legion members in our area, it would be the spirit of independence and freedom that drove us.

So Tiny had always known his position would be the first casualty if the merger went ahead.

But it wasn't just Tiny as the figure-head. Dazza had to go further, to weaken the club, breaking it up to reduce its numbers, ruthlessly driving out any member who could be an opponent or didn't make the grade in terms of loyalty and attitude. After all, the surest way to ensure control over the patch would be to wipe out all the potential competition for it. But he knew that Tiny would never drive this through for him.

So his only option was to impose a new leadership who would weed out anyone whose face didn't fit or who was thought to be too soft for the new regime. But it had to be someone who was loyal to Dazza, who knew that their power only came from Dazza's support and who would fall without it. Someone then who would be ruthless and active in promoting Dazza's interests in everything they did for their own power and protection.

Butcher fitted the bill perfectly. Unpopular and a ruthless bastard. He would be ideal.

Funnily enough, Butcher's crew would be a very different story if it ever came to it. There was a charter run by a single dominating individual. If you took him out it would be easy to replace him with someone else that you imposed and expect the rest to follow as they were likely to find it difficult to chose one of themselves to take charge.

But even leaving aside the how he was going about it, I still didn't get the why, and that troubled me more.

I was still wondering what Dazza was up to and why The Brethren had gone to all the trouble to acquire The Legion? There was still no sign of war with The Rebels, no sign as yet of the expected Rebel takeover of The Hangmen that Dazza had used as the reason for pushing the patch over. So I still wondered whether this had just been an excuse to get The Legion in, and whether Dazza had some private motives of his own.

The question still bugged me. Why would Dazza feel he needed The Legion and our territory? Why had he been so particular about needing Westmorland? We had some small towns and an awful lot of empty moorland, holes or no holes, nothing surely to get excited about?

But as it happened I wasn't the only one who seemed concerned about how things were shaping up, although for different reasons.

After only a month or so in his new colours Billy was complaining, loudly. Surprise, surprise, things weren't working out the way he had expected and he was moaning to me about it.

'What's the point of taking us over if he doesn't want to exploit the territory? You know I thought that when we patched over it would be the big time man, that we would really start to roll, I thought it would be my chance to really start to earn but no, now I'm stuck with this shit.'

That was one of the problems that Dazza would be having now across the piece I guessed as I let the whining wash over me. It was as old as the hills really. He had used people like Billy as his route in to taking over The Legion and now they would be expecting it to be payback time. But the problem was he could never satisfy them, he would never be able to give them as good a deal as they would be looking for in return for the help that they had given him, so inevitably they would start to resent him. Funnily enough I thought that he had a better chance of winning over the guys who had been anti but that he hadn't needed to hurt. After all, they had gone into this with no expectations of him, no assumptions that there would be favours done for them, so all he had to do really was to leave them alone, to treat them OK and in time they would become reconciled to him.

Whereas Billy as a supporter was complaining about how difficult he was finding it to make his nut now and becoming resentful.

The message had come down from Dazza clearly enough. One of the reasons he had pushed for the takeover was that he wanted the space our territory could provide. Space in the open countryside so that he could organise things that were difficult to do in town. The long and the short of it was that we weren't great territory for selling gear. Billy's and the other guys' operations had always been relatively small time deals and a change of patch wasn't going to change that. It was just the law of supply and demand and out here in the sticks with small towns and villages the demand for Billy's gear was never going to grow that much, whatever colours he was wearing.

No, what Dazza wanted space for was production. Not sales.

So he set up the first skunk house we'd ever come across. I was impressed.

It was an old farm house and barn high up in the valley. It was off grid, with an old lorry engine to drive a generator, liveable but a bit tumbledown and he was able to pick it up for a song with me arranging the mortgage for him. He staffed it with a bunch of Vietnamese guys who came up from down south somewhere who immediately got to work ripping out everything they didn't need. A couple of The Brethren took it in shifts living up there for a week at a time with a slick back tagalong to front for them, get the shopping in and stuff. He put out the story locally that the Vietnamese were builders brought in to do renovations working for the owners. They even used a battered white Transit van with a building firm logo on the side.

They insulated the house like you wouldn't believe. I've never seen so much Rockwool go up in a loft as these guys used. They

79

sealed up the windows and the doors until the place was tight as a drum. Then they rigged all of the rooms out with heaters, high intensity lights and hydroponic growing gear and installed an extra pair of 2,000 litre oil tanks out at the back to feed a massive new genny. This place was going to take a lot of power, they always did and it was one of the things that sometimes gave them away in town. But out here we made our own power. All we needed was an oil delivery company that would keep the red diesel flowing without asking too many questions, and so he also arranged to buy into Pogle's oil delivery business which meant a steady flow and a nice fat margin for Pogle of course.

And how did I know? Well it was because I was handling the money side for him. Buying up the properties, organising the companies.

From what he was asking me to do about placing orders in Oz I guessed he was in the process of setting up a Meth factory as well. I really doubted that he wanted to get into the canned peach importation business just for his health. My guess from what I knew about the Meth scene in Oz was that that was how he was planning to bring in the precursor chemicals. That, after all was one of the advantages of being part of an international organisation like The Brethren, those overseas contacts you could make at the annual world run, or the deals you could tie up through trusted intermediaries. And it would make sense to stick a factory out here in the countryside 'cos making that stuff stank to high heaven.

So with so much at stake on getting the production side up and running, Dazza wanted things kept quiet. He wanted to protect his new investments, to get them earning, so the last thing he wanted was any local trouble that might blow up in his face. In fact he could afford to lose sales locally by letting things wind down because he would make much more from wholesaling the product elsewhere. And that was hurting Billy and some of the others as they relied on local sales for their living.

'Well it's OK for Dazza, but how the fuck am I supposed to earn?'

So was that it? Just a need to control the guys and control the territory to have his factories? No I still just didn't buy it. He could have subbed a lot of that work out to the guys even if they were still

Legion patched. In fact it might even have suited him better to do it that way as it would have provided him with more of a cut-out, a deniability if it all ever went tits up.

'Why don't you ask him?

'Are you fucking kidding me?

'OK, I'll ask him.'

*

My chance came the following week.

Dazza had bought me a bike as a getting out of hospital present to replace the one I'd lost to Gut and his spanners and he organised a party to present it to me.

Like most of us I had a few bikes on the go at any time. For club runs and full dress business I had my Harley of course. It wasn't exactly in the club rules that you had to have one but it was pretty much expected. There comes a time in a man's life, for me it was aged about twenty-five, when a man needs a Harley, a man's bike.

Mine was a customised fat bob.

To me a bike has to be rideable. Choppers didn't get much coverage in *Bike* or *Superbike* as I was growing up and when they did they tended towards the baroque, all twisted steel springer forks and diamond coffin shaped tanks. For custom gear I had to buy copies of the American mag *Easyriders* as and when I could find them, and then *BSH* when it started. And over time my ideas about customising matured. Bikes are functional objects and for me their purest beauty lies in stripping them down to their purest practical elements. So that's what I think chopping should be about. I appreciate the artistry and work that goes into some of the more extreme choppers, but to me anything with over-lavish or intricate artwork or ornamentation misses the point, as does anything that takes the design elements to such extremes that they have compromised the purpose of the bike.

But it's a personal choice. A man has to build the type of bike he wants, it's the greatest expression of who you are, your personal design sense, your aesthetic. And some of the more extreme bikes are awesome works of mechanical sculpture, there's no doubt about it. Some are works of artistic genius, some can take your breath away or make you think about bike design in a whole new way. But sticking on a hardtail, a tombstone tail light, sissy bar and a pair of six inch over forks don't automatically create a work of biking art.

So it had to be a bike that rides.

I like the elegance of the 1950s Harleys, with their diamond shaped frame showing their bicycle heritage. The seventy-four inchers are also big brutes. From in front or behind you can always tell a Harley, even without the noise, just from the set of it on the road, the heft of the gearbox with its primary drive on the left, so that sense of massiveness is crucial to the bike's identity.

Bikes are also a bit of an iron horse, they're meant to have curves, so the shape of the seat, the depth of the mudguard over the back wheel, the thickness of the front tyre and the fullness of the tank are all important to the look.

And I like a clean look, with wires enclosed, nothing unnecessary showing, nothing flash or fancy. Attention to details, that's what gets the effect, the look.

So my personal choice is for a bobber type look, very much like a 50s bike, but stripped down and tidied up so as to be the core of what it is, white wall tyres, fatbob tanks, foot boards, a pair of cruiser bars.

But I was also into Jap muscle bikes.

There was no club rule against Jap bikes. Sure there were some hard cases who were dead anti. Guys of the 'Harley is the only bike' mindset, but for reliability and practicality you couldn't beat the UJMs. But they had to be real bikes, a basic frame, big engine, no crap. Anyone turning up on some spastic plastic Jap crotch rocket or dresser cruiser would certainly be in for a hard time.

For long distance fast motorway work I had kept a kwacker Z1300, a massive water-cooled wall of six cylinders under a brutal slab-sided tank. A big bulky bike, it was almost completely stock other than a paint job on the tank of Muttley.

For fun I had bought one of the old red and black CBX750s. In contrast to the Z it was slim and light, feeling more like a two-fifty to chuck around than a big bike. It was a bit of a toy, a bit of fun, not the sort of thing on which you would wear your colours when riding and I'd had a *Flying Tigers* paint job done on it, with shark's teeth along the bottom of the half fairing. That was the bike I'd lost to Gut's spanners. I guess that the red and black meant that it was Menace colours hadn't helped Gut's mood when I'd pitched up on it that evening.

And then there was my other love, *Ohka*.

White and pink delicately translucent petals of the sacred falling *Cherry Blossom* that never returns, were airbrushed onto the silver tank with its massive air scoops down either side, over a precisely inked thin technical drawing style plan showing the top and side views of a small single seater, straight winged aeroplane, the cockpit a greenhouse dome sitting squarely and uprightly amidships along the slim torpedo like body, twin tail fins at the end of a boom like tail plane leaving space clear at the end for three nozzle exhausts.

Naming a brutal single purpose bike like the four cylinder 1400cc V-Max after a Japanese piloted rocket powered flying bomb, the ultimate Kamikaze machine from the dying stages of World War II seemed apt somehow for the street dragster, the fastest accelerating, street legal production vehicle in the world when it was launched on an unsuspecting biking public. The top monster of its time, it was hellishly fast in a straight line, but didn't really do corners.

I loved it, even as I wrestled with it and it tried to kill me on the bends. It was a monstrous bastard that took brute force to control and quite often scared the shit out of me.

And now Dazza had bought me a Wing, an 1100, one of the last of the naked ones. All low down torque, 'Cos I know you like a good shaft up the back!' he pronounced to generally hilarity. He was right, I did. Plenty of grunt and the low centre of gravity meant that on a Wing and with a bit of attitude you could quite often surprise a few people about how fast you could hustle it along.

'Yeah, just so long as there's a black rubber at the end of it!' I joked back, I was really touched. I hadn't been expecting this, he hadn't needed to do it. 'Hey that's just really great,' I said, 'Thanks Dazza!' opening my arms for a hugged embrace.

And I really meant it. I was touched. And as I was now a Menace I had already decided that there was no other choice as since I already had a Muttley, this bike was going to have to be a Gnasher.

*

I waited until we were into our beers before I picked my moment to ask about Billy.

Dazza was sat on his bike while I stood next to him. He wasn't very sympathetic I have to say.

'Billy just needs to do what he's told. This is just a case of making the most of opportunities, it's nothing personal about him, it's just business.'

'What if he looks for other gear to deal instead?'

Dazza snorted at the thought of that. 'Come on, where else is he going to buy stuff from apart from me? How's he going to find another supplier? We don't exactly advertise do we? Someone that he knows he can trust isn't going to be a nark?'

'So you're not worried?'

'Nah. It's always the same. I've had this sort of shit over the years, people whingeing on that they don't like my product, that it's too cut, that they're going to find someone else. Well fuck 'em I say. They always come crawling back in the end.' He took another swig of his beer, 'makes me laugh sometimes really, how're they going to know it's poor or too cut? This crap people see in the films about testing gear and finding it's ninety-nine percent pure. It's just bollocks mate. Look at Billy for example. Whizzo couldn't pass woodwork let alone fucking chemistry, so how's he gonna know that what he gets from anyone else is any better? My stuff's too expensive? Well tough, just pass it on, like it or lump it. And they always lump it. Because in the end they can't find anyone else.'

'OK, but what if they could?'

'And if he did find someone else well…' Dazza just shrugged and left it hanging for a moment, the conclusion was fairly obvious really, 'Bringing competition onto the patch is hardly a very loyal act for a brother is it? Particularly when he knows what we've all got at stake.'

Dazza finished his beer and looked down at the bottle for a moment before turning and chucking it over the wall into the field next door.

'Billy's got too much of a mouth on him at times.'

'Hey, what's the problem? He isn't talking to anyone else.'

'Security's the problem. This is business. He shouldn't be talking about this shit to anyone you arsehole, you included. Don't you get that? All this shit is supposed to be compartmentalised. That way no one knows the whole thing and we can keep it tight.'

'What's compartmentalised? He ain't talking out of turn. All he's

84

saying is that you don't want him dealing so how's he supposed to make his nut? He's just bellyaching that's all.'

'So Billy wants some action does he? Well I've got him some that can let him earn his nut.'

Dazza looked at me as if thinking for a moment, then turned to scan the crowd of guys enjoying the warm afternoon sunshine in the courtyard, and then he reached down to open one of the panniers he had slung over the back seat of his bike.

'Oi Billy,' he yelled, 'come over here!'

I hear you want a job? He asked when Billy had joined us. Billy's eyes flickered between us and he nodded, 'Yeah Dazza, that would be great…'

'OK, I need you to go to the post office for me,' said Dazza holding out a parcel wrapped in brown paper, 'Use somewhere discrete.'

'Er, sure Dazza,' said Billy doubtfully, 'but…'

'Just do it,' Dazza cut across him, 'and then we'll talk.'

I couldn't help noticing that it had a Glasgow address. That was odd. Who the fuck would Dazza know in Glasgow?

But I knew better than to ask. If it was Dazza's business it was Dazza's business.

6   THE PLAN

Dazza had asked me over to The Brethren's pub down by the docks to see him. When I arrived I found him as usual through in his booth in the quiet lounge bar at the back, while his praetorian guard were stood or sat around the pool table in the public bar out front.

Dazza was talking as I walked through into his inner sanctum. He was in a good mood.

'Yeah, just heard the stuff got through safely. I love it when a plan comes together. We'll need to mix it up of course, different types of packet, different addresses, different post offices or just post boxes would be best I guess. Around here and out of area.'

'OK.'

'So that's the next one to go,' Dazza said gesturing to another parcel on the table.

'Where to this time?' Billy asked.

'Wales boyo, not that it's any concern of yours, and Billy,' he added as Billy reached for it, 'Wear some fucking gloves for Chrissakes would ya? D'ya want your dabs all over it you twat?'

Billy looked sheepish at the rebuke.

'Here,' said Dazza indicating the empty counter as he stood up, 'Nick one of the bar towels for now.'

'So Damage, welcome to my office again!' he smiled, extending his hand in greeting, 'Long time since you've been in here eh?'

'Yeah,' I nodded, looking around the otherwise empty room, 'Not changed much I see,' I said, noticing the same sewn up ripped seats and even grubbier stained swirly patterned carpet that I had last seen that day five years or so ago after Gyppo's death. We'd run with and partied with The Brethren many times since but having been out of the business I'd not been back in here since. He met me half way across the room and we bear hugged a greeting. It's not a fag thing, it's just we're brothers. And if you're really paranoid like we got later it also gives you a bit of a chance to feel if the other guy's wearing a wire.

We stepped across to the bar where Billy leant over and began rummaging behind the pumps as Dazza continued to issue instructions, 'Take a drive. Make sure you can't be traced.'

The landlord appeared and handed over a couple of bottles and a dry towel before vanishing again back to the public side. Not that with a room full of patched Brethren playing pool all day, there was a lot of what you might call the general public frequenting the bar on any casual basis.

'I'll hire a car.'

'Make sure it's clean.'

'I'll get a girlfriend to organise it. No sweat.'

Billy always had a string of girlfriends on the go.

'OK,' said Dazza turning to me once Billy had disappeared out of the door with a Guinness towel wrapped package under his arm, 'That's got him organised at least. Now all we need is more stuff to move.'

We? More? I wondered.

Beers in hand Dazza waved me back over to his booth where we slid onto the benches and relaxed.

'OK,' I asked, having taken a swig, 'So what's up? I take it this was a business call?'

Dazza leant back in his seat across the table from me where he could face the door and see anyone who might come in while we were talking, draping his free arm across the back of the bench while his right-hand gripped his bottle of beer on the table.

'What?' he exclaimed in mock disbelief, 'You mean to say that you don't think I'd just ask you over for a drink and a bit of fun? I'm truly, truly hurt.'

I laughed at his wounded expression and took another pull on my bottle. He cracked me up sometimes.

'Come on Dazza, pull the other one! It's me here not some fucking newbie. Don't forget I know you mate!'

He gave a wry smile. 'Yeah you're right, you got me. It's business. Now that it's over it's time to get to work.'

I shrugged back, 'Don't expect anything else mate after all these years. Anyway, what can I do for you?'

'D'ya remember that chat we had when you were laid up? You know, when you were in hospital.'

'What about it?'

'And what I wanted you to do for me?'

87

'Yeah.'

'Well, I need to talk to you about getting that going.'

'OK,' I shrugged, 'So what do you want me to do?'

'I need you to handle some money for me.'

'Clean or dirty?'

'Dirty.'

'OK,' I made a show of thinking about it, 'Well it could be difficult, but I've got some ideas.'

'I don't care how you do it so long as it works.'

'So how much are we talking about?'

'If things work out right, a fuck of a lot.'

'Thousands?'

'And more if we keep our shit together.'

'Cash cash, or just money?'

'What d'ya mean "just money"?'

'Bank transfers, cheques, that sort of thing, as opposed to real cash, notes and coins.'

He thought about this for a moment. 'Mostly money I guess, rather than cash then although there could be some of that as well.'

'Lumpy or steady streams?'

'Mostly lumps, although we might set some up as regular payments in on the drip.'

I nodded and put my empty beer bottle down on the table.

'OK, I'll see what I can do. I might need some seed money first though to set it up.'

'Much?'

'Nah. A few hundred I guess in the first instance, if that. Certainly no more than a grand.'

'That's no problem. I can stake that easy.'

'It'll also cost you though,' I warned him, 'banks and stuff. They'll all want to take their cut on moving money around. You won't get back everything you put in by the time it's been round the system enough times. Are you up for that?'

'Well it's a cost of doing business I guess. Just try and keep it to a minimum will ya?'

'Sure, don't want no fucking bankers making a mint on your dosh do we?'

'No we fucking don't!'

Given what he'd said before, what he was asking didn't come as a complete surprise other than that he seemed to be expecting to be handling some big numbers. To tell the truth I'd been giving it some thought ever since our first conversation back in the hospital, so I had some ideas already.

There were three problems as I saw it which basically were in, fuck it all about and out.

Firstly there was getting money into the banking system in a way that didn't arouse suspicion. For that I would need to open bank accounts, and the more of them the better, so that whatever was coming in could be spread around, and ideally those where money coming in wouldn't arouse suspicion. They could be a mixture of types. If I had some in the names of individuals, if we had some cash coming regularly on a monthly basis, that could be made to look like salaries going in. Then if I arranged some business accounts as well, lumpier receipts would just look like customers paying their bills. If we were going to be dealing with some real cash, then having some business accounts that you expect to have cash bankings, like a shop, a pub or even better a bookies, would be a good idea to cover this sort of stuff coming in.

But I had to come up with a way to get this organised whist minimising my tracks.

'So speaking of costs, what's in it for me?'

'Sure, we all gotta eat, I know that. I was thinking a percentage of what comes back clean?'

That made sense. It incentivised me to make it happen at the least cost.

'OK, that works for me in principle. So how much are we talking?'

'Ten percent to make it worth your while?'

I nodded.

'But it's on one condition,' he said.

'Which is?'

'If you do this then you're the banker, which means that you need to be clean. So I don't want your hands in anything dirty.'

'That's OK by me.'

'I guessed it would be, it's one of the reasons I asked you. So do we have a deal?'

'OK brother,' we shook on it like real businessmen, 'you're on.'

*

This was where my IFA business came in handy.

The following week with some of Dazza's seed cash I arranged to rent a flat in town in the name of one of my clients. Then as the new tenant, I called up the water board, the electric, the gas and the phone company and arranged supplies, only each time I called I used the names of a different client from whom I already had a signed authorisation to act on their behalf. So now I had an address with five different clients that I could soon prove lived there and I could go to work.

Dressed in my suit I went into five different banks across town that Friday and filled out application forms for accounts on behalf of my clients. Obviously I had their letter of authorisation to act on their behalf and from my records I had their prior address history where the bank forms wanted that. Since I was an IFA advising on mortgages and stuff no one in any of the banks ever thought it was odd that the clients that I was opening an account for had a different address from the one that was on my letter of authority. And when anyone did ask I just explained that this was their new place for which I had organised a mortgage.

And so by close of play on Friday I had ten accounts in the process of being opened, since each of my clients needed a deposit account as well as a current account. And of course they might then need accounts at another bank as well.

It worked beautifully.

Even later, when opening bank accounts became a bit more difficult with all the money laundering identification crap, the system still worked. Again with my IFA business, every time I advised somebody I had to collect all the know your client crap anyway, which included photocopies of passports as proof of ID, as well as photocopies of utility bills as proof of address.

So with the letter of authorisation that my clients signed to allow me to work on their behalf, opening some new bank accounts was still relatively simple. I continued to spread it around of course. Many of the local bankers were used to dealing with me, after all, I'd been doing this stuff for clients for years. I was also an IFA, so they were happy to trust photocopies of ID documentation where I had certified them as having seen the originals, they knew that customers wanted to hold onto their passports for obvious reasons. So a certified copy was fine, particularly when backed up by an original utility bill as proof of address.

Later on, I also started to ring the changes every so often, having Mr Bloggs move out, to allow Mr Smith to take over the lease so I could get even more people out of the same address. Of course I didn't want to do it too often, but as it grew I was ending up with around half a dozen names registered over time at each flat, which gave plenty of scope to open multiple accounts. You just had to do the maths and multiply it by the number of flats we had on the go to see how many accounts I had to play with.

I could actually have done more, I could have photocopied utility statements and overprinted them with new names to get more out of each flat, but the mix of photocopied passport and real utility bills was working well so why risk it by some cheap forgery? I could open enough accounts as it was and could always carry on doing so if we needed to. Besides, pretty soon Dazza was looking to get into property in a big way so eventually we became our own landlords, which was useful as it then started to give Dazza a legitimate source of income.

The same thing applied to companies. I bought them off-the-shelf, appointing Mr Bloggs and Mr Smith as directors and used one of our flats as the registered office. Then it was simple to open business bank accounts, and again once the money laundering regulations and the need for know your client identification documentation came in, I could use the same stuff used to open their personal accounts to vouch for their existence as directors and shareholders.

A couple of weeks later the banks' welcoming crap started to arrive at the flat so now I knew that I had some accounts opened.

'OK, we're up and running,' I reported to Dazza in early July.

'Great.'

'So what do we do now?'

'Now? Now we take a trip.'

He caught me in mid drink with, 'Have you got any golf clubs?'

and I laughed so hard I choked and I had the stinging sensation as the beer came back out through my nose. Fuck I was still laughing and gasping for breath as with an unsteady hand I plonked my bottle down on the table and wiping my eyes and my mouth with the back of my sleeve I tried to get my breath back.

'You cunt!' I gasped, 'Of course I haven't got any fucking golf clubs.'

'Here's some cash,' he said getting out a roll and peeling off some notes, 'go into town this weekend and get yourself a set.' My laughter died away. He was serious. 'Get some golfing type gear as well if you haven't got any.'

'Golfing type gear?' I wondered out loud.

'Yeah, casual stuff, polo shirts, that sort of crap,' he said offhandedly, 'Passport up to date?'

I nodded, taking the proffered cash.

'Good. Get some more accounts opened over the next week or so and I'll make the arrangements.'

'What arrangements?'

'We're off on a little holiday, in a fortnight's time I guess. We'll be gone for about a week.'

'Gone for a week? A week where?'

'Algarve I think. Should be nice there this time of year.'

And that was all he would say. I knew he didn't do things without a reason, but what the fuck was he up to now I wondered? And where the fuck did you go to buy 'golf type gear'?

He wasn't going to expect me to play for fuck's sake, was he?

*

I repeated the operation twice the following week and soon the bank details were flooding in.

So now I could get Dazza's contacts to deposit money into a whole range of different accounts, in different names. It was all done by telephone in the early days once Dazza told me who to ask for what, but later I switched to doing it all through anonymous hotmail accounts, just by sending them an e-mail with the details. All I had to do was check the balances in the accounts to see if the cash had come in when and where it was expected. Once it was in I could let Dazza know so he could get organised whatever it was he needed to and I could even confirm receipt back to the same number or to the same e-mail account.

The second problem, once the money was in the banking system, was fucking it about, arranging to hide it so that it couldn't be traced.

That actually wasn't so very difficult.

The key here was to simply move it around a lot which again came down to accounts. Moving cash from one account to another was a relatively quick operation, even in those days, and even overseas and back again. So with the cash in the bank I might split it up and transfer it to a whole range of other accounts in different banks, in different amounts, perhaps in different currencies, perhaps even in different countries by the time I got sophisticated about it. So now if the plod wanted to try and trace it they had to get access to the first account, which would take them time and court orders, only to find that they then needed to get access to the whole range of other accounts, which again would take them yet more time and yet more money and court orders, here and overseas or wherever; if they could get them overseas, knowing that by the time they got these the cash would be long gone, the electronic trails of criss-crossing payments and money orders spreading far and wide around the world in ever increasing numbers of jumps ahead of them.

Of course it could all be traced eventually if the plod had enough time, effort and resources to throw at it, but 'if' was the key. If you had enough accounts and places to put it you could leave such a confusing and difficult to follow trail that it would take them years to unravel. And the plod were never going to have the time for that.

So I always used some accounts only for money coming in and I kept others only for where Dazza wanted to have money coming out. The others were the money stream, just used for transferring funds in and out and around to hide the trail, cash being split up, sent in different directions, rejoining, jumping from account to account, country to country. A dividing winding silver stream of electronic cash, flowing in all directions, impossible to track.

But having cash and making it untraceable was one thing. Then you had to do something with it.

And as I got more into it, I became more successful in finding places to hide it. Everybody's heard of numbered Swiss bank accounts, and they're OK, but Liechtenstein's are better. But then I found that I could register a trust in Jersey which was completely confidential, much more secret than any Swiss bank account. I could deposit stuff in there and no one was ever going to be able to find out about it. And what's more, they were completely reversible so I could wind them up anytime I wanted, and just pull the stuff back out whenever I wanted to send the cash back on its way in its merry dance.

Then there were the safe-deposit boxes filled with cash or stones.

Then I would use the same ID documentation to open investment accounts, some funds were noticeably less fussy than others in wanting to check details and asking where the money was coming from. Pretty soon I had built up quite a network of accounts with investment firms who took cash on a very few questions asked basis. There was so much of it coming in that I didn't have time to manage it all so why not trust the professionals, I thought? After all, it's their job.

Pretty soon layering had started to become an increasingly full-time job.

We were building something fantastic here.

But there was still the third problem.

How do you get it back out again?

Well as far as possible I guess the answer is that you don't. The last thing you want to do is draw the plod's attention to you by having a whole load of cash that you can't explain, and Dazza was far too fly to make that sort of mistake.

Of course not all of the money that went in was pure profit. Dazza also had his costs to meet to his suppliers which was where some of the money danced away overseas. But even so there was a lot sticking to the sides right from the start as we got going. He was also quite happy to have the money working for him within the system or as investments. Dazza was a bit of an aesthete in some ways. He lived in a modest house a bit out of town and spent most of his time when he wasn't out on a run or at a party in his office at the pub, so it wasn't as though he had a particularly flash lifestyle that he wanted to fund. To a large degree he was happy to leave the cash in the system until I could find ways to diversify it out into investments in legitimate businesses or property. He was particularly keen to get some in South Africa for some reason, I arranged to buy a ranch for him out there through one of our dummy companies. I think he was planning on that as his retirement home.

Anyway the whole arrangement suited me.

I regarded it as good insurance. I was the money man. I knew where it all was and how to access it. Without me much of it would be lost so Dazza couldn't afford to lose me I reckoned. Not that I thought he would want to you understand, but it's always best to have some kind of back up.

And of course if he didn't know where it was, then there was no way he could keep tabs on whether it was all there or not, which was always handy if you were a bit careful.

*

Dazza called about the trip a fortnight later.

'Hi, how ya doing?' he asked.

'OK.'

'Good.'

'Where are you off to?' asked Sharon as I put the phone down. Cautious as ever Dazza hadn't really said much on the line. Just that it was on and the date.

'Somewhere called the Algarve apparently,' I told her.

'That's in Spain isn't it?'

'No, Portugal I think.'

'Can I come?'

'No, this is a Dazza thing. He just wants me along.'

'Why?

'Fucked if I know,' I said shrugging my shoulders, 'I just hope it's not to play fucking golf.'

'Not with Dazza it won't be,' said Sharon, 'it'll be business. That's all he ever does.'

'That's true.'

Even so I did have to wonder as we got off the plane and swanned through customs. Why were we here? Dressed like a couple of plonkers.

We checked into our business class hotel and met back downstairs in the bar for a beer.

'So what d'ya think,' asked Dazza as we wandered to a table on the outside terrace, 'eat here this evening or wander into town?'

I shrugged, 'Not fussed, whatever you want to do. I'm more interested in knowing what we're doing here and what this is all about?'

'Hey relax bro, all in good time.' He took a long satisfied drag on his cold beer and lounged back into his chair. 'You need to cool it OK? Just think for a moment what we've got here and how it looks. Here we are, just two ordinary guys as everyone can see, smart casuals, nothing unusual, we've obviously just slipped off the leash from the old dears at home for a week of sun and sangria or whatever the shit is. We've even brought a set of fucking golf clubs each, we're probably going to get a few rounds in. What could be more normal?'

'So this is what? Fucking cover? We're into spy shit now?'

'No, just good business. And sometimes for business you have to dress the part.' He finished his beer, 'Be patient, you'll see. Now, where do you fancy eating tonight. I'm told there's an English pub in town that does good fish and chips. Fancy it?'

We had a leisurely breakfast and sat around the next morning. I think Dazza was waiting for something but he didn't say what. I found that the hotel had access to a clay pigeon range just outside of town so we spent the afternoon with some shotguns blasting away. It was good practise, you never knew when it might come in handy.

We ate out again that night and had some beers. But mindful this was business we kept our heads, nothing too wild.

The next morning Dazza was in conversation at reception as I came down for breakfast.

'What's up?' I asked joining him.

'We're on,' he said, 'I'm just booking a room.'

'OK.'

I still didn't have a clue what we were doing here.

Dazza's contact arrived at about three in the afternoon. Burly guy, smartly dressed, Dazza met him at reception and they shook hands before heading off across the lobby to one of the hotel's little meeting rooms which Dazza had booked that morning.

As the door shut, I stayed sat in reception, a coffee on the table in front of me as I settled down to read the English language paper while

I kept an eye on the door for interruptions.

Dazza was in there for about an hour or so while I wondered why he had wanted me along? If it was just to have a bodyguard why not bring Butcher or one of his crew instead of leaving him in charge back home the way he had.

Then the door opened and Dazza reappeared, waving me over to join them.

Stepping into the room I could see that Dazza had been using the whiteboard. There was some stuff on it that the other guy was in the process of wiping off.

Dazza made the introductions as the big man turned to face us, 'Damage, this is Sergei; Sergei, Damage.'

'Hi, please to meet you,' he said in a heavy, almost comic book Russian accent.

'Hi.'

So it was business, hence the whiteboard. Dazza was obviously being extra careful. He'd only booked the room that morning and we didn't think anyone would know we were here so the chances of our or any local plod having bugged the room were remote, they just wouldn't have had time. But even so Dazza wasn't taking any chances. Plod couldn't bug a whiteboard for sound so it made for a safe way to 'talk' business.

Sergei turned back to the whiteboard and picked up a pen. 'OK,' he said starting to write, 'please excuse my English.'

I shrugged as I watched what he was writing. 'Don't worry about it mate, beats my Russian any day.'

Dazza looked pissed at that and held his finger to his lips. Now who needed to cool it I wondered, turning back to the board.

It was clear now at least why Dazza had wanted me along and why he'd brought me into the meeting. He and Sergei had obviously concluded their business and reached some kind of agreement whatever it was about. Now they needed to set up how payments were going to be made, which was my department.

Over the next half an hour or so, with a great swapping of marker pens back and forth between the three of us we worked out in more or less silence how we would organise it until Sergei eventually said, 'Is OK now?'

I stood back and looked at what we had written, arms folded, tapping the top of the pen against my chin as I thought it through. I knew we had to get this right now. You never knew how difficult meeting up to change it or deal with any subsequent fuck-ups could be. It was quite straightforward I decided, I couldn't see any reason why any of it would be a problem.

'OK, it works,' I pronounced.

'Sure?' asked Dazza.

'Yeah, I'm sure.'

'Great,' he said, clapping me on the back. 'That's good to hear. OK Sergei?'

'OK,' said Sergei, staring at the board with a cloth in his hand, as if to make sure he took it all in before he erased it.

Dazza wasn't here to socialise. Sergei didn't join us for dinner.

We ate out again, different place, table in the open. It felt pretty secure. 'How d'you know the Ruski? They're not Brethren are they?' I asked quietly.

For once Dazza seemed quite talkative. 'No. An outfit called The Wolfpack. Sergei was at the European run last year tagging along as one of their reps with the Krauts who are sponsoring them. They're trying out, looking for the charter for Russia and Trans-Dneiper, they know how the game's played. They need to show some class, need to get to know all the other charters and they need to show that they've got something to bring to the party.'

'So that's what's in it for them. Fair enough.'

'And the dosh of course.'

'Of course.'

'That's something I need to talk to you about. How we organise it our end.'

The next day was in many ways a repeat of the last.

As far as I was concerned it was the same deal. Dazza booked a room, a different one this time but still just off the lobby and I stayed out in the bar having a morning coffee and reading the previous day's paper as Dazza's next contact arrived.

Again Dazza waved me in after about an hour to meet a guy he introduced as 'Luis'.

Luis, if that was his name, was quite a contrast to Sergei. Short and slight with round glasses, wavy hair and a friendly grin, dressed in his civvies you wouldn't look at him twice. You certainly wouldn't have him pegged as the Pres of the local Brethren charter. But once you began to speak to him you quite quickly changed your mind. Luis was sharp, very sharp, and beneath that friendly tone, every so often a harder edge showed through.

They were talking as I reached the door so I overhead a snatch of the conversation before Dazza turned to make the introductions.

'Will it work?'

'It should do, my contact's very confident. He says that the guys he will be using were the ones that used to drop for the *spetsnaz*. Anyway what do you care? The first is a test with his gear, not yours. It's only the real thing after that.'

'At your risk,' Luis noted quickly.

'Sure, at my risk.'

'OK. As you say, it's at your risk,' said Luis, turning to greet me, 'I have my money, why should I worry?'

As before it was whiteboard work. But having gone through the process with Sergei yesterday it was quicker this time, even though whatever Dazza was going to be up to with Luis seemed as though it was going to be a bit more complicated than whatever deal he had going with Sergei.

Luis was talking about arranging schedules of payments. He wanted to know how quickly I could get access to and move sizable sums of cash. 'After all,' he said writing *we appreciate it takes time to move cash* on the board in not only excellent English but almost copperplate penmanship to finish his thought, 'we have to be realistic and practical.'

'Agreed,' growled Dazza.

I proposed that we set the payments up as trading between companies. All the normal stuff of importing and exporting, invoices, remittance advices, all that sort of straight up paperwork. At our end we could use a series of companies registered in the ever willing names of my clients at our rented addresses. From what Dazza and Luis were saying there wouldn't be that many transactions a year so if we spread them around the patch and broke the payments down into a variety of transactions they ought to pass largely unnoticed. What's more I'd arrange to have the companies liquidated every so often, solvently, so there was no fuss, no investigation, they would simply shut up shop and disappear so by the time anyone came looking they would be long gone, dead and buried, the trail gone cold.

That worked for Luis. He had trading companies he could use as fronts as well and it seemed that whatever plan Dazza and he had cooked up would involve some real trade as well which would help cover their tracks.

As with Sergei, this was obviously intended as far as possible to be a one-off meeting so again we sorted out communications as well.

Damage here is going to act as my front man on this. He handles all the money side of things, Dazza wrote. *You contact him or me direct on that but no one else.*

'That's OK, we understand.'

And operations? wrote Luis.

'Me.'

At first it was by telephone. Dazza had brought a list of phone box numbers. Of course we had phone lines in all of the flats but we didn't want to compromise them, so I had also arranged to rent a flat specifically to give us a phone to use just for this with no bank accounts attached to it. There was an answering machine that Luis could leave a message on when he wanted to talk to us, just a time and a code word to indicate which phone he was going to call us on. He would set up something similar his end.

Later, when we got tecchie, we moved to dummy Hotmail accounts which were great. Once you both had the password you didn't even need to send an email and run the risk of it getting intercepted by the plod. You just opened up the account, typed in a draft and left it for the other guy to read and reply to with his own draft. With the number of internet cafés around, not to mention the wonderful facilities provided to me as a resident by our local library service, I could ring the changes on where I accessed it from as well just to keep secure.

'Now what?' I asked as we sat in the bar later that evening having said our goodbyes to Luis.

'Now? Nothing. That's it, all done.'

'So what do we do now?'

'Kick back, relax, have some beers by the pool, chase some skirt if you want to. What am I? Your holiday rep? What the fuck do I care what you do? Just enjoy the rest of your holiday. We've got to do the rest of the week so just get into it. Tell you what, d'ya fancy doing the shotgun thing again tomorrow? It was a blast!'

It was weak but I still laughed.

And so we did. Christ Dazza even insisted we played a round of fucking golf on the Friday. I don't think it was completely for cover either. He could actually hit the fucking ball which was more than I could.

Dazza said I ought to learn. It would come in handy if I ever retired to Spain.

7   THE DROP

We got back to a crisis. Tiny was dead. And that was hard to take.

It hadn't been easy for me to make a choice when it had come to the vote, so I knew it would have been much harder for Tiny. OK, so we had partied with The Brethren over the years, gone on runs with them, hosted them at our clubhouse and at our bike show. But still Tiny didn't really know them, and Dazza in particular, the way that I did. After all, I knew Dazza from before, not only as someone to party with but as someone to do business with from my days of dealing with Gyppo, in a way that Tiny didn't.

And then again I didn't really have any position to lose in what would obviously be a new regime. OK, so I was road captain, but to be frank, given the hassle and the need to stay clean it wasn't a job that many guys wanted. Me, I could take it or leave it, so I wasn't too fussed either way.

But Tiny, like I said before, back then Tiny had been the P. If we went into The Brethren Tiny knew there would be only one P of the charter, and that would be Dazza. Tiny would be giving up a lot to go in.

But fuck it. He had taken a view and he had gone for it. Leaving aside his own personal position and interests he had voted the way a leader should, he had voted in what he saw as the best interests of the club. You had to respect the man for that.

And now he'd left behind a family; his wife, two kids and Jane, his righteous girlfriend.

*

I arranged to meet Billy at the clubhouse and leave my bike there. Billy had bought himself a big fuck off four-by-four, a top of the range Landcruiser and gave me a lift over to Tiny's place to see Sally and the kids. I got the impression that he hadn't wanted to run the risk of visiting alone. I didn't know why.

I soon found out.

I had wanted to go round, to offer some comfort, to let her know that we, the club, would look after her.

But she was distraught. She wouldn't listen. Kept cursing out the club and all it had done. It was as though she blamed us for what had happened. She screamed at us to get out, that she didn't want our dirty money. And that set the kids off too. Her folks arrived and we just didn't need the noise or the grief.

'Fuck it,' I said to Billy, 'Let's go.'

We sat largely in silence in the car on the way back. We couldn't say too much there obviously. Unlike the clubhouse which only people we knew visited, and which we swept for bugs regularly, you never knew whether somewhere like the car was secure. So I only spoke once he'd parked up again out front of the clubhouse and we were out of the car. It didn't seem like a conversation for inside either.

'So,' I demanded, 'something's up, isn't it?'

Billy looked away nervously.

'What's going on?' I insisted.

'I don't know, but I'm worried.'

'About what?'

Billy just shrugged.

'OK then, if you don't want to tell me you don't. Just don't come crying to me whenever it gets to be a problem.'

'I won't.'

'You fucking will, you always do. You know you do.'

'Yeah, suppose so,' he said sheepishly.

'Still, I always was the brains of the outfit,' I smiled. Another little victory. They all mounted up over the years.

'Yeah, but don't forget I'm the good looking one.'

'If you say so!' I laughed, changing the subject, 'So I've been meaning to ask, how are you getting on?'

'With what?'

'With the Dazza shit.'

'OK, but fuck it's some heavy stuff.'

'What stuff?'

'I can't tell anyone. Not even you man.'

*

We had a drink back at the club and Billy did a line. He offered me one and I shook my head, 'Not now mate, want to keep my head clear.'

'Well want a wrap to go for later then?'

103

'Yeah, that would be good, thanks,' I said taking the proffered small square of folded paper.

I left the question lingering unasked in the air between us as I tucked the tiny package into the pocket of my cut off until Billy waved his hand and said, 'Hey no charge mate, on the house.'

I nodded in acknowledgement. 'Thanks mate, I'll be getting back now, Shaz'll have dinner on the go. Fancy some?'

'Nah, I'm OK, I'm gonna call in on that new bird of mine in town. We'll probably hit the Chinky.'

'OK then, look after yourself.'

'And you.'

*

They were waiting for me as I rode through the village. The car parked down a side road, a dead end that slanted up from down by the river so that they could pull out behind me easily. As I sped past, leaning into the bend by the village green and setting myself up for the acceleration up onto the dark straight out and into the countryside again I clocked the headlights coming on in my mirror, followed a few seconds later by the flash of blues.

Shit.

I screwed the throttle on and tucked forward onto the bars as the bike leapt ahead. They would never catch me on the straight and I could make some space for myself as I thought furiously. I was carrying that wrap of Billy's.

Well Dazza, there's clean and then there's 'clean' I thought. But even at just a single wrap, I still couldn't afford to get caught with it.

On the bike I was confident I could outrun them for a while. They were making speed behind me so it wasn't a normal plod patrol. I think I would have spotted sarni stripes as I came past the turning so I guessed this was an unmarked box and they tended to be larger, faster, more serious motors. Losing that might be more difficult, but not impossible. I had been riding these roads for years, I knew every bend and every turn, and that, as the wind whistled past my head and my vision focused on the rushing circle of light and surrounding darkness streaming past me like a demented road movie on speed, was standing me in good stead now, even if I wasn't losing them fast enough behind me in the curves for my liking. Even so, there weren't that many alternative routes and doubtless they'd be on their squawk boxes already asking for their mates to join the party. I might get away but chances are they would have my number by now, and if they seriously thought I was going to be making a run for it they would quickly be organising back-up to block my available escape routes.

But all I needed was time, a bit of time just out of sight of the pursuing car, time to, sitting up and taking my hand off the throttle for just a moment, reach into the pocket of my cut off and catch the paper wrap between the fingers of my glove. Reaching forwards again to screw it on, the wind ripped the wrap from between my fingers and it disappeared into the blackness, falling behind me at ninety miles an hour as I rocketed through the next series of S bends with the blues now wailing two tones behind me. Until suddenly with a screech of brakes I hauled on the anchors, the back end starting to step out sideways as I scrubbed off the speed, the front wheel chirping and twitching as I jerked the bike off the road and onto a patch of waste ground at a junction. By the time the plod had pulled in beside me I had the engine and lights off and was waiting with the side stand down.

They were plain clothes, not traffic or local patrol. As they got out of the motor, the flashing blues gave an unreal illumination to the scene. This wasn't just an RTO thing I realised.

'Evening officer.'

'Evening Damage,' was the interesting reply from the guy getting out of the passenger side, so they knew who I was, 'Going somewhere in a hurry are we?' The driver was still inside the car, on the mic, reporting the stop I guessed.

Was this just chance I wondered, 'Just looking for a safe place to pull over officer,' I shrugged.

'Now there's a good citizen,' he said, as the driver got out to join us.

'So what can I do for you this evening, officer?' I asked as Wibble came round the bend on his way home and clocked us, nodding in acknowledgement as I raised a hand in greeting as he slowed down to ride by.

'Well you can take a bit of a ride with us,' said the copper as the roar of Wibble's bike accelerated hard away into the darkness. Well at least the guys'll know where I've gone, I thought.

*

The interrogation room back at the station was a familiar institutional green, with the usual fixed video camera and clock, metal framed chairs and standard metal and Formica table.

The two who had arrested me walked in. The driver was the more junior one. I recognised the older guy. He'd been the one that hassled me all those years before in the back of the Golden Lion although I don't know if he made the connection. He had a slim brown cardboard folder in his hand. They pulled out the chairs on the other side of the table and sat down in silence.

They wanted to talk to me. That was OK but I didn't want to talk to them, so I just waited to hear what was coming.

'So, Tiny was your mate wasn't he?' the older guy kicked off. He was obviously the man who was going to be doing the talking. 'Sorry to hear he's dead?'

I shrugged, 'Yeah, I guess.'

'You guess? I thought he was a mate, no more than a mate, a brother isn't it?

'Yeah sure, but hey shit happens and anyway, it's none of your fucking business.'

'Oh it isn't is it? And shit happens doesn't it? Well let's just see about that shall we? So,' he asked conversationally, 'what do you know about how he died?'

'Not a lot, I wasn't around when it happened.'

'Oh yes that's right. You were on holiday weren't you?'

'Yeah that's right.'

'That's convenient, isn't it? Having an alibi like that I mean.'

'Alibi? What the fuck are you talking about?'

'Tiny's death.'

'What about it?'

'Oh come off it Damage, don't play games with us. We know all about you and your little crew.'

I smiled to myself. I seriously doubted that. 'Who the fuck is playing games mate?'

'OK then, if that's the way you want to play it.'

Play what? I wondered, but kept my mouth shut.

'Tiny's death was no accident.'

'I've no idea what you're talking about.'

'I've got his post mortem report here,' said the sergeant, 'want to know what it shows?'

I shrugged. The easiest and best thing to do with these bastards I knew was just to say nothing, no comment until your brief arrived. I realised I needed to shut up. Not to rise to their bait. Still I was interested now to hear what they had.

The sergeant was looking at me, a quizzical eyebrow raised. He waited a moment longer.

'OK then,' he said acknowledging that no response was coming, 'so why don't I tell you anyway, just in case you don't know it all already?'

He sat back in his chair and extracted some papers and photographs from the file. 'Well it makes some interesting reading I must say,' he said, laying the photographs out on the table in front of me as he spoke.

'And a bit sad really. It's the bruising you can see that tells the story really isn't it? Throat, arms, chest,' he was pointing to the pictures as he laid the eight by tens down on the table in front of me. Then he looked up at me, 'the pills were forced down him weren't they? Somebody or bodies held down his arms and someone else knelt on his chest. I guess that's the one who actually stuffed the whisky bottle in and held it there while he choked on it, the one who stuck a clothes peg on his nose, the one who shoved the pills in and then clamped his mouth shut until he swallowed them so he could breathe. What I want to know is was that the same guy who stuck the needle into him to ensure he was finished off?[8]

He carried on staring into my face, our eyes locked, neither willing to break the stare. 'No comment I take it?'

---

[8] *Peter 'Tiny' Gresham, born 10 November 1945, was found dead on Friday 21 July 1994. Like Adrian 'Gyppo' Leverton previously, the post mortem showed a significant quantity of barbiturates and alcohol, together with an intravenous injection of heroin but no evidence of prior use of intravenous drugs. However the post mortem also revealed significant levels of bruising and the coroner's inquest recorded a verdict of unlawful killing. No one has ever been charged in connection with his death and officially the case remains open.*

I shook my head.

'Bodies, I guess,' he continued reflectively. 'He was a big guy so you'd have needed a couple of guys at least to pin him down I guess, just like before. We're having more tests done to see what exactly you and your mates shoved into him this time. So it'll be a while before we can release the body.'

'What before?' I asked despite myself.

'What d'you mean, "what before"?'

'You said like before, what do you mean by that?'

The sergeant leant back in his chair again with a snort of disgust, 'Don't give me that bollocks, you know what I'm talking about. D'you believe this crap?' he asked his assistant who just carried on staring at me and shook his head in silence. Bloody Trappist monk that one. What did he think I was going to do? Crack under the silent treatment?

Don't tell us you don't know,' the sergeant banged the table returning to his own style, 'don't play the innocent. I meant just like last time. Just like with your other mate Gyppo.'

I must admit I was stunned, but I think I kept a blank face as he demanded, 'It was you lad, wasn't it?'

Silence.

'Or someone doing you a favour?'

I looked at him quizzically. 'A favour?'

'Yeah, it'd be quite a favour wouldn't it? Your dealing partner's been at the powder too much and is becoming a risk and you fancy his bird. Can't say I blame you like, she's quite a looker isn't she? So you had him bumped off didn't you? Solves both things at once doesn't it?'

He sat back again folding his arms, 'And now there's Tiny isn't there? Rocking the boat was he? He couldn't have liked this new little deal you've stitched up with Dazza's mob. Put him out in the cold didn't it? So he had to go as well didn't he? Was that it?'

He waited again.

'Kinda convenient you and he were out of the country when it happened wasn't it? What kind of a fucking alibi did you think taking a golfing trip would be? Were you taking the piss or what?'

I shook my head. 'No idea what ya talking about, it's nothing to do with me.'

'Oh sure, just deny it,' he said in a tone of disgust, 'say nothing like your lot always do. Frankly I don't give a fuck about you scumbags. If you guys want to top the lot of each other then you just get on with it with my blessing.'

Just then the door opened and Jim our club brief walked in. Jim was a laugh, all big and clubby, pinstripe suit, plum in mouth accent and a bit of an 'Ah... Ah... my client... Ah...' stammer. But he knew his stuff and turned out for us every time, like he bloody well ought to the amount of dosh he made off us over the years. Anyway, he had me out of there in no time flat. They didn't have a thing on me, not even a DD charge as I'd only had the one beer and had passed the breathalyser with ease, they had just wanted to tug me in, shake the tree, see what fell out.

Some hope. I wondered why they had bothered.

'So what ah... ah... was that... ah... all about then?' Jim asked as we walked out of the station. So I told him what I'd picked up, they had pulled me in to allege that I'd been involved in murdering Gyppo and Tiny.

'D... d... did they now? Well, they ca... n't have had much of a... ah... ah case now can they then? Not with you just walking out the door like this?'

'No, they can't.'

'So, wha... wha... what are you going to do about this?'

I had been thinking about that myself. Particularly since it would have had to have been Dazza that had called Jim out this time of night to get in to see me. 'Need to let Dazza know what the plod's up to I guess.'

'I think tha..., tha... that's very... wise,' he concluded.

*

'Anyway, the plod are saying that Tiny was murdered,' I told him.

'So I heard from Jim. Why?'

So I told him what the cops had said about the post mortem results and the cause of death.

'Did you believe them?' he asked.

'They showed me photos,' I said flatly, thinking of the livid bruises against the flashlit blue skin and darkly faded tattoos in the pictures I'd seen, 'I'm no expert but unless they were faked or he's had an accident I don't know about before he snuffed it, I could see what they meant.'

'But didn't you tell them that you were away when it happened?'

'I didn't have to. They knew it already. Said it was a convenient alibi and that all it meant was that I'd arranged for someone else to do it while we were away.'

Dazza seemed to consider the implications of this for a moment.

'OK,' he said eventually, 'look, just keep it quiet for the moment will ya? I'll make enquiries, see what's going on.'

'OK, whatever you say, chief,' I agreed, adding offhand as an aside, 'Hey, thanks for sorting Billy out by the way, but you've sure got him crapping himself!'

'Why, what's up?'

'He's saying to me that you've got him dealing with some very heavy fucking people.'

'Christ almighty. What the fuck is he saying something like that for?' Dazza was suddenly very hard and aggressive. 'I tell you now, that little fucker needs to learn to keep his fucking mouth fucking shut or I'll fucking shut it for him!'

I was surprised at the vehemence of the response, 'Hey relax,' I protested, 'he didn't tell me anything.'

'He told you something, and that's one thing too many. And you know it, or you ought to.'

'Hey don't have a go at me mate. I ain't said anything to anybody.'

'Sure?'

'Of course I'm sure. I know what's what.'

'OK, but Billy now…'

'Oh come on, Billy just has a whinge every now and then, particularly when he's had a line or two and gets a bit antsy.'

'Yeah, well he's been doing that a lot lately. That's always a problem. I've seen it before.'

That was the second time I'd had a bad reaction from Dazza when I'd mentioned something that Billy was saying. I'd need to watch that from now on I decided. I didn't want to get in the middle of something dangerous unnecessarily.

*

110

Well so much for keeping out of it. I only had fucking Billy round my house the next morning.

'What the fuck did you say to Dazza? He's coming on really heavy with me!' he gabbled, as I opened the door.

Dazza had really put the scare into Billy I thought, as I ushered him into the house and shut the door behind him.

'I need to talk,' he said

'OK, but not in here,' I said, grabbing him by his cut off and hustling him in front of me and down the hall.'

'Oh hi Billy…' said Sharon as I wheeled him through the kitchen before falling silent as she saw the look on my face as I almost pushed him out of the back door and into the garden.

'You're close to Dazza but the only one I can trust,' he said, as I turned on the outside tap. Bugging people remotely outdoors is difficult enough, but the sound of running water would make it nigh on impossible if we kept our voices low.

'OK then, so what do you need to talk about?' I asked, looking at him appraisingly. He seemed nervous, on the edge, paranoid even and I wasn't sure how much it would be him and how much it would be the whizz talking. Perhaps, I wondered, Dazza was right about him?

He had collapsed into a chair, his whole body slumped back as if in utter defeat, 'What the fuck do I do Damage?' he asked at last.

'What about?'

'About Dazza.'

'Easy. You keep your mouth shut and you keep being useful.'

'That's it?'

'That's it!'

'But I am being useful, that's what's worrying me.'

'Look mate, either you're going to tell me what's going on so I can see if I can help or you're not, in which case you're just wasting my time and yours.' I left it hanging for a few seconds to give him time to think.

'So which is it to be? Time to decide.'

Billy had a hunted look, and then his head fell back with his eyes closed in despair. I had known him now for almost thirty years, since we were kids at school together. He was going to talk.

'Look mate,' I said softening my tone to an encouraging one, 'talk

111

to me. What's the problem?'

'Jesus Christ Damage mate, you've gotta help me.'

'What's going on?'

'It's Dazza, he is trying to get me fucking killed.'

'What do you mean?'

'Dazza… Dazza…'

He stopped for a moment, as though he was having difficulty actually formulating the words. I waited, it was coming, all I had to do was let it, 'Dazza…' then it came in a rush, 'Dazza has had me dealing in Scotland.'

'What on The Rebels' turf?' I couldn't keep the stunned shock out of my voice. Dealing into The Rebels' territory, right under their fucking noses was just about the best way I could think of to start an all out fucking war. If the situation was reversed, we wouldn't rest until we had wiped out their operation on our patch and taken our revenge for the insult. Christ almighty, what the fuck was Dazza up to?

'No,' a sound of anguish, 'you just don't understand.'

'Understand what?' I asked.

'You just don't get it do you?' Billy shot back with a flash of despair driven anger, 'He's not had me dealing on their turf. It's worse than that. He's only had me dealing with the fucking Rebels themselves!'

I was almost speechless for a second. I actually couldn't believe what I'd just heard.

'With the fucking Duckies? Are you out of your fucking mind?

It was as if Billy hadn't heard my question, he was too far gone in his own catastrophic imaginings of the consequences that could unfold as I tried to digest what he was telling me, the unbelievable news that Dazza was dealing with our sworn enemies. 'What the fuck are the rest of The Brethren going to do to me if they ever find out?' Billy wailed.

What indeed? I thought to myself. But instead I asked quietly, 'Did you know who you were going to see?'

'Of course I didn't fucking know. Dazza said he'd arranged a meet so I just went along and then three Rebels turned up. I thought I was fucking dead but no, it was all cool.'

I waited quietly. Now that he had started to talk he would tell it all. 'So how did it happen?' I asked gently.

'Dazza said he'd set me up with a meeting, just like the last one. No sweat, I thought. But then I've done it before for him a couple of times elsewhere around the country. Met up with guys, been a courier. Only this time it was up in Glasgow.'

'Christ, but you must have known that was Rebels' turf. You didn't wear your colours did you?'

'No I'm not fucking stupid. I just went up their nice and quiet like, booked into a hotel for the night and waited to be contacted like the times before. Like I said, Dazza had set it all up. I was just the messenger, I didn't know who I was going to meet.'

'No?'

'No, that's what I'm trying to tell you, it was The Rebels that Dazza had set me up with.'

I was still having problems with this, 'No way. You're fucking joking.'

Billy ignored me, 'So then there's a knock at the door. I open it and there's three of the bastards standing there in the hallway.'

'How did you know they were Rebels?'

'Because the main guy, the one who came into the room with me, just came right out and fucking told me! Jesus, I nearly crapped myself. He had one of his bodyguards with him, they left the other one outside in the hallway. I thought they were going to take me out there and then. But no, it turned out it was cool.'

'Did they know who you were?'

'Yeah they knew I was Brethren alright. The last thing the main guy said to me was that OK I had delivered my gear and would be taking back what I had to. But if I ever showed my face again in Glasgow, colours or no colours, I'd be a dead man. But the thing was, this time, they just didn't seem to care.'

'So what did you have to do?'

'Just the same as the other times, give them a package, and pick up something in return to go back to Dazza.'

'So what was it they gave you?'

'Just a list of addresses.'

'Addresses? What sort of addresses?'

'I don't know. They just looked ordinary to me, flats, houses that sort of thing. I didn't know whose they were and I certainly didn't ask.'

'And was that the same as the other times?'

'I think so. Yes. It was the same routine each time, hand over the package, pick up an envelope, deliver it back to Dazza. It's just this time I got a piece of paper instead of an envelope.'

'So you don't know what was in the envelope the previous times?'

'No I don't. But Dazza went ballistic when I handed the list to him. I thought he was gonna kill me there and then for having opened the envelope. It was all I could do to persuade him that I hadn't had a fucking envelope. I had to wait while he made a call to check before I was in the clear.'

'What would Dazza need a list of addresses in Glasgow for?'

'Don't know. A hit maybe?'

'Don't be fucking stupid. What's Dazza going to want to organise a load of hits in Glasgow for from here, not to mention all the other places you went to.'

'Perhaps he is just getting the info for somebody else?'

'Someone in The Brethren?'

'Sure, why not? Perhaps it's not his hit?'

'Maybe.'

'Well we'd have heard about it if it was a hit. I had the first of these meetings a month or so ago now, down in Wales. If it had been going to happen, it would have happened already wouldn't it? And we'd have heard about a dozen guys getting hit.'

I was sceptical, 'Yeah, if it's happened yet.'

'You'd want to follow up on those addresses soon if you are gonna do something. You know how quickly guys move on.'

'Maybe. But why would The Rebels be giving Dazza or anyone else a list of addresses to hit? They're hardly going to be setting up their own members are they? And if it was anyone else they'd be organising it themselves. They wouldn't be looking to The Brethren for help. That'd be the last thing they'd do. No, I just don't get it.'

And I didn't. It was another thing that didn't make sense. But, at the same time, if there was one thing I knew about Dazza, it was that he never did anything, no matter how crazy it seemed at the time, without a very good reason. It's just at the moment I couldn't see what it was.

'So what was in the package you took to them?'

'I only saw that once.'

'Well then, you saw it. What was it?'

'You wouldn't believe me if I told you.'

'Try me.'

'The guy from The Rebels opened it in front of me. It was only a fucking brick.'

'Of what? Coke?'

'No a fucking house brick you prat! What d'you think? It was a full K, paper wrap printed with a scorpion logo and everything.[9]

I gave a low whistle. 'Cali?'

This was serious shit. I didn't know much about coke. Whizz and dope had been my things when I'd been dealing and I'd got out before coke started to come in so much, but I'd heard of El Alacran, the scorpion. It was his logo.

'He pay you? This Rebel guy?'

'No, that was one of the odd things. He said, "Tell your man we'll get this checked out like before, and if it does, then let him know he'll get his cash the way he asked."'

Like before, I wondered, thinking about the packets that Dazza had asked Billy to post.

What was Dazza doing sending and handing out a couple of full K bricks of Cali branded coke?

And on credit?

To The Rebels of all people?

We were getting in deep here I realised, into some real shit. Billy was still talking, about how something was going on, something big, how Dazza had had some gear arrive that was fucking serious.

'What gear?'

'I can't tell you. He'd kill me, he really would.'

---

[9] *Cocaine is usually smuggled in compressed 1 kilogram wrapped blocks known as 'bricks'. Henry Loaiza-Ceballos, alias El Alacran, 'the Scorpion' was a member of the notorious Colombian drugs dealing Cali cartel and allegedly the man in charge of most of their military operations. Bricks in wrappings stencilled with a scorpion logo would be assumed to have been sourced from his part of the cartel.*

'Who would?'

'Dazza.'

Billy shook his head. 'Shit man, you should see what Dazza has got going down. He's just fucking incredible.'

'Like what?'

'I can't tell you man, Dazza really would kill me.'

'Don't be daft, he wouldn't.'

'No you're right he wouldn't. He'd have Butcher do it for him. He's becoming fucking nuts about security, even more so than he was before.'

Before? We kept coming back to that word again. Before. What did he mean? What the hell is going on here, I asked myself.

*

I saw a big payment coming into one of the accounts the next week. Banked in Glasgow. I let Dazza know about it and he seemed pleased. It meant message received and understood, I assumed.

PART 4
9 August 1994 to 15 September 1994

Clubs that are taken over are either used to being under a boss type already, or are used to freedom.

Damage 2008

8   THE DOUBT

I didn't hear from Billy for about a week after that. I guess he was just lying low for a bit. Shacked up with one or other of his birds I assumed. And then when he did call me I wished he hadn't.

He was down the station. And he needed Jim the brief. So I called Dazza and arranged to meet.

'What's up?' he asked as I walked into the café.

'I've had a call from Billy. He needs Jim, he's been arrested.'

'Arrested? What for?'

'He got stopped by the plod and they found coke and a gun in the car…'

'Oh for fuck's sake…' Dazza seemed exasperated, 'what's the fucking idiot think he's doing? I thought I told him to keep himself clean. Is that really so fucking difficult?'

'For Billy?' I asked.

He just grunted in acknowledgement. Then he lapsed into silence, staring out of the window for a few seconds as he gathered his thoughts. 'Jesus,' he said at last, 'he's so coked up these days and I know he's leaky. Look what he's been telling you.'

'What's he told me?' I objected, 'Sod all mate. I don't know anything and I don't want to know anything. I prefer it that way. He's just had a couple of moans that's all, he's never told me anything about whatever it is he's obviously doing for you.'

'Obviously eh?'

'Yeah, obviously. Come on now,' I said catching the expression in his eye, 'Don't you go making something out of that. Look, I asked you to give him some work, you gave him some, so obviously he's doing something for you.'

Dazza stared at me silently.

'So the question is, what do we do about getting Jim in there and getting him out?' I insisted.

Dazza nodded and pulled out a mobile, 'I guess you're right, leaky or not we need him outta there.'

*

The thing was, by the time Dazza tracked Jim down to where he was in Court, and got him across to the station, Billy was already in the process of being released on police bail.

'They let him out?' barked Dazza suspiciously once I'd got off the phone, 'what d'ya mean "they just let him out"?'

'He gave the plod a story,' I said, 'you'll like this, it's a real laugh.' In retrospect I don't know why I told Dazza the story. Partly I guess because I thought it was funny, partly I guess because he would get to hear about it anyway, but partly also, I guess, as a bit of a test, to see his reaction.

'He told them that they'd got him bang to rights guv as he'd stolen the car and so he didn't know anything about the coke and gun in the glove box. What d'ya make of that eh? Fucking brilliant.'

But Dazza was in a grim mood still.

'And you fucking buy that do you? I fucking knew it, he's singing. It's the only reason he's out so quickly. That's what they always do, they look to get you to offer them someone higher up the tree as the price of letting you off. Look, how did they get him in the first place?'

'He just got tugged…' I protested.

'Yeah right, he gets tugged and just by chance instead of traffic just writing some process they decide to search the car and find the gear and a piece? That's bollocks and you know it!'

'Maybe,' I conceded.

'Nah. There's no fucking maybes about it. There's no way traffic would pick that up. The only way that happened was a tip off from someone. Someone set Billy up to get off themselves, and now Billy's doing the same.'

'Now you're just being paranoid Dazza!' I protested, 'Billy's OK I tell you. Let me talk to him.'

'OK, OK,' he held his hands up and then stabbing his finger on the table for emphasis he added, 'Maybe you're right, and maybe you're wrong. But I'm telling you this for free. This is his last fucking shot. Any more fuck-ups and he's a dead man. When you are speaking to him, you make sure you tell him that from me.'

'I will.'

*

Despite what I'd said so confidently to Dazza, I wasn't really so sure myself. I would need to find out for myself if Billy was talking.

If Billy was at home of course. The lights were off.

I knocked and rang the bell. There was no reply so I rang again. Giving up on that as an approach I stepped back away from the door and as I looked up at the bedroom windows I saw a curtain twitch where it had been let fall.

So I shouted up, 'Come on Billy, it's me, Damage! Come down here and let me in you tosser.'

There was no answer so I went back to the door and leant on the bell.

It took what seemed to be an age before I heard him shuffling around behind the door and ask, 'Who's there?'

'It's me Billy!' I shouted.

'Are you on your own? No one else with you?'

'Of course I'm on my own. Now stop screwing about and open the fucking door willya?'

There was the sound of chains, then of a key in the lock, and then there was Billy, peering out furtively, checking left and right to make sure I was alone, ready to slam the door in my face if I tried to rush him.

'Christ man,' I said, 'you look like shit!'

And he did. His face was a pasty white, his eyes were bloodshot red and his hands were shaking.

'Yeah well, feel it too.'

I stood on the doorstep. 'Well?'

He looked at me, sighed and then held the door open wide for me to go in.

*

I passed Dazza's message on to a deflated Billy. He was up and down in spasms as I talked to him, really on edge. At one point I thought he was going to burst into tears on me. He really was on the downward spiral, I could see that. God I'd better keep him out of Dazza's sight or that would be it.

'But I don't understand mate, why is all this stuff about you such a big deal for Dazza?'

'It's because of what I know.'

'About Dazza and The Rebels?'

'That, and other things.'

'What other things?'

'I can't tell you.'

'Why not?'

The very thought of it seemed to hit him like a blow as he crumpled into a chair and hung his head in his hands.

'Christ man, he's going to kill me anyway. And you're his main man now,' he said almost accusingly, looking up with a flash of anger in his eyes, 'So what have I got to lose?'

I didn't say anything. His despair was on my side, I waited him out until it came in a rush.

'He's got big stuff going on, he's got a new route for gear coming in that he's just trialled and it works, so now his real shipments are going to start.

'So what's the real shipments?'

'I don't know.'

'When're they coming?'

'A month's time.'

'What, middle of September?'

'Yeah, almost exactly. The first one's scheduled for a Wednesday night.' His voice died off into a keening whine of 'Oh God, Oh God, Oh God, Oh God…'

'It's OK Billy mate,' I said grabbing him by the shoulders, 'It's OK, I'll tell Dazza it's OK, you're not talking. You just stay here.' I was thinking about how to handle this. Billy was on the edge of going to pieces and all the way over at times. I had to buy him and me some time while I tried to figure this out.

'You're going to lie low. And I'm going to tell Dazza that you've asked me to send a message. Have you got that Billy?' I demanded, pushing my face into his, desperate to get his attention. I needed to get him focused on me and to get what I was trying to tell him.

'I'm sending Dazza a message for you. That you suggest that Dazza changes it, whatever it is, to another place or time. So then he knows he's safe 'cos you don't know when it's gonna be. How's that?'

'I don't know.'

'Well I do. Don't worry, I'll sort this. OK Billy?'

He was just shaking his head. So I slapped him. Hard.

121

'Just fucking pull yourself together Billy. I told you, I'll sort this.'
He looked at me disbelievingly.
'You just have to stay here and stay calm. Have you got that?'
He mumbled something.
I tugged him to his feet.
'I said, have you got that?'
'Sure, yeah sure, I've got that.'
I let him go and he just sort of collapsed back into his chair.
'OK then. Just sit tight and wait till I get back.'

*

'Look Damage, face it, we've gotta problem.'
'What's that then?'
'Billy.'
'Billy?'
'He's talking.'
'How d'you know?'
'The cops catch him with coke and a gun and next thing he's out on bail after a cock and bull story like that? Bollocks, he's grassing us up. It's the only thing that makes sense.'
'How do you know he's a snout?'
'How do you know he isn't?'
'How do know anybody isn't?'
'You don't.'
'Hey I was tugged in too. Remember? D'you think I'm a grass too?
'No, that's different.'
'Why?'
'Because I know you,' he said calmly.
'What are you on about, you know me? You know Billy as well don't you? Maybe better than me, you've been using him long enough haven't you.'
'Yeah I've been dealing with Billy long enough. Long enough to know what he's like anyway.'
'So?'
'But I know you. The way you came in that day back then when you came to tell me you were out of the business. You know I've told you not many guys would come in to do that but you did. You were

122

prepared to take whatever came. That was the moment when I really knew you, that you were a stand up guy, that I would never need to worry about you ratting me out.'

That was quite a compliment.

'Whereas Billy, Billy's just bad for security. He knows too much, he's using too much, he's just become too much of a risk.'

And deep down, despite the fact we were mates, I now knew Dazza was right about Billy as a risk. The plod would always press for info, always be looking for someone to give up someone higher up the tree in return for a ticket. And I did have to face it, Dazza was spot on, Billy was becoming heavily coked and unstable. However old a friend Billy was, Dazza's suspicions weren't unreasonable, they were just wrong, I thought.

But they also risked turning into a self-fulfilling prophesy if Dazza ended up scaring Billy so much that he felt he had nowhere else to go for safety but to the plod.

I had to have one last try. I owed Billy that much.

'Dazza he's OK, he's not talking to anyone, let alone the plod. He's got himself barricaded in his house. I've told him to stay home and lie low, not to leave the place until he hears otherwise. There's one thing though.'

'Yes?'

'He said to ask whether you still wanted him at the thing next month or whether he should stay home or just clear out completely?'

'The thing? What thing?'

'He didn't say and I didn't ask. He said you'd know and you might want to think about changing the date so that he didn't know it.'

'What? Why?'

'Change the date for when whatever it is, is going to happen. That way he won't know it so there's no way he's a danger to it.'

'Christ, so now he thinks that I think there's a risk he's a grass, and he has to prove to me he isn't? I don't like that Damage. I don't like that at all.'

'Look what's the guy to do? He must know that we're suspicious about him because he gets lifted. He wants to make sure you're secure and to prove to you that he's no problem, only then we're suspicious that he wants to prove he's OK! It's Catch 22 mate. Keep

123

going round this loop and you can never trust anybody over anything.'

Dazza paused, then shook his head and laughed. 'Who said I ever did? Anyway I can't change the thing. It's all set up now. So he's not talking, but he's talking to you?'

'Well I'm the only one he can talk to and get a message to you aren't I? You asked me to talk to him don't forget. And anyway he isn't telling me anything, he's just getting me to play Postman Pat and pass on a message that I know fuck all about.'

'Relax mate, I'm not having a go at you. Right then, tell him he can come and go. I don't want him locked up inside his house, it'll just look suspicious. Tell him he can get on as normal other than business. He can go to the shops, down the boozer, over to his birds', whatever the fuck it is he does. But he stays clear of anything to do with business or the club and he stays clean until the heat is off and I say so. Is that clear?'

'I'll tell him.'

'You do that.'

Dazza sat back. I started to get up to go but he stopped me in my tracks with a question.

'Did you know Billy's been up to meet with The Rebels?' he asked me casually, catching me completely off balance.

'No shit?' I said turning back to meet his cold-eyed appraising stare, the tone of shock in my voice would have been real enough. 'He can't have, surely? Not even Billy would be that fucking stupid!'

'Yeah, he's been dealing with them,' he said quietly.

'Are you sure?'

'Absolutely sure.'

'Christ,' I said, after a pause which seemed to just about cover it, what with Dazza not volunteering that he was the one who'd sent him up there in the first place, 'So how d'ya find out about that?'

'Through Butcher.'

'Butcher?'

'Yeah. I've had him and his guys tailing Billy for a while. See what's going on, who he's been talking to.'

'Christ,' which again seemed to cover it. I was thinking furiously, partly about my recent meetings with Billy. I thought I had in effect told Dazza about all of them so there wouldn't be anything to arouse his suspicions about me.

Of course all I had was Billy's word for it that Dazza had sent him to deal with The Rebels. So could Dazza be right? Was Billy just so terrified because he'd been found out, because of what The Brethren would do to him for dealing with The Rebels? Was he just making up a line to blame Dazza? Was he just trying to concoct a story to protect himself? But if so, how would putting Dazza in the frame help him?

Besides, I remembered the package I'd seen Dazza give Billy to post, addressed to Glasgow, and the cash that had come into the accounts, probably just about right for two Ks of coke I reckoned.

No, Billy's story fitted. It certainly fitted much better than some bullshit about Butcher tailing people and Billy taking it into his head to wing it on his own with The Rebels.

'So what are you going to do about it?'

'Nothing, I just haven't decided yet.'

*

I passed Dazza's message on.

Billy was so wound up that he was crying with relief by the time I'd finished.

'Look, what the fuck is going on here? I can only help you so much if I don't know what the score is.'

He was shivering, 'I'm scared, just so scared.'

'You have to trust me.'

I sat down opposite him and just stared at him. Immobile and immovable. I'm not going anywhere I told him, without saying a word. Not until you start talking.

'I'm all that stands between you and Dazza. So what's it to be Billy? What's it to be?'

So eventually, he told me just what it was he'd been a part of. What Dazza was really worried about.

'So what happened?'

'It was the week after Tiny died, in the evening.'

'The week after we got back from Portugal?'

'Yeah, middle of the week, Wednesday night I think. There was Dazza and Butcher's boys and me. Dazza had told me to organise a van, a Transit or something similar, and to meet him at the clubhouse.

125

We were all to go clean, no patches, nothing traceable. When I got there, Butcher was waiting. He had brought along a load of those big square battery torches, you know the ones? The big jobs?

'Anyway he bunged those in the back of the van and all the guys piled in to it and an old long wheel based Defender that Dazza had brought along. Dazza opened the gate into the field out the back of the clubhouse and led the way up the track and out onto the moors. It was rutted and bumpy, but once on top it wasn't too bad. It's been dry recently so it wasn't muddy and I guess someone must look after it for driving the shooters around.

'We must have gone about half a mile or so, possibly a bit more, so we were right on top, you know where it's flattened out. It was about ten o'clock so although the sun had gone down, the sky was still quite light, you know that sort of turquoise. It was beautiful when we stopped, you know you feel like you're on top of the world up there, nothing but you, the sky, the wind, the birds. As though there's not another person in the world.

'Dazza never told us what we were doing so we just hung around the van and the Landie while he and Butcher took nine of the torches and set them out across a flat piece of ground beside us in a big cross shape, about 50 yards wide.

'Then they came back and told us we were gonna have to wait. So OK, we waited. Had a smoke, chatted a bit, but other than Butcher and Dazza, obviously nobody else knew what was going on, or if they did, they weren't talking.

'After about an hour or so it got much darker and Dazza said it was time to get ready. Dazza, Butcher, Wibble and I were to take one arm of the cross each. The other guys were to take the Landie and head back down the track to make sure no one came up. So we split up and I walked over to my arm of the cross. Butcher had put the torches on their backs on the ground so that when they were switched on the light would shine straight upwards which seemed strange at the time. According to Dazza my job was to wait until his signal and then switch on the torches in my arm of the cross then get the hell out the way.

'I didn't have a clue what he was on about.

'So there I was standing in the dark feeling like a complete plonker when I hear the sound of an aircraft in the distance. It wasn't a jet, not one of those fighter boys that come screaming over every so often. No this was a big prop type, something like one of those big military jobs, the Hercules or whatever it is. And as it gets closer, I'm more certain that it's heading towards us.

'And that's when Dazza shouts to us that we're to turn on the lights. So Butcher hits the central one and I do my two and get the fuck out of there because this thing is coming straight for us and it's down to only a couple of hundred feet and still dropping. I chucked myself face down on the ground as it came roaring overhead and there was a tremendous crack and a crash behind me above the howling storm of noise and wind from the rotors as it swept overhead. Looking up I could see that its back door cargo ramp was closing as it headed off down the valley.

'Looking across I could see Dazza and Butcher were already on their feet and running towards where the thump had come from. In the continuing back draught from the plane I could see something billowing black against the dark blue of the sky. When I got there a moment later what I saw was a sort of specialised pallet. It was bigger than what you'd normally see, reinforced, with sort of metal skids. At the back, Butcher was already reeling in what looked like a couple of parachutes. I guessed that they had dragged the pallet out of the back of the plane so that it could drop from such a low level and the pallet with the skids was designed to absorb the impact.

'I mean this looked like specialist military gear to me. And that plane, it was in civvies, and it was a military type, but it just wasn't one of ours.

'Meanwhile Dazza had his knife out and was already cutting away the straps that held the cargo crates onto the pallet. As I got closer he shouted at me to get the van. Wibble was going round dousing and collecting the lights.

'I backed it up and we loaded all the gear into the van as well as the pallet and the shutes. Man, there were some heavy bastard boxes there. Dazza called ahead to the guys in the Landie to make sure the coast was clear and we headed back down to the clubhouse.

'Dazza was sitting next to me in the van for the ride down the hill which he made us do without lights. I guess he wanted to keep an eye

127

on the stuff. He seemed quite pleased with how it had gone. I asked him about the plane. He didn't give me much, he just said it was a big Russian job, an Antonov or something, and it was off to land at Glasgow, clean as a whistle if anyone wanted to check it when it got there.

'You've got to hand it to the guy. He's a brilliant operator. Complete fucking genius.'

I could see it now. And Billy was right, it was genius. I could see why he needed us and Westmorland as well. The Tyne Gap had been an aircraft route for years, uncontrolled airspace not covered by air Traffic Control and up here across the moors the RAF and army helicopters were forever practising low-flying, so no one was going to notice one more low-flying aircraft one night. With all the clutter from the hills you'd guess that any radar operator would lose a plane flying that low and certainly they wouldn't be able to catch the pallet being dropped.

Up on the moors no one, except in the aircraft overhead, was going to see the lights of the torches arranged in a giant X to mark the spot, and if anyone did find their way up to investigate, other than some broken heather and some tracks there wouldn't be anything left to find.

And I knew that it was booked as an ordinary commercial flight. Of course I knew, I'd booked it. My fingerprints were metaphorically speaking all over this. Machinery parts from Russia landing legitimately at Glasgow with all its paperwork correct.

We all knew that sending stuff was always the easy bit of any run. Customs most places were never that bothered about checking stuff going out of a country. The difficult part was always getting stuff in, which was where Customs were always interested. Airports and ports were the choke points on any route so that's where Customs concentrated. Only with this plan there was no need to try and smuggle anything past Customs or through the airport checks, it had already left the plane en route. So long as the pallet had never officially been booked on the plane when it left, no one would be looking for it or miss it on the plane's arrival.

Billy was right. Dazza really was a fucking genius, I thought.

'So that's what's happening again next month?'

'Yeah, another drop. But all I know is that it's going to be different stuff this time.'

I'd been sending some heavy cash to Luis's nominated accounts in Portugal for Dazza recently. And if Dazza's method had worked for gear from Russia, then there were no reasons I guessed that it wouldn't work just as well for gear from Portugal. So if I knew the when, where and how, the only questions were what and why.

But as far as Billy was concerned, I still needed to know two things.

'Billy, Billy listen to me,' I said, grabbing him and pulling his face up to mine, 'listen to me, there's stuff that I need to know. And I need to know it straight.'

'Yeah, sure, like what?'

'Well the first is, are you talking?' I overrode his expressions of innocence and kept hold of him, 'You're my bro, I can help you but I need to know. Don't lie to me. This is your one chance do ya understand that?' He nodded and mumbled something.

'I didn't get that Billy,' I said threateningly, 'Now are you or aren't you?'

He protested again.

'Because if you are, you've got one last chance to tell me, get out of the house and get the cops to protect you.' He looked up at me, his face frozen, 'if you aren't, then you just need to stay clean.'

'Look mate, I'm not fucking talking alright! I fucking swear to you!' he suddenly shouted at me, 'and you can tell that to Butcher or any other fucker that wants to know.'

I looked into his face and then let go of his jacket so he could step back from me.

'OK, I believe you.' And I did. 'I just had to be sure.'

There was a moment of silence between us, then he collapsed back into his chair. 'Christ man, for a moment there I thought you'd come to kill me.'

I just shook my head. 'I'm just here as your bro. And if you just play it the way I tell you to then I'm going to get you out of this.'

'Christ mate, thanks. You know I'm going to owe you my life mate after this.' I just shrugged.

'What else was it you wanted to know?'

'You said there was gear that had been dropped. Tell me about that, did it all land OK?'

'Seemed to, it ended up just past the cross and all the packaging seem to have survived.'

'So did you see it? What was the gear?'

'No. It was still all in its crates when we were at the clubhouse. Dazza had the guys get them out and then he told me to take the van and make sure I lost the pallet and the shutes so they wouldn't be found. So I stuck them in my garage and had myself a bit of a bonfire at the weekend. But I do think I know where the stuff is.'

'Where?'

And he told me.

*

I couldn't afford to be spotted so I needed some wheels that wouldn't be recognised. I called Sharon and told her to borrow one of her mate's cars for the next evening.

'Is it gonna be OK? I wouldn't want to get them in any bother.'

'It's OK, it'll be fine, nothing to worry about. Just a Sunday evening drive in the country. The motor'll come back completely clean.'

'Promise?'

'Promise.'

'Alright then. I'll call Julie and see what I can do.'

I took the back road, sweeping wide out to the west before it dropped down into the valley running south into the hills parallel with my normal route up and over the top of the moors. Eventually I turned off onto a small side road that snaked its way up into the hills, following the winding course of a steep sided river valley, before at its end rising up to join with the clubhouse road at a junction about half a mile past its entrance. So just before it started to climb I pulled over into the shadow of a field gate entrance about a quarter of a mile before the gate to the club's drive and killed the lights. I pulled a small but powerful torch and my jemmy out of the bag I had bunged on the back seat of the little Peugeot 106 that no one from the club would recognise if they noticed it parked up. But to start with the moonlight would be enough to let me find my way.

It was Wibble who had given it away apparently. He had been

whingeing on the next time Billy had seen him at the clubhouse. He was all, 'It was alright for you, you bastard, you got to fuck off with the van. Left me, Butcher, and the boys to hump the gear down the hill.'

'Down the hill?'

'Yep, that's what he said.'

'Into the woods?'

'That's what I'm guessing.'

We'd both grown up out this way. As kids we had walked and cycled and explored. And one of the places that we'd camped had been the woods across the field and the road below what was now our clubhouse. And so we both knew what was there.

The land that came with the clubhouse was a huge slice of the hillside up from the road and past the clubhouse to where a dry stone wall and rickety gate marked the end of the field line and the start of the moors proper. Below the clubhouse the land stretched down to the road, and then down again below the road towards the lower road that followed the snaking course of the shallow rocky river. The stretch between the two roads was heavily wooded and so as a club we never used it much, except as a handy additional source of firewood for party bonfires. It was one of the regular chores for the strikers to be sent down there with axes to chop stuff up to make sure that there was always a ready stash in hand for the summer parties.

I climbed over the gate and was instantly hidden from the road by the darkness of the trees beyond. I hadn't been here for years but I was sure I would remember the way easily enough as I headed along the overgrown remnants of the old mine path, two huge piles of tailings growing on either side of me. Opening some crates when I got there was going to be interesting.

As I felt my way through the trees on that old familiar path it seemed to me that too much business, too much serious money had rotted what we were about. I think Billy saying that he had thought I was there to kill him had shocked me more than I had realised.

That wasn't what we were about. Not in my book.

OK, so back in the old days, Gyppo, Billy and I had been in business, we had dealt a bit of blow and a bit of whizz, but the main thing about being in the club had been about belonging, about being with your mates.

Now though, through Dazza I was involved in serious dosh and serious shit, and when the stakes had become as high as this, the game had got serious for everyone involved. It was becoming play or be played. How had it come to this, I wondered, that our loyalty to our club and our bros could end up with Billy being scared I'd come to kill him?

But in reality, it was inevitable, I knew. I had seen it ever since the outset. And so ironically had Billy, although he had always assumed that he would be on the inside rather than out in the cold. But with too much cash available to the top guys in the club from escalating into serious business, it was no wonder that the old solidarity had rotted out of the club. What we were about had been perverted. Loyalty was no longer a two-way street, but something that a ruthless inner clique could exploit for their own profit.

Dazza had needed to clean house alright. But it hadn't been for the good of the club. It had been for the good of his deal, it had been to ensure the coast was clear for his big scheme, whatever it was.

I had reached the low opening of the mine entrance. Right then, I thought, now we'll see.

The hills round here were riddled with holes from lead mining that had gone back hundreds of years. There were shafts hundreds of feet deep which had generally been capped off with concrete for safety to stop sheep and people falling in. Then there were the old drift mines, levels going straight into the hillsides. The more public ones were generally fenced off or had metal grilles across them to keep wandering Joe Public out. But there were still plenty of unblocked openings to underground tunnels if you knew where to look. And we knew that one of these was in the woods.

Billy and I had joked with Dazza that this was one of the reasons that The Brethren had been interested in our territory. Holes could be useful.

We were right, but for the wrong reasons.

Torch on, I splashed into the entrance. These mines were always dug running slightly upwards into the hillside so that water would naturally drain out and even today a continual stream of cold water flowed out of the dark entrance and cut its way down the hillside to join the river below.

The crates were there as I had expected, piled up about forty or fifty feet in from the entrance. They were at the first junction where the tunnel divided into two at right angles where the old timers had started to follow two separate veins through the surrounding bedrock limestone and had left a little raised platform at the junction that was therefore dryer than the floor.

I gave a sigh of relief.

I knew there had been a chance that Dazza would have had them moved, but I hadn't thought it had been a big one. After all, if it was Billy talking that Dazza was concerned about, then as far as Dazza was aware, Billy didn't know where they were and getting guys together to move them somewhere else would have seemed more risky than leaving them where they were.

They were safe enough, no one ever came here. There were nutty guys who liked exploring these old holes but this was on private property and there's no way that the club would have ever given anyone permission to explore the woods, Dazza or no Dazza.

As I suspected, the crates had all already been opened once to check the contents, so no one would notice my jemmy marks if they came back to look at them.

I fitted my wrecking bar under the lid of the first one and prised it up.

'Oh shit!' I said out loud. And then I prised the lid off another, and then another, not quite believing at first what I was seeing.

By the time I'd finished, it was quite a haul.

The first and second crate I had opened were AK47s. But there was more.

A crate of longer barrelled rifles with telescopic sights.

A couple of boxes of handguns with matching silencers.

Ammunition.

Military style walkie talkies.

What I assumed was a supply of plastic explosives.

But the pièce de résistance had to be the two RPG7s with a supply of rockets.

So that's what the dosh to Sergei's accounts had bought.

As I stood and stared around me at what I'd uncovered I gave a low whistle, 'What's he planning? To start his own fucking war?'

I toyed with the idea of helping myself to a gun but decided it was better to leave it be.

But then, I asked myself, as I started to carefully replace all the lids so that no one could tell I'd been there, if he's dealing with The Brethren's main enemies The Rebels, then who the hell's it going to be against?

9   THE TURN

Billy wasn't at Prayers on Monday. I assumed he was following Dazza's instructions and just laying low.

Early on Wednesday afternoon Dazza picked me up from home in a black BMW.

'Get in, we're going for a drive.'

'New car?'

'Hired for the day.'

He clearly wasn't in a chatty mood.

We only went across town, climbing up the back road. Uneasily I realised we were heading towards Billy's place, a feeling confirmed when Dazza turned off into the estate of detached executive homes high on a hill overlooking the town where Billy had bought himself a four bedroomed house with the cash from his dealing. We parked up a little way before we got to the house but from where we could see the front door and Dazza killed the engine. Stay there he said, hopping out of the driver's door and into the back seat.

A moment later Butcher appeared from out of a footpath on the other side of the road and came strolling along the pavement to slide in behind the wheel beside me.

'OK?' asked Dazza.

'OK,' said Butcher, without looking round.

'Now what?' I asked, wondering why Butcher hadn't taken off the pair of thin black leather riding gloves he was wearing.

'Now we wait,' said Dazza

'Are we watching Billy?'

'What the fuck does it look like we're doing? Now shut up will you?'

'That's him,' said Butcher about an hour later reaching for the car keys, as a hundred yards or so down the road Billy came out of his house and walked across the road to where his car was parked.

We edged out into the road behind his car as he headed off round the corner and slipped out into the light traffic on the main road, taking up station a couple of cars behind him as he headed down the hill into town. Dazza and Butcher obviously wanted to keep close enough to see which way he was going but far enough back not to be spotted which was why I realised that he, or more likely someone on Dazza's behalf, had hired, a car that Billy wouldn't know.

'What are we looking for?' I asked.

'He's heading towards the cop shop isn't he?'

'Oh come, on he's just heading into town. He could be going anywhere.' I said, although yes, he could be, I thought as he turned right at the junction at the bottom of the hill onto the main shopping street; or out to Enderdale.

We turned right as well, still keeping our distance, but up ahead he was still just in sight, caught as the traffic bunched up again at the traffic lights. The cop shop was dead ahead across the lights, while left was out towards Enderdale and the clubhouse.

From where I was sitting in the stationary car I couldn't see whether he had any indicators going, although knowing Billy and how he drove a lack of them could mean anything or nothing. The lights changed to amber and then flicked to green. The car at the front of the queue pulled away straight ahead. Billy was second in line. I held my breath. Billy's car moved forwards and then to my relief he pulled left and disappeared round the corner.

Most of the traffic headed straight over with only a couple following Billy. Butcher ran the lights just as they switched to red. The road wound round a couple of snaking bends as it worked its way slightly uphill so at first we couldn't see Billy ahead of us but Butcher gunned the car through the twists to catch up with the car ahead and as we eased round the last bend and onto the long first straight up out of the valley we could see Billy's car about quarter of a mile ahead.

'OK, next one,' said Dazza cryptically to Butcher who just nodded and then about a mile further on Butcher braked suddenly and pulled into a lay-by. Dazza was out of the car before we stopped and Butcher pulled straight back out onto the road without a word, accelerating hard to make up the seconds he had lost on Billy's car which was out of sight around the next bend. Glancing back I saw Dazza pulling open the door of a car parked facing back into town and sliding inside before we disappeared around the corner. It was just Butcher and me on Billy's trail now as his car came back into sight up ahead in the distance.

We hung back maintaining station for a few minutes with two cars between us and Billy. Then, as he drove, Butcher reached into his jacket pocket and I heard the familiar tune of a mobile phone being turned on and then a couple of beeps as Butcher picked a number that he'd preset.

'Here take this,' he said handing me the phone.

'OK.'

'What's the reception like?' he asked.

'OK at the moment,' I told him, it could be quite patchy out this way but at the moment I had five bars showing.

'Dial when I say so,' said Butcher, watching as Billy's car disappeared round a tight bend ahead and headed out into the open countryside along a lengthy straight.

Butcher pulled over again, this time into a field entrance as Billy's car pulled away into the distance. There were no other cars parked around that I could see so I guessed Butcher wasn't going to play the same car changing trick as Dazza had pulled.

'Aren't you going to follow him?'

'No need. I know exactly where he's going. Dial the number.'

I pressed the call key.

From about a mile in front of us I suddenly saw a ball of orange black flame billowing into the sky, followed a second or so later by a boom that seemed to echo across the rolling open fields from where a pillar of black smoke started to form.

'Beautiful,' said Butcher reaching over to pick the phone out of my hand. You know the really cool thing is he continued conversationally, 'you don't even need to pay for the call!'

I couldn't say anything.

'Told you I knew where he was going,' said Butcher, smiling at me as he pulled the car round in the entrance to a field, and headed back towards town.

'Damn those fucking Rebels.' He shook his head.

'Wha…?' I started to ask distractedly.

'The Rebels. That's the sort of thing that happens when you start treading on their turf.'

We drove quietly back towards town, turning off the main road on the outskirts just as the blue flashing lights of the cops, ambulance and Trumpton sped past us, all heading the other way. Butcher spent an hour or so working our way cross-country through back lanes to across the other side of the dual carriageway and then he headed east towards the city along roads where there was no chance of cameras.

He dropped me off in the outskirts and I caught the Metro to the central station and then the train back to town.

Butcher kept the phone. He said he'd get rid of it.

But of course it would have had my fingerprints on it.[10]

*

The cops had kept Tiny's body for almost a month now. They'd done two post mortems like they couldn't work out what had killed him, and then finally they'd released it to his wife Sally.

As a club we'd taken over the funeral arrangements. It would be a full dress affair with Brethren riding in from all over the country, and some reps coming from overseas chapters. It was a solidarity thing, as well as a chance to catch up with old contacts, have a bit of time for face to faces where guys wanted them. I wondered whether Dazza had taken the opportunity to ask Sergei or Luis over.

The funeral was on the Saturday so we had a few guys arrive the Thursday, but most made it up during the day on Friday, first stop being the clubhouse to check in, say hi, and grab details of plans for the day, or to hang around to see who else was turning up or just kill some time.

By Friday evening the clubhouse was full, fuller than I'd ever seen it, with guys squeezed in everywhere, in the bar, in the poolroom, sat on the stairs sharing joints, upstairs in the meeting room. The scrum around the bar was half a dozen deep and the strikers behind it had their work cut out keeping the booze flowing until the party started to break up in the early hours but it was a strange kind of party, solemn like, a quieter mood than usual. This was a serious run, a paying of respects, not a party event, so most guys had turned up riding solo,

---

[10] *William 'Billy Whizz' White, born 8 June 1964, was killed instantaneously on Wednesday 17 August 1994 when a bomb made from military style explosives went off, where it had been attached under the floor of his car with magnets, while he was driving through open countryside. The bomb had been detonated by remote control, apparently using a mobile telephone.*

No one has ever been charged in connection with his death and officially the case remains open.

even those that would normally double pack, so there weren't many chicks around which I guess made a bit of a difference. By the time I left at two or so some guys were crashed in the bunk rooms at the clubhouse, others had arranged to crash with members around the region. It turned out that a few guys spent the night on mattresses on the floor in the back of the Charter's crew bus. The Freemen had booked out a country club hotel for themselves of course which must have given the place a shock when their booking had rolled up mid-afternoon on Friday in a twin column of rumbling menace Harleys.

I opened my eyes at eight or so on the Saturday morning and then closed them again.

Outside I could hear the rain pelting against the windows and see the leaden dark sky that told me it was set in for the whole day. It was going to be a miserable fucking day, just pissing it down continuously, for a miserable fucking event.

'Christ!' I said eventually, with a reluctant resolve pushing away the covers before swinging my legs out onto the floor and padding my way across the landing to the bathroom for a good long piss. I stood in the shower, swaying and turning so the hot jets of water sprayed across my skin, defrosting me and washing away the cold of sleep.

I rested my forehead against the tiles and closed my eyes as the hot water cascaded down my back, before after an age, with one hand I finally popped the top off the hanging bottle of shower gel, squeezed a dollop onto my hand and began to wash.

I wasn't looking forward to today. I really wasn't.

Showered, dressed and a quick cup of strong black coffee with two sugars later I started to feel a bit more able to face the world, although my mood hadn't improved much.

Sharon repeated her offer to come with me to pay her respects but again I turned her down. It wasn't that I didn't want her there, or even that I didn't appreciate her concern or desire to be there. I knew she had liked Tiny as well. It was just that it wouldn't be right. This was going to be a club funeral, a serious club full dress event, we were burying one of our brothers, and so it was really club business, so from that sense she and any of the other old ladies just didn't belong there.

I pulled on my gear at about nine or so and stepped out of the

139

house and into the grey gloom of the insistent, persistent rain. I had pulled on my scuffed black waterproof trousers but was resigned to the fact that I was going to be soaked through all day. I'd get Sharon to drop me some dry stuff off at the clubhouse later I decided as I slipped the key in the bike and felt the rain soak into my scarf.

We were meeting out of town to form the cortège. As road captain I'd been heavily involved in the organisation. With Dazza's blessing I'd even set foot inside the cop shop to let the plod know the plans as we didn't want any hassle from them, not that we'd have got it, they would have known better than to try and dick around the whole of The Brethren in the mood we were going to be in at a funeral of someone like Tiny; but also so that they could get organised to direct traffic and arrange escorts and stuff. With all the bikes that we were expecting and the speed that we would be travelling at behind the hearse the cortège would take quite a while to pass through any given point so the plod would need to arrange to hold up traffic at junctions for us and wave the stream of bikes through traffic lights so as not to interfere with the convoy. It just made sense, and in a weird way it was something the cops understood. I guess it's that sense of loyalty to your own, the thing that comes from a sense of being something set apart from the ordinary civilians. It's one thing that we on our side and the plod on theirs sort of have in common.

We'd told them to expect a few hundred bikes so we'd agreed a rendezvous point where we could form up out of town. When I got there, it was a surreal sight. The plod had coned a lane about a hundred yards long off one of the wider stretches of road and bikes were already arriving to form up, with The Brethren strikers standing silently towards the front of the lane, reserving without a word space for the club's turnout whilst further back the other clubs sorted themselves out in order of relative status. To keep traffic flowing there were a pair of jam sarni striped boxers on their stands at either end of the coned off lane, blue lights flashing and their riders in fluorescent yellow rain gear marshalling arriving bikers into the coned off lane while waving on citizens in cars who were slowing down to a crawl as they rubbernecked at the sight as they came past.

I wheeled across the road in a U turn and slid my bike into station at the front of the line. As road captain I, and Dazza as P, beside me, would normally be lead bikes, but today we had Polly as UK P with us as well, so Dazza and he would take the honours up front and this once I'd set us off and then slip in behind them to follow in second place. Leaving the bike slumped on its side stand I joined some of the other early arrivals huddled under the trees at the side of the road for a shared smoke and to watch the show as over the next half hour or so the column filled up and the rain came down.

'Are our friends coming to show their respects?' I asked Dazza quietly.

'Nah,' he said, 'thought about it but decided there's no need.'

I nodded. The cops would be watching us. No sense in giving them anything to see unnecessarily.

'Aye, aye, something's up,' said Dazza glancing towards where one of the coppers had leant into the fairing of his bike, and appeared to be in conversation although from where we were all we could hear was the crackle of his radio but nothing intelligible.

'Roger that,' we heard him say and then he turned to walk over to where we were standing.

'OK guys,' he said, 'I've just had word. The hearse and family cars are ready to go so it's all on if you're ready?'

'Yeah, I think so,' said Dazza dropping his fag on the ground.

'Right then. We'll give you the escort into town as arranged. Once we're rolling I'll radio ahead so the hearse can pull out to let you form up behind when we get to the undertakers and then we can all roll on to the cemetery. OK by you?'

'Fine by us,' said Polly, pulling on his lid and turning to lead us back to our bikes, 'Gentlemen, start your engines.'

We felt rather than saw the wave of attention as the guys from further down the line saw us move but to make it official I raised my arm in the air and rapidly waved my hand twice round in a circle to indicate 'mount up' even as I saw cigarettes being dropped, conversations breaking up and lids being pulled on. As I started my own bike, without turning round I could hear a ripple of noise as starter motors whirred and engines burst into life with a roar, each adding to the suddenly growing cacophony of sound from the pack behind me as riders flicked off chokes and blipped their throttles to warm their bikes up.

141

I pulled my goggles down over my eyes against the rain and wiped across the front of them with a gloved finger. Better, but the oncoming headlights of the cars still starred crazily together with the flashing blue lights of the cop bikes and their bright brake lights.

I could see the lead copper, the one who'd come over to speak to us, he was sat on his bike, half turned, waiting in his seat for us to be off. Well fuck it, I thought. Let him wait till we are good and ready. This was our show, not his.

And Dazza and Polly were waiting beside me as well, Dazza looking straight ahead, Polly glancing down at his dials for some reason. They were both just waiting, waiting for me and my signal. Because I was road captain, this was down to me. Taking the weight on my left leg and bracing my bike upright I stood up in my seat and looked round over my shoulder, back down the line of bikes. It looked as though everyone was up and started, a solid line of lids stretching back as far as I could see, and right at the back the flickering lights of the police beemers where they had moved out into the road to hold the traffic and let us out. Well sod them, they could wait too, I thought.

I raised my arm and felt hundreds of pairs of eyes on it. I held it there for a moment and then waved it forward and down, hearing the increase in noise as reflexively, everyone edged up their revs in anticipation of the off.

'OK, let's go.' I nodded to Dazza and he and Polly nodded back and slipping their clutches, they eased off and out into the road without looking behind or glancing at the coppers. We'd go at our own speed. They could form up on us. I slipped in next to Butcher as sergeant at arms behind them and behind us first the club and then the others slowly started to roll in disciplined pairs.

There had been words in a sort of chapel of rest at the entrance to the graveyard. The crowd was too big, so only The Brethren and family made it inside. It wasn't too much. Just some words about Tiny and what a great bloke he was and then we, his brothers, carried him to the graveside.

We had shovelled the earth in over Tiny and the guys were starting to break up into bunches for the ride back. Polly, Dazza and I stood by the graveside waiting. As the national and local charter Ps and as the road captain we were still in charge, this was still our event. So we stood there as the rain continued to softly fall, insinuating its way into every sodden crevice and chink in our armour, while engines started outside the gates and the crowd thinned.

Dazza and I lit up, me cupping my lighter against the wet. Polly didn't smoke.

'Well now, what the fuck's going on here?' Polly asked conversationally as we reappeared in a puff of smoke, 'Did I need to pack my tin fucking helmet or what? There's way too much action going on round here for my liking, given what's going down. I thought you were going to keep things nice and peaceful like, Dazza, up here amongst the sheep?'

'Yeah, well I was. Only trouble is we've got a black one.'

'Sheep?'

Dazza nodded.

'Who?'

'It's Butcher.'

'Butcher? Why? What for?'

Dazza sucked on his fag and looked around to ensure that there was no one else close enough to overhear.

'Personal beefs, as far as I can make out.'

'Tiny?'

'Yeah.'

'So what happened?'

Dazza shrugged. 'I left him in charge and he just seems to have lost the plot and went too far while we were away,' he said indicating me with a dip of his head, 'I asked him to clear up and it looks like he's just used it as an excuse to settle his own accounts as well.'

Yeah right, I thought to myself as I stood there in silence listening to him as the rain drenched us, that's complete bollocks. What about Billy? What were the chances of Billy really being just one of Butcher's personal beefs that you really hadn't known about when you got out of the car. And what about 'before' I wondered, what about Gyppo? What really happened that night?

'Anyone else involved?' Polly asked.

'No.'

'What you going to do?'

143

'The necessary.'

'You'll take care of it?'

'I'll take care of it.'

'Going to tell people?'

'What's there to tell?'

Polly nodded. 'I suppose you're right. They'll get the message anyway though will they?'

'Sure they will.'

Wibble was coming over and Dazza and Polly left off as he reached us. There was a muffled conversation and Dazza left us with a 'Be back in a mo' to go with him to sort something out, although to be truthful, with everyone having now made it back to their vehicles there really wasn't much to do other than make our way back to the clubhouse ourselves.

But Polly still remained standing beside me, we were the only two left in the graveyard now. I had the impression that it wasn't just by chance.

'It was a bad business that car bomb,' he said quietly and matter of factly, as if carrying on a conversation which in reality we had never started, 'That mate of yours, Billy. Bad for business.'

'Everyone's getting on just nicely now,' he continued, 'so why would anyone want to stir up shit like that? Why start a war when no one needs it? We need to get rid of whoever did that, whoever it was.'

What did Polly mean I wondered? What did he know, or simply suspect?

'Well taking out a Rebel's not going to help keep the peace is it?' I proffered cautiously.

He shrugged, 'True, but like I said, whoever it was, we don't want the heat on us, particularly not just at the moment, if you know what I mean.'

I got his drift of course.

'*If he who rules a state cannot recognise evils until they are upon him…*' Polly started.

'*…then he is not a truly wise man,*' I finished for him.

Polly looked across at me appraisingly, 'Oh, so you know it?'

'Yeah.'

'Have you read it?' he asked, and I nodded.

144

'Is it good?'

'Yeah,' I said, shutting my face down to cover my utter astonishment at the question, 'haven't you?'

'Nah,' he said dismissively, looking away, 'it's just something I picked up somewhere that rang true. Heard it's good though.'

He hadn't read the fucking P! I couldn't believe it. You twat, going round quoting crap that you don't really understand, as he turned back to face me.

'Yeah. He had some smart stuff to say.'

'Like what?'

'Oh loads of things,' I said looking him straight in the eye, 'like *the only proper study is war.*

Polly nodded, 'Hey I like that, what was it, *the only proper study is war?* That's good. That makes sense to me. Go on then, I'm listening, what else does he have to say then?'

'Well,' I said thinking furiously, 'how about *the unarmed man is never safe from armed servants.* How do you like that?'

He just looked at me for that one, his face a mask.

'Or *you can be hated just as much for good deeds as bad ones.*'

'Well now they're all true enough,' he said slowly, gazing back squarely at me, before his eyes slid across to look towards where Dazza was standing at the gates talking to Butcher. 'You know, I think I might have to get round to reading it one day after all.'

Bad for business I thought, as he turned to go, and I flicked the butt of my fag off into a muddy puddle. Was business really all it was about now? We used to be about something different.

Looking at Polly and listening to him it was true enough I decided, *a good man soon comes to ruin amongst the bad. So if you want to remain in charge, you have to learn how not to be good.* But that was not one to tell Polly.

It was just life.

Men see what you appear to be, very few see you for what you really are. Now I saw what Polly was.

Dazza caught me, grabbing me by my elbow just as I was getting ready to leave and leaning forward to speak quietly into my ear so he couldn't be overheard.

'Look Damage, normally I wouldn't involve you in this but

Sprog's lunched his bike, Bagpuss ain't around, I used Wibble last time and I need to ring the changes a bit but there ain't too many guys I can trust to do this shit and get it right.'

'Sure, what d'ya need?' I asked as I pulled on my cold sodden gloves.

'Post some stuff for me will ya? Wibble'll have the parcels tomorrow in his motor and can meet up with you to hand over the stuff. I want you to take it out and do it somewhere your way. It's the usual deal.'

I nodded and swung my leg over the bike.

I got the gear off Wibble later the next day in a lay-by to make sure we weren't being watched and stuffed them into a bag slung across the back seat of the car I'd borrowed, before heading out across country to some out of the way sub-post offices. There were three parcels, two to Glasgow addresses and one in South Wales. They were brick sized and I sent them first class, but not recorded, no one in their right mind would want to sign for something like that the other end. The posties asked if the contents were worth more than thirty-nine pounds as I handed them over to be weighed and I shook my head, if only they knew. Dazza was definitely in business.

They'll give you a proof of postage Dazza had said. Bring it back to me, he had instructed.

I suppose it was his way of checking that I'd actually sent something. He could then let his contacts know to expect it so that they would have someone at the address who could take a parcel when it arrived. After all, they really wouldn't want to have to go down to the sorting office to ID themselves and pick it up would they?

It also meant he could check it had gone to the right place since they wrote the post code and house number on it, and it meant he could check that I was actually mixing it up, using different post offices and not getting lazy and just banging them all through the same one.

He was smart was Dazza.

Of course he wouldn't know that I'd actually sent what he'd given me, but again once his guys the other end took delivery I guess he'd hear soon enough if I'd interfered with the parcel or tried to pull a fast one.

The other thing I guess he couldn't know was whether I had copied down the addresses on the parcels although since they could always have been a test I in turn could not know for sure that they were the real deal. They could be dummies that would wing anything that came in back down to him so he would soon see if I tried anything on with them, or he could be getting word back about what had arrived. That was part of the trouble that we were now getting into. How could anyone trust anything that anyone else ever did? The stakes were getting too high and the possibility of and consequences of any mistake or betrayal were so serious that you had to think through every step very carefully.

But then you also couldn't be seen to be thinking through things too carefully. Because that in itself might arouse suspicions. What are you thinking? Why are you thinking it? What are you planning? Why are you being so careful?

In place of the old absolute bonds of trust, brother amongst brother, something new was growing. Something that I didn't like and didn't want to be part of.

A sort of inevitable institutionalised paranoia.

In a situation where someone like Dazza would want to err on the side of caution no one could ever be completely safe. In fact the higher up the tree you got, the more you knew, the more risk you represented, the more exposed you probably were.

No, you would have to be pretty fucking stupid to punt anything off to them to suggest a bit of private enterprise. Still, you never knew when any bit of knowledge might come in handy did you?

*

Sharon noticed when I picked up the slim book from the bedside.

'Hey you aren't reading that again? Don't you ever get bored with it? You must know it off by heart by now!' she joked.

'Yeah, just about,' I grunted, reaching for the pair of reading glasses I had taken to leaving on the cabinet and settling them down on the end of my nose as I started to leaf through the well thumbed pages to find the short section I was after, no more than a paragraph long early in the book, my eyesight was starting to give me problems with reading the small print by the dim light of the bedside lamp.

'There's just something in here I want to find,' I said, flicking through the pages. 'It's something that's been bugging me and I just want to look it up.'

'Bugging you?' she said sharply, catching the tone of my voice, swivelling round in bed to look at me with concern, the duvet slipping down to expose her shoulders as she reached out her arm to lay her hand on my shoulder. 'Hey now, what's up? What's the matter?'

My hands fell into my lap taking the opened book with them as I rolled my eyes up towards the ceiling and stared vacantly at a cobweb that was waving gently in the updraft of warm air from the reading light.

What's the matter? I thought. What's the matter?

What a fucking question.

What a whole set of fucking questions.

Where do you start?

What do they want?

What the fuck am I involved with?

Who the hell could I talk to about it?

It was club business.

I believed in brothers loving each other but when did it cross the line? When did your love and loyalty to your brother mean that you are just being exploited by him?

'I've never seen you like this love,' I heard her say as if from a distant planet and my mind wheeled round in a vicious circle of conflicting emotions. Where did my loyalties lie? Who really were my club and my brothers? What did I owe them and what did I owe myself? Where was the freedom that being part of a freebooting club had always meant to me?

She just waited silently, a look of concern on her face. I lifted my left arm to give her a space and reached across with my right to take her hand from where it rested on my shoulder and pull her gently across towards me. Without a word she moved over to nestle up against me, her arm stretched across my chest, her head resting on my shoulder as she waited for an answer if one was going to come. She knew that it was up to me what I wanted to say. That there was nothing she could say which would make me talk. She could just wait and hope and see what I felt I could tell her, when I felt I could say it.

148

'It's Dazza,' I said at last. It felt as though the words were being wrenched out of me with pliers.

'Of course it is,' she said gently, 'I knew that. But what about him?'

'He's using the guys.'

'Using them? How?'

'He's using their loyalty to the club and to each other to exploit them.'

'But he's not used you to do anything you don't want to do has he?'

'No.'

'Then what's your problem?' she challenged, 'It's up to all the guys to decide for themselves what they will or won't do isn't it? You all make your own choices and live by them don't you? That's what you always do.'

She was right.

'I don't understand. You're an outlaw biker. You've always been about being free and not taking any shit from anyone. So what's all this crap with Dazza?'

The crap wasn't with Dazza, that's what she didn't get yet. The trouble was Dazza. Dazza and what he was capable of. What he was capable of and what it meant for us.

And by us I didn't mean the club. I meant Sharon, and me.

I meant Gyppo, admitting to myself for the first time what had really been festering away, growing like a tumour in the dark of my mind.

Like Gyppo, the whacked out, paranoid, raving speed freak that I had last seen losing it that night where Dazza, his supplier, could see it.

Deep down I had to admit to myself, I had never completely believed Gyppo's death was an accident.

But now it was all happening again. *Like last time,* the copper's voice came back to me.

'Listen, I knew Gyppo sure did downers but did he ever really do smack?'

'Not while I was with him. Why'd you ask? Why bring that up now?'

But you weren't at the end were you, I thought? But for once in my life I did think before I opened my mouth, and having thought, I bit my tongue and kept it shut.

'Nothing. Just thinking about Tiny that's all.'

Even now, four or five years later, the wounds were too fresh and too painful for hurtful words.

'Don't worry about it,' I said as I turned out the light and we lapsed into silence.

*

I was later than usual for prayers on Monday. Fat Mick was on duty indoors when I got there, the others had obviously already all gone up. 'Hey, have you heard the news?' he asked as he buzzed me in through the steel door.

'No? What news?'

'It's Butcher.'

'What about him?'

'He's been topped.'

'Topped? Christ, how? When?'

'Shot sounds like. Somebody took him out round the back of his shop. Execution style it sounds like.'[11]

'Bloody hell, do we know who?'

'Well you need to see Dazza about that.'

'Dazza? What's he got to do with it?'

'You'll find out,' he said with a grin. There was no love lost there for Butcher from Fat Mick which I could understand. Still, for all his faults, Butcher had been a full patch and Fat Mick was still a striker so he ought to show some respect, 'He's upstairs in the meeting room, telling the guys.'

And so he was. He was being careful about the words that he

---

[11] *Ken 'Butcher' Moore, born 2 April 1948, was found dead on Monday 29 August 1994 in the cold store of his butcher's shop having been killed it's believed on the Saturday evening. He had been handcuffed and been suspended by the cuffs from a meat hook in the ceiling. He had then been shot twice at point blank range with both barrels of a sawn off shotgun and police had to rely on fingerprints for identification. The gun was found at the scene although it had been wiped clean of fingerprints.*

Again, no one has ever been charged in connection with his death and officially the case also remains open.

actually used, we swept regularly, and there were only full patches present, but hey you never knew, but the message was clear. Butcher had been left in charge, Butcher had exceeded his authority, Butcher had used his brief to settle personal beefs and Dazza had as a result been forced to come back to take over personal control and sort things out. And no one was left in any doubt about what sorting things out meant. Butcher had crossed the line and now Butcher had paid the price.

I got fined for being late into the meeting of course.

*

She and I both know there's some music I just can't listen to.

It's fairly obvious that if I start to want to listen to the Wall, or the hollowness of Bauhaus, or some Mötorhead, that I'm going into one of my self-destructive cycles.

'What's up?' she asked as I killed the grinding guitars and we hit the sack.

I could see the worry in her eyes. But I just didn't know how to tell her anything.

I knew that I had killed Billy. I don't just mean that I pressed the button. I mean that I had been responsible for him getting killed.

Billy had known what he was talking about alright. Dazza would have got Butcher to do it.

Or me.

It was what I had been trying to, or not trying to talk to her about the previous evening. We were being used, Dazza was using our loyalty to set us up as his own personal support club.

'Listen, you know I wanted to look something up the other night?'

'Yes.'

'Well I found it.'

'So?'

'So, I wanted to tell you about it.'

'OK, but why?'

'Because it's the only way that things makes sense to me.'

'So what's to tell from your old book that makes sense of where you are today?'

'Well, let's see what you think then. Have you ever heard of a guy called Cesare Borgia?'

151

'Borgia rings a bell I think, something about poisons perhaps?'

'You're thinking of Lucretia, his sister.'

'OK.'

'So Cesare, who was also called Duke Valentino, he was the Pope's son.'

'The Pope? You mean like the Holy fucking Father? Like the Vatican?'

'Yeah, second son actually. They think when he was twenty or so he had his elder brother knocked off to eliminate the competition although no one ever proved anything. This was way back at the end of the fourteen hundreds, start of the fifteen hundreds, things were way different then.'

'Christ almighty! What a family.'

'And Borgia wasn't even one of the anti-Popes, he was the regular one, but it was all political back then, the church was a real power, and the Pope had armies and stuff just like any of the other princes.'

'Wow, I never knew that. So what about this Valentino then?'

'Duke Valentino. Like I say he was the Pope's son and his dad Alexander the sixth wanted to carve out a kingdom for him in Italy. But he had a problem, he couldn't give him one of the Church's own states as that would antagonise too many of the other powers and he didn't have many natural allies as none of the other princes wanted to allow the Church to get stronger by having the Pope or Cesare grab more territory.'

'So what did he do?'

'Simple, he stirred the shit. He did as much as he could to create turmoil amongst the other Italian states, all sorts of crap, and then gave the French king a divorce in return for the loan of his armies to Cesare so that he could make his first conquest of a place called the Romagna.

'So then Cesare's taken Romagna and what does he find? He thinks the people who ran it before were weak, and to a degree he's right, in that anyone can do what they like, there's factions, chaos, you name it. So he decides, like you do, that it needs to be pacified, so that all his subjects will obey him and he can do what he wants.'

'So what's he do? Go in with the big boots?'

'No, he doesn't. That's the clever part. What he does is he appoints someone else to rule it for him as his lieutenant, a guy called Remirro de Orco. Now this guy is a real hardnosed bastard and Cesare gives him *carte blanche*, tells him do what you like, but sort it out, no holds barred. And of course he goes out and does it.

'But then Cesare sees that not only has Remirro done enough, but that leaving him with so much authority might also be dangerous for Cesare. He also recognised that Remirro's ruthlessness had become hated and some of that was rubbing off on him as well, so he had to do something about it.'

'Like what?'

'He decided to show that all the violence had been Remirro's doing and not his, so everyone would think that everything bad that had happened had been down to Remirro. So one morning the city wakes up to find Remirro's body hacked in half in the main square with the bloody knife left beside it.

'Everyone was so relieved that Remirro was gone and so impressed by how brutally and effectively it had been done that they were happy to give Cesare the credit, because of course, from then on everything was peaceful because Remirro had done all the dirty work that was needed before he got topped.'

'And you think that's what Dazza did to Butcher? That Butcher was Dazza's patsy?' she thought about that for a moment, 'But that means...'

'That Dazza was responsible for all the deaths?'

'Yes?'

I nodded.

'What Tiny? And Billy too?'

'Yes, directly or indirectly. It's the oldest trick in the book, isn't it? Delegate all the dirty work to someone else and keep your own hands clean, because then you can then blame them, have them take the fall when you need them to.'

She hadn't yet made the connection back to Gyppo but that was now firmly in my mind. I didn't know how long it would take her to make the leap but she would soon enough.

I could see now how Dazza had always planned to use and then get rid of Butcher. It was all so obvious in retrospect. Just like Cesare he was presenting him now as a bad apple, as having been excessive in his cleaning out. By spreading the word amongst the guys that everything that had happened was down to Butcher's personal beefs, he had ensured Butcher took all the blame for everything that had happened and then Dazza had come back in to take him out and claim the credit for restoring peace and prosperity. You could see the way his mind worked. He was brilliant.

The question was though, as she asked it, what was I going to do about it now?

'So if he has taken out Butcher does that mean that everything's now over?'

'I don't know. Possibly,' I conceded.

'So, should you just keep quiet?'

'Stay out of it d'you mean? Avoid any trouble?'

'Yes, I suppose so.'

'I don't know if I can do that. Not after what's happened to Tiny and Billy.'

'But if things are quiet shouldn't you just let it go? After all Butcher, who's the guy who actually did it, is dead. And you don't actually know that Dazza actually ordered any of it. He wasn't even there when Tiny got his was he? He was with you out in Portugal or wherever it was?'

She was right of course. Again. But I had already made up my mind.

'You know you should never let something go just to avoid trouble.' There was no avoiding trouble, I knew. All you ever did by not facing up to it today is to delay it until later to someone else's advantage. Better to deal with something now when it's small than have to face it later when it's bigger or more of a threat.

'But why not just wait and see so you're sure? Why risk trouble now for the sake of it?'

'It's not for the sake of it. It's because it's necessary. Today I have a position, today I can trust to the power I've got. Who knows what will happen tomorrow or the day after? Dazza might get weaker, fine, but who knows, he might just as well get stronger. In fact given the hand he's got to play at the moment that's the most likely scenario. And if he does, what have I achieved by waiting? I've just fucked up. But if I go for it now, well, we'll just see what happens won't we?'

No it was far better to just go for it now, and see how the pieces then fell.

There was a resigned silence, and then in a quiet voice she asked, 'So what happened? To your bloke Cesare in the end I mean? Did he keep his kingdom?'

'No he didn't. He got unlucky. He did everything he could to ensure that he was secure, except that he hadn't allowed for the chance that he would fall sick and he was very nearly on his own death-bed when his father died. So he couldn't control who was elected as his dad's successor as Pope and took over the Church's armies and that was that really.'

'It just goes to show I suppose,' she said reflectively.

'Show what?'

'That you can't always control everything.'

She was right there too. There was even a theory that his father had accidentally poisoned both of them, but I thought that was just a nice story.

*

Butcher's pet Spud had got his patch. Dazza saw to that.

It was the first patch I ever saw awarded with a Bonesman's badge already on it.

I guess they were Spud's rewards. It was pretty obvious what for.

10   THE TALK

The cops pulled me in again, this time over Butcher getting it. I don't know why they seemed so keen to get me in the frame for everything. I was thinking about telling them how I'd been on the grassy knoll.

'Come on son, everyone knows that you hated Butcher.'

'Do they really? Now who would say a thing like that? Who's this everyone who's so chatty?'

'Yeah, like I'd tell you that? Let's just stop playing games shall we? We both know something's building here.'

'Something?'

'First the takeover and then all those guys kicked out. Then Tiny gets it, then someone blows your mate young Billy to kingdom come and now Butcher gets blasted. It's not looking too clever for you guys at the moment is it?'

'Yeah well, perhaps I'll be able to sell the guys some life insurance.'

'What d'you reckon Sarge,' the younger one chipped in laconically, 'is that enough of a motive?'

'Listen, you little scumbag,' the sergeant hissed leaning forward and stabbing the table aggressively with his finger to underline his points, 'Like I told you before. Personally, I really don't care if you lot take all of each other out, in fact nothing would give me more pleasure than to sit back and just let it happen. However sometimes unfortunately you just can't mix business with pleasure, particularly if there's a chance that this'll get out of hand.'

He sat back in his chair with a disgusted expression on his face like I was something that he'd just stepped in on the street, 'Fucking car bombs for Chrissakes. Innocent people could get hurt and I don't want that on my patch.'

'In fact I just won't have it, d'you hear me, Damage? So you take a message for me. You take it to all your guys. This stops, right here, right now. Understand?'

I looked at him blankly. 'Are you planning to charge me with anything officer?'

'What? No. Not this time.'

'Then I'm free to go I take it?'

'Yes and get the fuck out of my sight. But just remember what I said.'

'Oh I'll remember alright officer.'

'And remember to tell your mates?'

'I'll let them know we've had another one of our little chats.'

'Now you do that son. You just fucking do that.'

*

'I don't fucking believe it. Lifted again! For fucking Butcher this time! What does he think I am, Murder Inc?'

Dazza laughed, 'Don't worry about it mate. They're just trying to wind you up.'

'Yeah, I know.'

'Are you worried about it?'

'Nah, course not. Just it's a pain in the arse y'know?'

'Yeah, it must be,' he commiserated, 'Still, while they've got this downer on you, even more need to make sure you stay clean. No sense giving 'em any excuse.'

'Yeah, you're right. Still, I'm thinking about getting away from it for a bit.'

I'd checked the accounts, more dosh had come in, so I took a chance.

'Sprog and Bagpuss're still out of it. D'ya need any more post doing out my way?'

'Nah, it's OK thanks, I'll get Wibble to take a trip up North to take care of it.'

'OK, it's just I'm thinking about taking Sharon away next week, bit of a break, y'know? So if yer gonna need me that's fine but I need to know so I can work round it.'

'Well OK then. Are you at prayers on Monday?'

'Of course.'

'Turning up on time this time?'

Now he was winding me up I knew, but all the same, there was the continual watchfulness, the hypersensitivity to detecting the merest hint of slipping commitment, a weakening of the faith and loyalty that meant I couldn't let it go unchallenged.

'Yeah, give us a break will ya? I'm like late one time and it's a hanging offence all of a sudden?'

'Well then, if I'm gonna need you it'll be Wednesday so I'll let you know then.'

'Chances?'

'Probably not, like I said, Wibble should be able to handle it this week and Sprog and Bagpuss should both be back in action next week so I'll be back in business.'

'OK. Cool.'

'You going to the funeral?' He meant Billy's.

There didn't seem to be any reason to deny it.

'Yeah. He was my oldest mate.'

Dazza nodded. 'Yeah, you ought to go whatever. Would look strange if you didn't.'

It was another grey morning as the hearse rolled in quietly through the cemetery gates followed by a couple of cars although at least it had kept dry.

You can tell a lot from the turnout for a funeral. In contrast to Tiny's there were only a few for Billy, and nothing and no one from the club, not even a wreath. It was a family do not a club event. Family and girlfriends. And standing at the back, me.

Dazza had put the word out about Billy's Rebels connection, about his Glasgow trip. He was giving that out as part of Butcher's beef with Billy. That was why guys from the club had stayed away of course. No one wanted to show up for a guy who'd been dealing with The Rebels, it was almost as bad as being a grass in some ways, not just because it was dealing with the enemy but because of the danger it meant he had been bringing everyone into. You could understand how they felt. We were ready to go to war with The Rebels as and when we ever needed to and accept whatever the consequences were. But to hear that someone in the club had risked stirring up all that kind of shit just to do some dealing of their own, well that was hard to stomach.

The family had gone for a vicar, the works. Billy's mum and dad were standing beside the grave. She was crying. He had been staring into the middle distance as though he was a million miles away from the here and now of the grass squelching underfoot and the smell of damp earth from the grave. As the coffin was lowered into the ground she turned and buried her head against his shoulder, her body rocking with sobs as he dragged his attention around to her in slow motion and enfolded her within his arms and let her cry. I could see his mouth move but I couldn't hear what he was saying.

It was a full sized coffin they had used, all varnished pine and brass rail and handles. I wondered how much of Billy they had actually found to put inside it. Seemed a bit of a waste really.

As the preacher droned on I switched off and carried on thinking about the situation. Dazza's mistake I decided was in how he had done it, he'd made the mistake of not moving to base himself at the clubhouse.

He had faced a problem in taking over The Legion. With the exception of Butcher's cohort, we had always been a democratic club, used to being consulted, to making our decisions as a club, by vote. We had had that freedom, it was part of our club's DNA. But then Dazza had taken over and his model was very much a top down one, of command and control, that he was in charge, that the club would work as a team and that meant we would all do exactly what he told us to.

And the problem with that was there was always going to be a potential for conflict between the way he was going to run things and what the guys had been used to. We wouldn't forget very quickly how our club had run; within the members from the old Legion, that memory of freedom would remain strong. So if any conflict arose, a challenge to Dazza which could call on that emotion would be a powerful force that opponents would swiftly rally round. As I saw it, that was why Tiny had had to go of course, he was the obvious figure-head or rallying point for any such challenge, and so Dazza had had to have him taken out completely, whatever story he was now spinning to the guys.

Of course, to really ensure peace he should have destroyed us all in such a way that we could never threaten him again. But that was very much the nuclear option and would have meant that while he might have got the territory, he would have wiped out the resources by way of bodies that came with it. And without bodies how realistic was it to think he could hold an area that big without someone else moving in?

No, keeping most of us was a risk that he had been forced to take.

But then to manage that risk it would have been best if he had based himself in the territory, changed to operating from the clubhouse so that he was very visible to the guys who were there, so he could be a living breathing, constantly visible symbol of his own authority to them, not some absentee landlord sat in his pub over in the city that unless they were part of the inner circle they only saw at every other Prayers if they were lucky.

There were lessons to be learnt there. But they were all old ones that I had read so many times before from *The P* and knew off by heart. If you are going to hurt someone, you should crush them so thoroughly that there is no chance of them ever recovering sufficiently to be able to rise up and take revenge. And if you are not going to hurt someone, just leave them in peace and security so long as they know it is you they have to thank for this as their protector.

So I could try playing the old club card if I wanted to, I could raise the watchword of liberty to obtain support I would need within the old Legion club to take him.

But that was just the old Legion guys, what about the others, how would I deal with them?

As I thought it through I decided that in contrast with Dazza's problems in taking over and holding The Legion, taking and holding Dazza's charter was going to be easy precisely because he had run it like a dictatorship.

It was a much simpler question of decapitation. If I could take out Dazza and his top guys then the others would follow a new leader easily enough. So it had to be a coup d'état, done hard and fast, and executed so ruthlessly, completely destroying anyone who was to be harmed, so that as the memory of it faded, the rest of the guys would carry on in peace.

The priest was winding down the service now. I caught the ashes to ashes, dust to dust bit which seemed a bit ironic given the circumstances but no one else seemed to be giving the words a second thought.

This was going to be high stakes stuff.

I knew the theory of what I was going to need to do. I had worked out a plan as to how I was going to do it. Now what I needed were the tools with which to put it into action. And that was one of the reasons

I was here today.

I raised my head and stared across the grave; past the mourners clustered around, yet stepped back from the gaping wound in the earth; over the green tarpaulin covering the mound of dirt waiting for the mini digger to be trundled out from the shed at the back of the field once everyone had gone, to shovel it back into the hole; to where a large figure dressed in dark clothing was standing watching the ceremony from a distance.

Our eyes met, our faces were blank. Slowly and deliberately I nodded to him and after what seemed like an age of his eyes boring into mine, Gut did the same.

The priest was done and the people by the graveside broke up into ones and twos, turning to go and walking or stumbling away from the graveside, onto the gravelled path and crunching their way in slow quiet knots to the cars waiting at the entrance.

Gut and I were still standing where we had each been during the service and it was only as the last of the mourners reached the gate that we advanced to meet each other on the path.

I took out a packet of fags and offered him one. He took it and I flicked my Zippo for us both to light up.

'So what's happening now?' Gut asked by way of making conversation as he exhaled a cloud of smoke.

'They're all going back to Billy's folks place. His mum's laid on some food and stuff.'

'You going?'

I wasn't sure how I felt about it. I shook my head. 'Don't think so.'

'Why not?'

'Don't think it would help. I guess they still blame me for getting him mixed up in all this stuff in the first place.'

He nodded.

'So what's this about then?'

'What?'

'All this,' he said gesturing to the empty graveyard. 'I mean where's yer fucking Brethren brothers now, Damage? Billy gets blown up by The Rebels and none of the wankers turn up for his funeral. I mean what's that all about then?'

'I'm here aren't I?'

161

'Yeah but you and whose army eh? You're not here officially are you? Skulking at the back, no club wreath or nothing. You'd have thought if The Rebels snuffed him then all the more reason for the club to step up for the funeral in a big way. I mean it ought to mean war right? You don't just do that to someone in a club, any club, never mind The Brethren and the reputation that they have to protect and expect nowt to happen. I mean they'll have to be gearing up to do something won't they?'

I dropped my fag and ground it out with the toe of my boot, before staring back into his face.

'Yeah, strange isn't it?'

'Is it war?'

'No, it isn't.'

'Well why the fuck not?'

'Now that,' I said smiling at him, 'is a fucking good question that far too few people are thinking to ask.'

'Well I'm asking it now.'

'Yes you are, and I think I want to tell you why.'

'Well, what's stopping you?'

'Don't want to be repeating myself that's all.'

He raised his eyebrows quizzically.

'See Popeye much these days?' I asked casually.

That immediately put him on the defensive I noticed. 'No, you know we don't, not since you bastards disbanded us. That was part of the price of calling the dogs off. You know that.'

'Still, I bet you're still in touch. Would make sense wouldn't it?'

'Are you trying to trap me or something Damage? Stir up shit between us and The Brethren? Get the truce called off? What are you up to here? What do you want?'

I just smiled at him. 'Me? Nah mate I'm not up to anything like that. Like I said, I'm here aren't I? When as you so accurately observe, the rest of The Brethren aren't. Now don't you find that just a little bit peculiar? And I'm telling you that I'm thinking about filling you in on some club business. And don't you find that a bit odd as well? So what do I want? Well I might as well hang for a sheep as a lamb. I want to meet with you and Popeye.'

'Really?'

'Yeah, really. Somewhere safe, somewhere private.' I could see he was hesitant.

'Look I know what you're thinking, but this isn't a trap. You choose the time and the place to suit you. Pick me up and take me there if you like so I can't set you up. It's up to you. I just want you to hear what I've got to say.'

He looked at me appraisingly.

'I'll think about it.'

'You do that. But Gut, don't think about it too long.'

'I've heard that before. And I didn't much like it then either.'

'Yeah, I know. And I'm sorry about that. But for what I think is going down, we need to talk in the next few days or it'll be too late.'

'Will it now?' He finished his cig and dropping it on the grass took a moment to grind it into the dirt with the toe of his boot before looking back up at me.

'OK,' he said at last, 'I'll see what I can do. I can't promise anything about Popeye though.'

'Yeah, bollocks. Call him. I'll wait.'

*

I caught Dazza at the bar of the clubhouse before Prayers on Monday night.

'How'd it go?'

'Oh, it was OK I suppose. For that sort of thing.'

'Many there?'

'Nah, just family and a few local friends really, although there was one interesting face.'

'So who's that then?'

'Gut showed up.'

'Did he now?'

'Yeah. He and Billy were always friendly, so he was just showing his respects.'

'How d'you know that?'

'I spoke to him.'

Dazza laughed. 'Really? So how'd that go then?'

'It was fine.'

'Considering the last time you met, he had you jumped, stomped and put in hospital?'

'Yeah well. That was just business wasn't it? It was nothing personal. And now since they disbanded we've got the truce so I didn't see there was any issue from my side.'

'Guess not then. How about from his?'

'He seems OK. We're still not top of his list of favourites but then you wouldn't expect that, but so long as he's left in peace I don't see we'll have any trouble out of him.'

'I hope not.'

'Well they've not patched up again have they? Or thrown their lot in with The Hangmen or anybody else? So if they're not getting reorganised like that then there's nothing to worry about.'

'Guess not. So what did you two find to talk about then?'

'Oh not a lot. Billy mainly, what some of the other guys are up to these days, just chewed a bit of fat really.'

'Nothing else?'

'Nah. Just thought it was worthwhile making contact again since he was there. You know despite everything that happened, he's good people and was always useful. If we ever got him back onside he would be an asset.'

'Yeah,' Dazza said reflectively, 'I always rated him and I was sorry he ended up on the other side. But they way things panned out I think it'd be tricky looking to bring him in now, even if he wanted it. But never say never like. Oh well, I was wondering what you two had had to chat about over a smoke.'

Of course that was why I had told him. I had assumed that he would have been having the ceremony watched to see what went on, so I had got in with my story first. No use giving any grounds for suspicion.

*

The pickup happened the following day.

A battered white Transit van pulled up parallel to where I'd just parked my motor down the road a bit from my house where I'd found a space and a voice yelled 'Oi' from the open passenger window and a jerked thumb indicated the side door of the van. 'Get in,' said the voice. I didn't recognise either of the guys in the front. Without thinking about it I walked round the parked car, pulled on the handle and stepped up into the back of the van.

164

This was it.

I don't know where we went. They put a bag over my head and I sat on the floor of the van, my back against the wheel arch as we rocked and bumped our way along for what seemed like an age but in reality was probably no more than an hour or so until with a final sharp swerve as I guessed we turned into a driveway and rattled down a rutted farm track to a yard where with a slight skid on some loose gravel, we drew to a halt. There was a banging of doors and the sound of shouting voices.

'You followed?' was one I recognised.

'Nah, don't think so.'

'OK then, get him out and inside.'

And then there were hands, pulling me to my feet and shoving me out of the van and stumbling through a doorway and into what I saw when the bag was whipped off my head was an old farmhouse kitchen.

Facing me was Gut, and next to him was Popeye, as pissed off as ever it seemed about what had happened.

'You've got a fucking nerve Damage, wanting to meet up with us like this. You really have after all that's happened.'

I shrugged. 'Maybe.'

'Maybe? Maybe? What's to stop us just fucking doing you right now, right here?'

'Not a lot I guess, other than wanting to know what I've got to say.'

'Why would we want to know anything that you've got to say?'

'Because why would I have come here like this if I didn't think it was worth you hearing?'

'How d'you know what's worth hearing to us?'

'I don't, but that's just the risk I have to take isn't it?'

'Well now you've taken it,' broke in Gut, 'So I for one am interested in hearing what he's got to say.'

'So?' I asked Popeye, who fumed at me for a moment.

'OK,' he said finally, 'Go on then, say your piece. I'm listening, but it had better be good.'

'Well, the first thing is, you guys were right.'

'We were?'

'Yeah.'

'Well that's just great but now what do you want to do about it?'

'I want to go back to being us.'

'But that's impossible,' protested Gut, 'You know that.'

'Is it?' I asked, already knowing all the things they were thinking, 'Why?'

'Because we can't go back you tosser. None of us can, even if we wanted to. You know that and I never thought I'd hear you come whining to say something like that.'

'Yeah well, I don't mean going back. I just mean going back to being us.'

Gut was puzzled about where I was going with this, 'Well you're a minx[12] and we're either disbanded or in bad standing so just how do you think that's going to work, even if we wanted to?'

'This is all bullshit,' jumped in Popeye, 'what the fuck are we standing here listening to this drivel for?'

'No it's not,' I said calmly in the face of his outburst, 'I'm here aren't I? You know me and what I'm like. Why else would I be here?'

'God knows, perhaps you're just trying to set us up, give Dazza the excuse he needs for war,' he said.

'Dazza doesn't need an excuse for war. He can bring it on anytime he wants, you know that. You turned down The Brethren, that's reason enough in his book.'

'Yeah, but how do we know we can trust you and anything you say?' Popeye continued. 'No, if we're gonna trust you you're gonna have to do something to show us that you're really on the level, something to prove that you're not doing this for that fucker Dazza.'

I'd half expected this of course. Putting myself in their shoes, of course they would be bitter, angry and suspicious. I was here wearing a Brethren patch after all, a patch they had fought against when I had taken the other side in what was a war as bitter as only a civil war can be. They were always going to take a hell of a lot of convincing that I was on the level.

'OK,' I shrugged.

---

[12] *Disparaging nickname for The Brethren based on their black and red colours, from Minnie the Minx as opposed to Denis the Menace.*

'OK? What d'you mean, OK?'

'I mean, yeah, OK, I'll show you.'

'How?' Popeye demanded

'You got any strikers at the moment?'

'Might have,' he said cagily.

'Are those the guys that picked me up? They new?'

'Yeah, we're recruiting, figure we need some numbers.'

'Would anyone else in the club recognise 'em?'

'No chance.'

'Good. I'll need 'em in town on Wednesday. And I'll need a bike, not one that anyone will know.'

'I can organise that,' said Gut.

Of course I knew he could.

'Anything else?'

'Possibly somewhere to lie low for a while for the rest of this week. I need Dazza to think Shaz and I have gone away.'

'We can arrange that as well,' said Popeye.

'Right then, we're on.'

*

Sprog, Bagpuss and Wibble were Dazza's regular couriers, picking up the gear from him or wherever he told them to get it from, and taking it to be posted. With Sprog and Bagpuss out of action that just left Wibble, or me as a stand in since Dazza was obviously careful about who he was using for this. And from what Dazza had said it looked as though come Wednesday Wibble ought to be carrying.

At about two in the afternoon, the strikers let us know that Wibble was on the move. They followed him discretely as he visited a house in the east end of town, emerging with a heavy looking bag that he chucked in the back of his car, before heading out into the countryside. Out of town, as I had suspected, he turned north, heading up into the borders country where for much of the trip, the roads north would funnel him onto the main A road.

I fired up the kwacker that Gut had supplied and set off to intercept him. I had on a borrowed lid and jacket so that Wibble wouldn't be able to recognise me from my gear or tell who it was behind the scarf, but I had on my colours so that he would see the patch when I overtook him.

I caught him as the road rose up and down in roman straightness over a series of ridges, zooming up from behind to take up station out in the road beside the driver's side of the car. I looked in to check it was him at the same time that I could see he had clocked the patch and gave me a grin although I could see he was a bit puzzled that he didn't recognise the bike. I indicated that he was to follow me and he nodded in acknowledgement, so I accelerated from beside him to swing in front of him. Then for a few more miles I led him further out, further north along the main road he had been taking anyway. Further away from the daytime town and suburban traffic and into the quieter countryside. About twenty miles out we were taking another series of sudden crests when I indicated left and jabbed my arm at the upcoming turn just to make sure he understood. This was the moment, this was where the plan either worked, with Wibble deciding to follow my instructions, assuming that Dazza had sent me, or ignored me, carrying on to where he was planning to go anyway.

I slowed for the corner and gently dropped the bike through it, holding the speed just sufficiently to ensure it stayed upright and then coasting slowly, bike barely rolling, my eyes fixed on my inside mirrors until with satisfaction I saw his flashing indicators and the nose of his car turn the corner to follow me.

He was trusting me and following. That was good since it was going to make things a whole lot easier. If he hadn't then we would still have done it, but it would have required a whole lot more force and violence.

It was about five minutes later and a few miles off the main road that we took him. He was still behind me as I cruised along, leading him into the spot we had picked and he still followed when I indicated to pull into a lay-by that ran off the road behind a screen of trees, one of those old meanders of country road, cut off by more modern straightening and gradually forgotten except as a place to park and piss.

It was only when you got into it that you could see that the exit was blocked by the white Transit van which already had Popeye and some of his crew piling out of it.

It was an ambush. Wibble didn't stand a chance.

With a sudden roar two bikes came screaming down the road

behind us, appearing out of nowhere.

Wibble seeing what was happening desperately slammed the car into reverse and looked back over his shoulder as wheels spinning on the gravel he tried to get away from the helmeted hoard rushing towards him from the van. But just then, the bikes roared up beside him and I saw the passenger on the back of the first bike rise up in his seat and bring an axe swinging down from on high at the car, smashing into the windscreen in a huge starring crash, while with a darker, deeper roar, the front of a lorry in dirty fluorescent colours swung into the lay-by, closing the gap behind Wibble and cutting off his escape route out onto the main road. The car swerved in its crazy career backwards, half turning as though he was planning to try facing back out, before jolting as the back wheels hit and went up and over the kerb before tipping back as the whole car slid down off the road into the drainage ditch six feet below the side, and the van and lorry closed in around it.

Popeye and his strikers plunged down into the ditch beside the car, opening doors and bundling the dazed Wibble and his bag out of it. They got the gaffa tape on him while he was still too out of it to put up much of a fight and three of them carried him, starting to kick and struggle as he came to, a pair of them following him into the back of the van where they had thrown him and pulling the doors shut behind them. Popeye slung the bag onto the passenger seat of the van and jumped into the driver's seat.

And all the time I sat there, incognito behind a skull bandanna, in stranger's clothes and on a stranger's bike.

Gut meanwhile had jumped out of the cabin of his wrecking truck and was working with one of his guys to get a tow rope on the front of Wibble's motor.

'Right, let's get out of here,' he said to me, heading across to join Popeye in the van. He jerked his thumb at his driver, 'It's OK, it'll just look like he's doing a recovery if anyone comes along. He'll take it back to my place and we'll lose it.

Good old Gut I thought, as his massive bulk clambered up into the van. Never one to miss an opportunity. Popeye eased the van past Gut's recovery truck which now had its amber lights flashing and I slipped the clutch and tucked in behind to follow him while the other

169

bikes made themselves scarce.

I didn't know where they were planning to take us although I guessed that it was likely to be the place they had seen me before. I just had to go along for the ride at this stage and hope to hell that my plan was going to work out.

It was an old farmstead, isolated a way up the coast. A tumble down barn and an old farmhouse, barely habitable.

We were gathered around the table in the familiar looking kitchen, just Gut, Popeye and me, the others were either with Wibble where he had been bundled away, or keeping an eye out outside, Wibble's bag sat in front of us.

It was time to find out how much he was carrying, so I picked it up and emptied the contents onto the table.

There were four parcels, two addressed to Glasgow, one to South Wales and one to somewhere in the Midlands which was new. But then I'd noticed a new payment coming through recently banked somewhere around Brum, so maybe that was it.

'Who's in Glasgow then? asked Popeye.

'The Rebels,' I said off-handedly, as I looked the parcels over. About the right size I thought.

'What d'ya mean The Rebels?'

'I'll tell you in a moment,' I said, getting out my knife and flicking it open.

'And what's in 'em?' asked Gut suspiciously.

'Well now,' I said with a broad smile as I picked up a parcel and slit open the jiffy bag it was in, 'let's just have a little look-see, shall we?'

The stuff inside was wrapped in brown paper and bubble wrap which was a moment to cut away and then there it was, a genuine Cali brick, with the scorpion logo printed across the paper wrapping just the way Billy had described.

'Is that what I think it is?' whispered Gut as I handed it to him and picked up the next package.

'Yep, and I'm betting they are all the same.'

'Fucking hell,' said Popeye and I plonked the next one into his hand. 'I don't think I've ever seen so much gear. And you knew he had this?'

'I didn't know how much he would have but I was pretty sure he'd be carrying.'

'So what do we do with it?'

'You hold onto it for the moment. You stick it somewhere safe where it won't be found and don't mess with it, we're going to need this later. But meanwhile I need to keep the addresses off these parcels,' I said, cutting the front panels off the jiffy bags and stuffing them inside my cut off.

'What for?'

'For contacts,' which wasn't really an answer but seemed to do for now.

'Now what?' Gut asked as I closed my knife and slipped it back in my pocket.

'Now I need to speak to Wibble.'

'Speak to Wibble?' You've just helped us knock off a Brethren courier for four bricks of finest Charlie and now you want to blow your ID? Are you nuts?'

'Yeah, that's exactly what I want to do.'

'It's your funeral.'

'Yeah it is, isn't it?'

Down in the cellar, Wibble was gagged and blindfolded with silver grey gaffa tape, and watched over by the two strikers.

'Take the tape off his eyes,' I instructed.

'Are you sure?' the larger one asked surprised.

'Yeah, I want him to see my face.'

'OK, if that's what you really want.'

'Well he's heard my voice now hasn't he? So what's the difference?'

The striker bent down and none too gently caught the ragged edge of the tape and ripped it off Wibble's face. There was a furious look in his eyes and also one of shock as he saw not only me, but also Gut and Popeye.

I squatted down on the floor in front of him. He had been chained to some old pipework by the looks of it and his hands had been gaffa taped in front of him.

'Listen Wibble,' I said conversationally as I sat down on the floor opposite him and leant back against a post, I might as well get comfortable 'cos this was gonna take a while, 'that's right, it's me Damage. Look, sorry it had to be this way, it's nothing personal, it's just business that's all, and once I've got this thing sorted out you'll be free to go.'

His eyes told me he didn't believe me, didn't give a fuck and would quite gladly rip my balls off if he had half the chance.

'Look Wibble, I need to talk to you so I'm gonna get 'em to take the tape off your mouth but don't start shouting the house down or it goes straight back on again. Understood?'

There was just his furious glare.

'Understood?'

He just stayed stock still.

'I'll take that as a yes then,' I sighed, nodding to one of the hulking looming strikers to get it off him.

There was a hesitation, without looking round I could sense the striker looking to Popeye for instructions, which must have been nodded because the striker leant forward and ripped the tape from across Wibble's mouth releasing an 'Oh fuck!' of pain and a stream of muttered obscenities.

'Are you OK?'

'Fuck off Damage you cunt.'

'Look Wibble, you've been in a shunt. I'm asking if you're OK?'

He looked at me appraisingly. I could see him thinking. He was confused, he couldn't work out what was going on here. But he was smart. That was one of the reasons I still liked Wibble. He had a bit of brains, he had potential if he learnt how to use it properly. I was prepared to take some time with Wibble. He looked at the odds and decided that he hadn't got much choice but to play along with me for now, see where this was going. Like I said, the smart move.

'I'm OK,' he said at last, 'few lumps and bumps but I've had worse.'

'Good.'

'So what's this all about then Damage?' he asked. He had balls as well which I liked. Ambushed, chained up in a cellar and surrounded by enemies and what did he do? He tries to give me a hard time. Defiance. Class. Good stuff. 'Why've you knocked Dazza off like this? You know that's what you've done don't you? And with these bastards of all people?'

There was a growl from behind me but I put my hand up to stop it.

'And don't give me this shit about letting me go. You know you can't do that. As soon as Dazza finds out what you've done he'll have you.'

I just shrugged and smiled at him. I wanted to talk to him. I needed to so as to give the guys what they needed. But I also wanted them to hear this. I hadn't told them yet and they needed to know the whole story.

'Yeah, I know. Just like he had Tiny done. Just like he had Billy done too,' I said, over his rising tide of objections. 'Just like he had Gyppo, oh but I forget, you wouldn't have known Gyppo would you? Dazza croaked him before your time didn't he?'

'What the fuck are you talking about?' he seemed genuinely puzzled, 'The fucking Duckies killed Billy, everyone knows that. And Butcher killed Tiny, and Dazza had him taken out for it.'

You had to hand it to Dazza. He really knew how to work things sometimes.

'No you're wrong.'

'What d'ya mean I'm wrong?'

'You're wrong about just about everything, about Tiny, about Billy, about Butcher and about Dazza. You see, you and the other guys just don't really know what Dazza has got going on, you just don't see what he's doing.'

'And you do I suppose?'

'Yes I do.'

'So what do you know then that I don't?'

'Well, for a start I know that The Rebels didn't kill Billy. Butcher did.'

'Bollocks!'

'And he did it on Dazza's instructions because Dazza was worried that Billy would grass him up. He had Butcher plant a bomb made of plastic explosives Dazza got out of Russia and set it off with a mobile phone call while driving a black BMW that Dazza had hired.'

'How the fuck d'you expect me to believe any of that bullshit?'

'Take it from me. Believe me or not. I just know that that's the way it went down.'

173

'And Tiny?'

'Tiny was murdered. The cops pulled me in on that one. Tried to pin it on me.'

'Yeah I know all that. But Butcher did it, we know that too, he made him o/d. And then Dazza took him out for it.'

'Butcher, on his own? Think about it fer Chrissakes, how's Butcher gonna do that to Tiny on his own? Butcher did it alright I grant you. But only after someone else held him down and some fucker knelt on his chest stuffing barbs and vodka down his throat. And whose crew d'ya think that was? Who could do a thing like that?'

'Butcher, like I said.'

'Yeah Butcher, OK, but why?'

'Like Dazza said, he had a beef.'

'Maybe. But quite a convenient beef for Dazza don'cha think? Taking out The Legion's old P, the one guy that we might all have rallied round if there was going to be any challenge for Dazza's spot at the top of the tree? The ex Legion guys would have outnumbered the original Brethren charter members don't forget, so which of the two would have had the most loyal backers?'

Wibble had obviously never thought about any of this. It always amazed me how people could go round not noticing what was so obviously just in front of their noses. I guess some people just don't get it, just can't see things and how they work.

'But Dazza sorted Butcher for that!' Wibble protested.

'Yeah sure he did.' They were all about ready I thought. 'Listen Wibble, can I tell you a story?'

He just looked at me blankly.

'OK, have you ever heard of a guy called Cesare Borgia?'

Wibble shook his head but his eyes never left me. He was probably wondering what the hell I was going on about now?

'It's a good one,' I said, 'might remind you of something. So if we're all sitting comfortably? Then I'll begin.'

So I told him, and the waiting listeners behind me, the story I'd told Sharon the other night. The story of Cesare Borgia and Remirro de Orco. Of doing the dirty and then taking the fall. They weren't daft guys. They might not have been able to see it before, but by the time

I'd finished they sure got the point of the story.

'But that just can't be right,' protested Wibble, 'Dazza and Butcher were good mates weren't they? Dazza wouldn't set him up like that?'

Even as he spoke I could hear the doubt creeping into his voice.

'But don't you see? That's just it,' I overrode him, 'that's why Dazza could set him up.

'Butcher thought he and Dazza were mates, that's why he was prepared to take chances for him. But this isn't just friendship anymore is it Wibble? It's business. And in serious business, at the end of the day friendships are expendable aren't they?

'When it got to the point where Dazza needed a scapegoat, Butcher was perfect. After all, no one's going to think that Dazza would deliberately sacrifice his closest mate and ally would they?'

'No one but you.'

'No one but me and my dirty little mind.'

There was silence in the cellar. I knew I had won.

'You're going to stop here now with these guys. They're gonna keep you here and secure for a few days but otherwise you'll be OK.'

'Why?'

'He's becoming a mad dog, Wibble,' I said, standing up, 'he's taking down good guys, guys who were our brothers, and he's got to be stopped.'

'So what are you going to do?' he asked, looking up at me.

'Simple. I'm going to stop him.'

As I turned to go Gut and Popeye were facing me with the two hulking strikers off to one side. 'These the guys who are gonna be guarding him?'

'Yeah.'

'They know what to do?'

'Yeah, don't worry about it. We'll look after him.'

'That's what worries me. They'll do what we agreed?'

'Yeah.'

'Well I'm gonna tell 'em anyway.'

Popeye just shrugged impassively.

'OK,' I said to the two guards directly, who stiffened up as I spoke, 'look after him, he's good people. I don't want him touched, you understand? He's a full patch Brethren and you're strikers and you're gonna treat him with respect, you understand me? If you want to keep your gonads, you keep him here but you keep your hands off him and you keep him fed and watered? Got it?'

They looked at me, and glanced across at Popeye in confusion as I continued to stare at them.

'I said have you got it?'

From beside me I heard Popeye's voice. 'It's OK lads. Do what he says.'

'OK,' the larger of them said, 'Whatever you say Boss.' I just didn't know which of us he was saying it to.

Back upstairs in the kitchen and with the door to the cellar safely barred I turned to Gut and Popeye who had followed me up.

'So, if he ever speaks to Dazza again he'll have to tell him about this to save his own skin right?'

'Yeah.'

'And if he does, I'm a dead man. Agreed?'

'Agreed.'

'So now do you believe me?'

They looked thoughtful and glanced at each other. And then Gut said, 'Well yeah, I guess so.'

'Great,' I said with evident relief, 'so now can we cut the crap and get on with doing what we need to do?'

'OK, so tell us, what's really going on here and what are you up to?'

So I explained to them what Dazza was up to.

The first drop had just been a test drop. Of guns coming out of Eastern Europe to check that the systems would work and to give Dazza the firepower to protect himself it he needed it. But then the main stuff would be starting, of Charlie, in large quantities, coming via Portugal. That was what Dazza was really about. Setting up a route for large scale Charlie imports.

Using Portugal was clever. Spain with its traditional and long established trading links to the Spanish speaking parts of South and Central America had always been the main entry route into Europe for Charlie. Some came in using mules but the really big stuff, the major shipments came across the seas from Columbia, often off loaded offshore onto smaller boats that could scoot in at speed to land the stuff all up and down the coast or sometimes take it into Morocco where things were even easier, and it could then slip across the Straights.

The only problem was that as a result, Customs were now hot on Spain, where a load of weed used to come through from Morocco as well.

But Portugal had never had the same links, so it hadn't been used as a transit point. But you had to ask yourself, how difficult would shipping stuff from Columbia to say Brazil be? And from there, or even straight from Columbia, to Portugal would be as easy as hitting Spain, so it was a natural when you thought about it, while with its long coastline, it would be easy to land stuff.

'What did Billy say the plane look like? asked Popeye. I gave him Billy's description.

'Sounds like an Antonov at a guess,' he said, 'that would be Russian.'

'That makes sense, I suppose. The gear I found was all Ruski stuff as was Dazza's contact. He said something about his guys used to drop for the *spetsnaz*.'

'Well that'll be the crew then. They'll know what they're doing for sure.'

'You see, that's why he needed us and what we had. It was the space he was after. That it's empty is an advantage not a drag. He needed somewhere that he could pull this off and he sure as hell couldn't do it in town so that's why he made the land grab.

'And it's a great method. The air charter's all legitimate.' I knew, I booked and paid for some of the flights through the dummy companies I'd set up for Dazza. 'Stuff out of Portugal landing at Glasgow, and of course by the time it lands, the plane's completely clean, there's nothing for the plod to find on board.'

Popeye nodded and said 'LAPES. Came across it when I was in the forces[13]. You'd be amazed the sort of shit you can drop with the

---

[13] *Low Altitude Parachute Extraction System (LAPES) was invented by the American air force during the Vietnam war and is designed for dropping supplies from an aircraft when they either cannot land or the target area is too small for a normal parachute drop. A set of drogue parachutes are released which pull the load from the rear cargo hatch of the*

right kit and have it land safely. It's an awesome sight to see.'

'He really is a clever fucking bastard isn't he?'

'But how's he going to shift that much product? The local markets couldn't take it that's for sure.

But I already knew the answers to that.

He'd already set up his distribution method, he was sending the stuff by post. It was easy, cheap, and difficult for the plod to try and track.

All his customers had to do was rent places, flats for six months, a house, even a PO Box. Just so long as Dazza had the address he could just post the gear there. All the customer had to do was send someone in every so often when a package was expected and wait for the postie to come by with it, and then disappear again. Simple, but brilliant, like most of Dazza's ideas. Flats would be favourite I guessed, they were cheap to rent, no one would notice people coming in and out and you could keep a few on the go to ring the changes, never using the same one more than a couple of times max. How were the cops ever going to clock on to the stuff arriving?

And if you broke the bricks up into smaller quantities that could go in ordinary jiffy bags or whatever, they could never monitor every post box in the country to see you sticking the stuff in to send it either.

Cash could come back in to Dazza the same way using the flats we had set up for the banking side if necessary, or Dazza could just have the customer pay it in direct into one of the acceptance accounts.

And that's why he'd used Billy to tie up with The Duckies. He had built his machine for getting it in, he'd figured out how to move it about, but what he needed now were customers, and customers on a national basis. He could use other guys in The Brethren across most of England but by establishing connections with The Rebels he'd got Scotland and Wales as well. By using The Brethren's sworn enemies Dazza had built himself a truly national franchise.

'OK,' said Gut, 'but I don't get what you want us to do about it?

---

airplane and then help to break the load's skid on impact. With the right specification pallets the technique can be used for quite large objects even up to small armoured fighting vehicles. There is a video clip on www.youtube.com of the Australian air force dropping a tank using this method.

We can't go back to how it was before. You can't leave The Brethren, you know that, not with what you now know, there's no way Dazza could afford to let you go. And if he ever finds out what you've done I don't give much for your chances.

'And if we restarted, how could we hope to fight the whole of The Brethren? We didn't think we were strong enough to take them on before and that was before we lost half the guys to 'em?

'The only way would be to join up with another of the big six, like The Rebels.'

'But even that wouldn't work would it?' I objected, 'Dazza and The Rebels are in business together now. D'you think The Rebels would want to rock the boat by taking us on? No chance.'

'We could join someone else.'

'Like who? Join up with The Hangmen?' I asked.

'Go crawling to those cunts – no fucking way!' Popeye was vehement.

'If they'd have us,' I pointed out, 'they might not want to provoke The Brethren either.'

'So we've no choice but to fight? Even if we can't win?' Popeye persisted.

'Who says we can't win?' I asked. I had wanted them to work through things themselves before I pitched my idea. They both looked at me knowingly.

'Alright Damage,' said Gut, 'out with it. Stop jerking us about. You've got a plan haven't you?'

'Might have,' I said, smiling.

'Come on you old cunt then, tell your uncle Gut all about it.'

'Wait a minute!' Popeye was still sceptical. 'Why the fuck should we trust you?'

'If you want to take him on and win then I don't think you've got much choice.'

'Why?'

'Why? Because I'm the guy who knows what's going on here, that's why. I'm the guy who knows what and where it's going to happen. I'm the guy who knows what he's bringing in and what to do with it. And I'm the guy who knows where there's enough stuff hidden to enable us to take him on and win.

179

'With me we can take him. Without me, you don't have a fucking hope. So what's it going to be Popeye?'

'We?'

'We.'

'And what happens afterwards?'

'I've thought about that too.'

'I bet you have.'

So I told them what I had in mind and they heard me out in silence.

When I'd finished, Gut and Popeye looked across at each other for a moment, and then broke out in wide grins, Popeye too, I was delighted to see, and before I knew it we were in a three way bear hug and slapping each other on the back.

'Good to have ya back Damage.'

'Sorry about back then at the yard.'

'Forget it.'

One of Billy's old contacts ran a blob shop in Sunderland. Sold poppers and more under the counter. Had stuff for the gay bondage brigade as well. Just the place to get half a dozen pairs of handcuffs in case we needed them.

I would get Popeye to sort out a builders merchants and a hardware shop for the rest of the necessary. Might as well spread the load, beside which, made more sense that way.

*

There were messages on the answerphone from Dazza when we got home on Sunday. He was furious, demanding that I call him as soon as and asking if I had seen Wibble. I picked up the phone and dialled. He shouted at me to get out, ask around and meet up with him to tell him what I'd found out.

'No one's seen him. No one that's letting on anyway. So what's up?' I asked, when we met a couple of hours later.

'It's that little fucker Wibble. That's what's up. He's ripped me off and now he's done a runner.'

'Has he? Taken much?'

'Only four fucking bricks. That's all.'

I gave a low whistle. 'How d'you know he's done anything?'

'He'd not been back to me with the postage stuff as normal so I sent Sprog round his place to check. There's no sign of life, his car's gone and his girlfriend says he's not been home and she don't know where he is.'

'She sure about that?'

'Oh I think Sprog was pretty certain she'd told him everything she knew alright by the time he'd finished. He'll have made sure of that.'

He would as well I knew, with a mental apology to Wibble for what would have happened to his bird. She was quite a tasty chick I knew. I hoped Sprog hadn't messed her up too bad.

'No, he's done a fucking runner with the gear. Now what the fuck am I supposed to tell my buyers? Shit, if I ever lay my hands on the little bastard he'll wish he'd never been born.'

I wouldn't want to be in Wibble's shoes if Dazza did ever catch up with him. Whatever story he had to tell him about what had happened, he wouldn't have much time to tell it. And anyway, as courier, Wibble knew he was responsible for the stuff while it was in his care. That was just one of the rules of the game, the way it works, otherwise you could have couriers 'losing' all kinds of shit. If he'd let it go he knew that it was up to him to get it back or pay Dazza off, and without robbing a bank there was no way in hell that Wibble would be able to step up for the value of four bricks. It was one of the reasons I had been quite relaxed about talking to him in the first place.

11   THE HIT

Under cover of darkness and using their anonymous white Transit van, I took the guys to the mine on Tuesday evening. I thought it best to wait until the last minute. Again there was a risk in leaving it so late as the stuff could have been moved but I still didn't think it was a big one, and if any of Dazza's crew did go down there, the last thing I wanted was for them to find they had no stash. Even if they didn't cancel the drop, they would be armed to the teeth from elsewhere.

As before we dumped the van a way down the road, close to the nearest farm so that it wouldn't raise any suspicion. I had brought a couple of shovels and I handed one each to Gut and Popeye as we left the van while I shouldered a roll of rope.

'What are these for?' Gut asked.

'You'll see,' I said leaving him none the wiser, but I guess thinking that Dazza's stuff was buried and we were going to need to dig it up.

The reality was that they were to dig us out if the mine roof came down. I'd had a good look when I'd been in the other night and I hadn't liked what I had seen. Things hadn't improved any since Billy and I played down there twenty odd years ago as kids, and they were dodgy enough then. These old drifts were safe enough alright once you got properly underground. From about twenty to thirty feet in they were carved out of the solid rock, hard limestone, and so that wasn't a problem, other than where the old guys had chipped away upwards, following a vein of ore. Then they would stack the spoil on wooden shelving above the tunnel as they went ever higher because it wasn't worth the effort to cart out worthless rock when they didn't need to. So sometimes these would collapse as the supports rotted away sending the deads cascading down into the tunnel below. But that was only a problem much further into the hillside than we were going.

No it was the entrance I was worried about. Before it got to the solid rock, the entrance tunnel was just driven through the earth and scree of the hillside, with the roof supported on timber pit props, but timbers that had now been stood with their bases in the cold running water draining out of the mine for over a hundred years, or maybe even two. In going in you were betting your life on what could be some pretty rotten timbers.

If you knew what to look for you could see them elsewhere around the area, scars in the hillsides where the entrances to old tunnels had collapsed in over the years since they had been abandoned.

I led them to the entrance, and they followed me underground.

'Wow, SVD Dragunovs!' Popeye sounded impressed as he yanked the lid off one of the longer boxes and peered inside.

'What are they?' I asked. I didn't really know much about guns.

'Sniper rifles, semi-automatic, integrated telescopic sight,' he said, putting it to his shoulder and sighting out down the mouth of the tunnel, 'supposed to be good.'

'Yeah, but this is what we need for what we're gonna do,' said Gut, turning an AK47 over in his thick hands, 'Kalashnikovs!'

I had pulled a pistol from yet another box and was screwing in a silencer that had been stowed beside it.

Popeye looked over. 'Makarov,' he said, 'nine millimetre, standard Warsaw Pact side arm. He's really got himself all the shit hasn't he?'

'He has now,' growled Gut. 'How much do we take?'

'All of it.'

'Aren't they going to spot it's missing?'

'They won't. And even if they did, if it's all gone it's a bit late then isn't it?'

'We'd risk losing the element of surprise,' Popeye pointed out practically, 'and they might tool up from somewhere else.'

'True, but trust me. They won't know a thing about it until it's too late. That's what that's for,' I said swinging the torch round to shine on where I'd left the rope I'd brought.

Popeye called in some of his boys that he'd brought along and in pairs we lugged the boxes out of the mine and down to behind some bushes off the path by the low dry stone wall beside the road where they would be out of sight if anyone came by while we were working, but be easy to load when we pulled the van round. As we worked in relays Gut elected to remain with the growing stack, standing guard in the shadows of the overhanging trees with a loaded pistol, as he said, 'Just in case.'

Working quickly we emptied the mine of Dazza's arsenal.

'Is that it?' asked Gut as Popeye and I together heaved the last crate to the bottom of the path.

'That's it,' I confirmed, as I caught my breath.

'Right,' said Popeye who hardly seemed mussed, 'I'll get the van.'

'OK,' I said turning to go back into the woods, 'come with me,' I said to the bigger of Popeye's strikers.

'Hey. Where are you two going?' asked Gut.

'To cover our tracks. See you in a few minutes.'

Back at the mine I set to work. I had checked the entrance when we first arrived, looking for rotting supports. And as I had expected I found plenty which was great because now they were going to work for us. Carefully I looped the rope around a couple of the worst looking ones on the left-hand side of the tunnel about twenty feet or so in and played the rope outside. Then I ran the free end of the rope back into the mine again, securing it to some dodgy looking supports on the other side of the passageway.

Outside again I picked up the loose loop of rope that I had left lying on the ground and which was now connected at either end to the wooden props.

'Feeling strong big lad?' I asked, handing a length of the loop to the striker and taking in the slack, 'because now mate, we are going to pull. On the count of three.

'One.

'Two.

'Three.'

And with that we both gave a mighty heave on the rope that brought it cracking taut. There was an ominous creaking from somewhere in the mine and we heaved and strained at the rope but nothing moved.

'Alright,' I said letting my grip slacken after a minute or two of fruitless tugging, 'perhaps we need to work on it. Get a rhythm going or something.'

'Yeah, sort of jerk it.'

And so again on the count of three we heaved away, only this time we were rocking back and forth, building up a series of shorter, sharper tugs, back and forth. Not trying to drag the things out in one go, but trying to dislodge them, work them free. And then I felt something different in the rope, a vibration, a movement that had not been there before. 'Here,' I hissed swinging round towards where the striker was pulling on his side of the rope down the tunnel. 'Quick! Give us a hand pulling on this one!'

Grasping what I meant, he dropped his handhold on the rope where he was and turning round grabbed at it just behind my back, wrapping the slack around the bulging muscles of his arm and shoulder as we leant back into it like a demented tug of war team, and as we did so, suddenly it started to move. With an abrupt crack the rope went slack and we both went sprawling backwards into the mud while from down the hole in the hillside in front of us came a dark growling roar of collapsing debris.

Once the noise had stopped I picked up my torch and cautiously made my way inside. I could only get about ten feet or so before the way was completely blocked with wet looking rock and soil. The roof had come down alright, the only question would be for how far and the only way to find that out would be to dig your way through it which wasn't going to be a five minute job.

Reaching down to the floor I cut the rope off where it stuck out from the entombing mud and buried the loose ends under piles of mud and stones.

Popeye had come running back up the path from where they'd been loading the van when he heard the noise and hissed at us, 'What the fuck was that?'

So I showed him what we'd done. 'Now when they came to look for the gear they'll find the roof's come down and they won't be able to get at it.'

'Won't they be suspicious?'

'Possibly. It's a risk. But it's been raining a lot recently, the grounds sodden and heavy which always makes this sort of thing more dangerous. Anyway I've told Dazza that people coming down these things can disturb the supports so he may just think that it's something they've caused themselves. Don't forget, they're not expecting any trouble.'

*

I felt as though I was riding like a dark angel of vengeance as I headed up over the moors, the thunder of the bike rolling behind me and the darkening skies following me, the thrum of the engine and the road vibrating through my hands, the gloom of the fading moorland reflecting dully in the chrome of the engine, contrasting with the matt darkness of my boots, faded jeans, scuffed leathers, cut off, and my matt black painted open-faced helmet.

Everyone was always at the clubhouse for Prayers on Monday evenings of course, and for parties, but plenty of us used it other times as well. There was always a striker on duty, for security, but most evenings, and plenty of days too, you'd find some or other of the guys hanging around, playing pool, spannering on bikes or just chewing the fat over a beer in the bar. I tended to look in a couple of times a week, it depended how the week was going, what Sharon was up to and whether she fancied a ride out. So when I pitched up at around eight that evening I slipped into the bar just like normal. I was deliberately early and I settled in for what I knew might be a long wait but I didn't want to stand any chance of missing Dazza when he arrived.

He and his crew turned up an hour or so later in a rattling convoy as an old Landie like Billy had described and an anonymous white Transit parked up outside the clubhouse. Well they weren't on until much later I guessed so there was no need for them to be early.

I had picked a corner in the bar where I could see through to the back of Fat Mick who was monitoring the CCTV and the main door next to him so I had a good surreptitious view of everyone who came in that evening. Dazza was first through the door, closely followed by Spud. They must have come together in the Landie I reckoned. Then the guys from the crew van followed them in, Doggie and Bagpuss from Newcastle and Scottie from the late lamented Butcher's crew over on Wearside. Dazza's inner circle.

We were in business. I was sure of it.

Dazza glad-handed a few people. He looked relaxed, well he could afford to be. He had plenty of time, he was on safe ground, he had his guys around him and in a few hours time he was going to see the culmination of all his planning, with the first successful delivery of his gear from Luis.

Dazza could feel he was on the brink of the big time.

'Hey Damage!' he called as he walked into the bar over the sound of *Freebird* on the juke box, 'what brings you out here in the middle of the week?'

'Hey Dazza!' I could ask you the same question I thought, but I'd better not.

'Shouldn't you be at home shagging that tasty bird of yours? I would be if I was you.'

'Yeah maybe. But I have to give it a rest sometime you know.'

Dazza laughed. 'That's a good one. Well if you ever need a hand I'm sure the guys'll be glad to help out.'

'What?' asked Spud appearing next to him with a couple of opened bottles, one of which he handed to Dazza, 'what Damage's bird? Yeah she's fit. Be glad to.'

Reversing my hold on my bottle so I could swing it at him like a club I jumped to my feet and with my free hand grabbed Spud. With our history I could take a joke like that from Dazza. But I was fucked if I was going to take something like that from a little wanker like Spud, Dazza's pet or not. He was a short arse and I towered above him so I bent my head to speak straight into his face.

'You ever even think anything like that ever again and I'll break every fucking bone in your body!'

'Oooh touchy!'

'Leave it Spud, I mean it!'

'C'mon Spud,' Dazza intervened, 'stop winding Damage up and go and start getting the shit organised.'

'OK Boss,' said Spud as we eye fucked each other, 'just as soon as Damage here lets go.'

I dropped my hold on him. 'There you go Spud, run along now.'

'Oi!' said Dazza, 'You know the rules. Either take it outside or leave it out and that means both of you. Got it Damage?'

'Yeah I've got it.'

'Well then.'

'OK,' I said, settling back into my seat as Spud, still glaring at me, turned to find Bagpuss and disappear out of the door.

Dazza pulled up a chair and slid into it opposite me.

'You OK?' he asked quietly.

'Yeah I'm fine.'

'So what was that about? 'Snot like you?'

'Oh nothing. He just gets on my tits that's all.'

'Who, Spud? I wouldn't worry about him,' Dazza said expansively, 'don't let him get to you mate. He's just muscle that's all. Like I always said, you're one of the ones with the brains.'

I smiled.

'Don't get me wrong,' Dazza continued, 'he's got his uses has Spud. But really, you and I both know he couldn't think his way out of a paper bag.'

He took a draw on his beer and looked around. 'Who's in tonight?'

'Not many. Fat Mick's on cameras, Andy and Porky are through next door playing pool, apart from them it's just the guys in here,' I said nodding across the room where Little Matt and Prof were shooting the breeze with Pete who was on duty behind the bar.

'No one upstairs?

'Not that I know of. Hey Pete,' I yelled to make myself heard over Lynyrd Skynyrd, 'anyone upstairs?'

'Nah. No one's been up since I've been here.'

'When was that?'

'About six or so.'

'Thanks,' said Dazza.

'Why d'you ask?'

'Oh nothing much. It's just I'm going to need the clubhouse later tonight that's all.'

Need it empty was what he meant of course.

'Business?'

'Business,' he confirmed.

By half ten or so he'd moved the guys out so it was just him, Spud and Scottie, Fat Mick and me still sitting with Dazza in the bar; Bagpuss and Doggie had disappeared half an hour earlier on foot down the track, I guess they had been sent off down to the mine.

And then from the hallway I heard Spud telling Fat Mick to get lost.

'But I'm on cameras!' he protested.

'Not now you're not. I'm taking over this evening, so take a hike.'

'OK,' he said, 'if you're sure.'

So then there was one. Me.

A few minutes later Bagpuss and Doggie were back. A bit out of

188

breath and flustered they held a whispered conversation with Dazza which brought a sharp 'Shit!' and 'You're sure?'

'Problem?' I asked.

'No,' he said without turning round, 'nothing to worry about.'

Dazza thought it over for a moment or two and considered his options. 'Well it is what it is I guess,' he said.

Bagpuss whispered a suggestion in Dazza's ear, I guess he was suggesting that they get tooled up from some other source but Dazza dismissed it with a crisp, 'No, we ain't got the time.'

'And anyway,' he continued, 'we shouldn't need it. No we'll go as we are. We'll just need to be extra careful that's all.'

'Hey Damage, he said turning to me, 'slight change of plan. I might need you to give a hand with security tonight. Is that OK?'

'Sure,' I said nonchalantly, 'whatever you need mate. You know that.'

'Thanks Damage, that's great.'

And with that the stage was set.

We had planned to hit them either at the clubhouse or as they went for the drop. Popeye and his lads had approached over the fields, Gut and his guys up the track from the road. It was now just a case of when and how.

Dazza didn't fill me in on what he had going on. I wouldn't have expected him to, the less I knew the better for both of us.

'So what d'you want me to do?'

'I need you to team up with Spud.'

'Spud?'

'Yes. He's on security. Can you do that?'

'Well…'

'This is business, Damage. I need you to leave your beefs with him out of this. D'you understand me?'

'Yeah I get it. You don't have to worry about me.'

'Good man, Damage. I knew I could rely on you.'

So I went and sat in the hallway where Spud and I watched the cameras in uncompanionable silence. And then we waited. Eleven came and went.

At about half past Dazza came through and quietly announced, 'Right then lads, it's time we got organised.'

'D'you want us to check outside?' I asked, seeing a chance.

'Wouldn't hurt I suppose,' he said, 'yeah why not?'

'Come on then, Spud,' I said standing up and grinning at the fact that a trip out into the cold night air obviously wasn't something that Spud fancied, but at the same time wasn't something that he could now refuse, 'grab us a couple of torches.'

Outside with Spud I walked past my bike. As we did so I slipped my hand into the unlocked saddle bag thrown over the rear fender on the side away from the clubhouse entrance, my fingers feeling under the jacket dumped in there for the notched touch of the pistol's grip. Unseen in the darkness I pulled out the long shape of the silenced weapon and, my arm hanging loosely by my side, I walked on after Spud around the end of the buildings and out of sight of the main CCTV cameras covering the yard and the door. There was one up on the end of the lower barn that faced down the track towards the road but being high it had quite a large blind spot just in the shadow of the building.

Spud had stopped to look down the track and was just starting to moan about how there was no one there and it was freezing and why didn't we get back inside before he froze his nuts off when I stuck the end of the silencer to the back of his head and cocked the gun. That froze the little wanker in his tracks alright.

'Don't move a muscle you fucker or I swear to you I'll plug you right now,' I whispered into his ear as with my free hand I flashed the torch once, 'get on the ground face down and put your arms behind you.'

Seconds later Popeye appeared out of the darkness.

'We're on security,' I hissed as Popeye whipped out a roll of gaffa tape and kneeling down across the small of Spud's back swiftly gagged him before beginning to secure his arms. 'Take him down. I'll tell them he's on patrol.'

Popeye was working quickly. Now he was binding Spud's ankles with tape as well.

'I'll get back inside.'

'OK, go!'

Take it outside Dazza had said. Well it had been my pleasure I thought, as I turned away.

Stepping back into the light of the courtyard there was one more thing I needed to do before I headed inside, so I opened the door to the outhouse.

'Where's Spud?' Dazza asked, as I shut the door behind me.

'He's taking a walk around to check the place out. He'll be back in a few minutes.'

'Bugger. I want to get started upstairs.'

'Well why don't you get on if you want to?' I said, standing by the desk with the monitors, the long cold shape of the gun with its silencer pressing into the small of my back where I had stuffed it into the waistband of my jeans. 'I can watch the cameras till he gets back.'

'Yeah, OK then. We'll do that.'

Dazza and his crew assembled upstairs. As soon as I head the last clump of boots heading down the landing I turned out the hallway light, and slipping open the front door's latch, I flashed my torch twice in quick succession towards the corner of the barn where I knew Popeye would be waiting.

As an ex-marine, Popeye had naturally tended to attract other ex-service guys into his cohort. So he and some of his guys formed the assault and clean-up team. At my signal he came scurrying across the yard carrying a sledgehammer, followed by three figures. They were all dressed in dark coloured boiler suits, boots and black balaclavas, their hands and exposed bits of faces blackened with cammo paint. Popeye and the first two of them had pistols drawn as being better for close up work, the backup guy had an AK47 for firepower if needed. Gut and a couple of his lads meanwhile were acting as security, parked at the foot of the drive to make sure no one got in or out, and were then going to be transport for the drop.

I pulled the pistol from under the back of my cut off and slipped off the safety catch. Leading the way, silently we crept up the stairs and along the darkened landing towards the meeting room door.

There was no one on guard outside, they were all in the room.

I stopped and listened for a moment at the lit crack around the door. There was no sound of conversation, just odd words every now and then in query or acknowledgement. Dazza would be using the whiteboard again I reckoned, to make sure nothing could be overheard. Even in here he was being cautious about the risk of bugs.

That might be useful for us though, I thought. He would be going through the final drop plan again on the board so there was a chance that there might be some info on it which would be of use to us as well. Behind me Popeye and his team stood in silence in the darkness of the corridor. Stepping back from the door and to the left to make a space I waved them forwards with the end of my gun, and pointed down to where there was a loose floorboard that would creak if stood on. Carefully and deliberately, Popeye stepped over it to stand in front of me while the two other guys with pistols formed up on the right. The AK47 lurked in the gloom of the corridor.

We tensed. We all knew this was it. The guys were watching me.

Three, I mouthed silently.

Two. Popeye raised the sledge hammer.

One.

With an explosion of noise Popeye let out a fearsome yell and swung the sledgehammer crashing round into the door with all his whipcord force, bursting the lock from its jamb. As he did do the two guys to the right shoulder charged the swinging door, bashing it inwards and almost falling into the room to the left and right on the other side, guns out, while behind them Popeye flung the hammer to one side and we charged in after them with the AK47 guy bringing up the rear.

Inside the room Doggie, Bagpuss and Scottie sat, chairs drawn up in a loose semicircle facing Dazza who was stood, dry-wipe pen in hand to the left of the whiteboard. At the crash of the door bursting open I had a momentary impression of their four faces turning towards us, mouths open in complete astonishment. I stood still while Popeye and his guys' momentum carried them on, shouting instructions as they rushed the guys in the room, using the element of shock and pure armed aggression to force them up and against the wall, spread-eagled at gun point before they really knew what was happening, while Popeye swiftly ran a practiced search, patting them down for guns while his boys stood back, guns at the ready so as to be able to plug anyone who moved.

'They're clean,' he said stepping back after a moment. And then, 'Good job guys,' to his lads.

As I just stood there and watched, it had all taken just a few seconds from start to finish. And we hadn't even needed the handcuffs.

I walked into the room and up to the start of the line where Bagpuss was standing. Without saying a word I put the muzzle of the silencer to where the back of his neck met the roll of fat of his skull and squeezed the trigger. The gun gave a kick in my hand, there was a cough from the silencer and before he started to slump I was squeezing the trigger again into the back of Scottie's neck. As I swung the gun around for the third shot, Doggie had started to turn towards me to see what was happening to the guys beside him. A startled 'Hey!' had start to form in his mouth before the gun popped and kicked again in my hands as I shot him in the temple and took a step back to let his body collapse on the floor in front of me as well.

Dazza stood there rock solid facing the wall and just muttered 'Oh fuck!'

'Yeah, that's right,' Popeye said triumphantly, before I waved him quiet with a lift of the gun and stepped across to be right behind Dazza.

I had learnt my lessons from history. To be safe from revenge, there was only one course of action open to you, to destroy utterly anyone that you had moved against so they could never, ever, rise against you.

As I moved across, gun now lowered to my side, Dazza moved too, slowly dropping his hands from the wall and turning around to face me.

'I'm not turning away,' he said matter of factly, 'If you're gonna do it you're gonna have to do it to my face.'

'Alright,' I said, 'but there's some things I want to know first.'

'Such as?'

'What happened to Gyppo?

'Christ mate, that's ancient history. What d'you want to know that for? Want to know who did you the favour?'

'Favour?'

'His bird. You did alright there didn't you?'

'You bastard! And Tiny?'

He just shrugged, 'What's it matter now?'

'It's the same thing. I just want to know.'

'So what's with all the chat then Damage? Killing time?'

'Maybe.'

We stared at each other for a moment in silence. Then Dazza said in an exasperated voice. 'Look, if you're going to do it, just fucking get on and do it.'

'OK then Dazza,' I said, 'if that's the way you want it.'

'I do.'

I raised the gun and placed the muzzle of the silencer right between his eyes. He didn't even blink. He really was something. I fired. A red purple hole appeared in his forehead, the skin singed blackish around the edge from the flash and he slumped silently towards the floor as his legs buckled beneath him and his head lolled forwards onto his chest.

Reaching down I shot his prone body twice more in the back of the head and neck. As I leant over him I whispered so that none of the others could hear, 'That was for Gyppo you fucker.'

'From both of us,' I added silently.

'OK, you know what to do?' I said turning to Popeye.

'Yes. We'll see you there. Now get going,' he replied.

*

I walked around the corner of the lower barn and flashed my torch down the track towards the trees that obscured the road. There was an answering flash and a few moments later the sound of an engine starting and then headlights came on as a long wheel based Landie started up the track.

Now all that remained was to take delivery of the drop.

We did it just the way Billy had described it, right up on top of the moors where the ground flattened out into a rolling boggy mossy upland crossed by the occasional sheep or shooter's track. Up here we were easily out of sight of the road and so we laid out our torches in a cross and then sat in the Landie to wait.

'How'd it go?' asked Gut.

'Fine.'

'No problems?'

'No problems.'

'Good. Now let's just hope the rest works out OK or we're all fucked.' And with that he lapsed into silence.

We took it in turns to stay outside on sentry duty. We needed to hear the plane as quickly as possible so as to make sure we had all the torches lit in time. Half an hour passed. Then an hour.

'What's up? D'you reckon their coming?' asked Gut. 'How long do you think we give it?'

'Relax, they'll be coming. Dazza was there wasn't he?' I pointed out with more certainty than I actually dared to feel. This was when I would find out whether I was right about what Dazza had been planning. 'He was obviously expecting them.'

'OK,' he said reaching into a bag in the back of the van and pulling out a Thermos. 'So we wait. Meanwhile no use getting cold. Coffee?'

'Now you're talking!' I said delightedly. That was one of the great things about Gut. He was just so practical and domesticated. I would never have thought about it until too late.

He was just starting to pour when one of his guys pulled open the door with a breathless, 'It's coming!'

'Shit!' said Gut spilling his drink as we leapt out of the Landie. The guy was right, I could hear the approaching drone of a distant plane's engines quite clearly now.

'Quick!' I shouted, 'get the torches on!' as bodies dashed in each direction, beams of light shooting upwards into the misty air as they hit the switches.

The approaching noise grew louder and louder. It was definitely heading our way. And then the plane came swooping in, low over the horizon, roaring overhead at what felt like only a few feet above our heads in a tremendous blur of screaming noise and vast overwhelming bulk before with a massive whoompf noise three black parachutes suddenly billowed against the sky above us, followed almost immediately by a rattling crash as the load's sledge was jerked backwards out of the plane and off the roller on the rear cargo ramp and into the air... before smashing down violently onto the ground, and skidding wildly until it came to a halt; while the plane, suddenly lightened from its load climbed back up into the sky and away, its rear cargo door closing as it did so and its noise quickly diminishing into the distance as it flew away from us and off, on towards Glasgow and its entirely innocuous landing as an innocent cargo flight.

As we stood and listened to the receding roar of the engines, we were all too surprised to move for a moment. And then with a shout, Gut suddenly started to run towards where the sled had finished up wedged against a mound of turf.

It had worked, I thought to myself as I walked after him. Just like Billy had said. It had really fucking worked!

By the time I got there Gut had his knife out and had opened the outer packaging. We were all crowded around, wanting to see what was inside. Wanting and not daring to hope that I had been right.

But I was.

Neatly stacked and secured in their packaging were those white wrapped packages that I was expecting.

Fuck me, we had a metric tonne of coke. A thousand bricks.

It took a surprising time to load into the back of the Landie.

*

The yellow of the sodium lighting danced on the black water of the dock as I met up with Popeye at about five am. There was no one else around that I could see. He was in the wheelhouse of his fishing boat and his crew cast off as soon as I got on board.

He had used those big builders' dump bags. You know the ones, the sort they deliver a cubic metre of sand or whatever in, or there's some bigger ones, a metre and a half long, I tell you they're just made for the fucking job.

They had stuffed each of the bodies into one before they had a chance to stiffen up. The bags made it easy, with four handles that helped them carry them down to the van like a purpose-made body bag. They had trussed each body with rope to securely wrap the bag round it and then the handles gave something good and strong through which they had passed the chain that secured the bag to its weight of concrete blocks that were going to act as weights to anchor them down when they went over the side. We would be going way out but even so we didn't want to take any chances. We didn't want any of these fuckers putting in a surprise reappearance on some beach somewhere.

'Any chance that anyone saw anything?' I asked Popeye, looking down at the floor of the after deck where a blue tarpaulin was lashed across one side concealing the bags.

196

'Nah, no one about this time of morning,' he said, as we cleared the harbour entrance.

'Won't people notice you going out?'

'Not really,' he shrugged, 'often make an early start to get out to where we need to. Don't sweat it. It's all OK. Just enjoy the ride.'

Out in the North Sea and away from the shelter of the land it was a bit rough for me. So enjoying the ride wasn't really on my agenda.

About half an hour out Popeye cut the engines and came and joined me down below. 'We're far enough out now and it's still dark so no one'll see us, so I reckon we get on with it here, OK?'

'OK by me,' I said, 'It's your call. Lead on.'

Together with two of his guys, Popeye stripped back the tarpaulin and they quickly set about disposing of the bodies. The two guys picked up either end of one of the first of the sagging silent bags and balanced it in the middle on the boat's rail while Popeye lifted the anchor up on its chain and played it down over the side and into the water. Then Popeye let go of the chain which immediately snatched at the bag, tugging it out of the guys' hands and tipping it over the side and into the water with a splash before disappearing in a flurry of bubbles.

'Very neat,' I complimented Popeye, 'You done this before?'

'Occasionally,' he grinned.

'So, *tonight he sleeps with the fishes*.'

'You watch too many films you do mate,' Popeye said as he and his guys reached for the next bag.

Swiftly another three bags followed the first over the side leaving just one lying on the deck. But this one was different. This one was still moving.

I gave it a kick right about where I thought its kidneys would be, just to get its attention, and then squatted down on deck beside it as Popeye and his lads stood next to me.

'Spud,' I asked, 'Spud, can you hear me?'

There was a groan from within the bag which I decided to take as a yes.

'Spud, are you into ancient history?

'I am,' I continued without waiting for an answer, knowing that while he could hear me from within the bag where he lay trussed,

197

with the gag of gaffa tape all he could make were muffled grunts and screams, 'I'm really into the ancient Romans. I was going to do history at Uni. Did you know that? No I guess you didn't.'

The guys picked up the mummified Spud by his shoulders and feet.

'They were great. Really hard core at times when it came to dealing with people and very big on duty and loyalty. D'you know they had this penalty for patricide? That's strictly not just someone killing their father but also someone who betrays their country or kills someone they should regard as sacred. Do you get that it's sort of an extension of the father thing, so killing someone you ought to owe a duty of loyalty to is sort of the ultimate betrayal. So d'you know what they did with patricides?'

The bag was bucking frantically now in the guys' hands as they began their swing and Spud writhed and struggled against his bonds.

'One.'

'They had them bound in a sack with a cock and a snake to symbolise their treachery and ingratitude, and then they were thrown into the Tiber to drown.'

'Two.'

'So what d'you think of that, eh Spud?'

'Three.'

The lads reached the end of their last swing and with my nod they let go and the blue bag with the bound Spud suddenly went rigid as it arced over the side of the boat with what sounded like a terrified scream before landing in the water with a great splash, while simultaneously further astern Popeye heaved the attached weights over the side, the short linking anchor chain rattling as it rolled over the gunnels. The bag floated on the surface for a moment, thrashing about before the plunging weights jerked it momentarily upright and then pulled it down into the depths in a rush of bubbles.

No one spoke.

It was really ironic, I was imposing a punishment for betrayal on Spud for having taken out someone I'd gladly have done myself. Partly it was because I hated the wanker, but mainly it was to send a message, I wanted the word to get around how betrayal would be dealt with. I wanted to be feared.

We stayed out most of the day. Had to make it look like a real fishing trip after all.

Gut chopped all the vehicles over at the Boneyard. They'd never be seen again.

So we'd done what I'd sold to Gut and Popeye. A reverse takeover, us taking The Brethren's charter rather than the other way round.

Now we had to make it work. We had to get back in business and quickly.

That evening I sent a message to Luis confirming safe receipt of the gear. I also asked him to begin to organise his next shipment. Later I would let Luis know that I was in charge of the operation but for now all he needed to know was that the route was working and we would be looking to take more as soon as it could be organised. After all Luis wouldn't really care who his customer was so long as they paid and were reliable. Business was business.

I had Gut post Wibble's bricks on as well as if nothing had happened. But in with each one went a note.

I told them to keep this address clear from now on so I could use it to contact them and that we would work out any other changes needed later. To confirm that we were still in business they were to pay fifteen pounds and eleven pence into the bank account, and if they wanted to talk, pay in stuff in a couple of lots to show me the digits of a phone number.

Fifteen pounds eleven pence came into the account banked as cash the following week.

They deducted it from their next payment, which was only fair I suppose.

*

'Now what?' asked Gut.

'Now we wait.'

'For what?'

'A call.'

'You think they're gonna just call after this?

'No. I know they're gonna call.'

199

PART 5
24 September 1994 onwards

To take over a club you need skill and ability; or just plain luck; or you have to use force, either your own guys, or someone else's.

Damage 2008

12   THE RECKONING

I heard the roar of the approaching bikes from way down the valley long before I saw them. And then I watched as the three Harleys appeared from between the trees and headed up the road that curled its way along beside the rocky bed of the river, before heading straight up the hill and leaving the shelter of the valley below for the bleak exposure of the moorland where I stood waiting.

At the top of the hill, where the road crested the rise in a dip between the gently sloping higher ground on either side, opposite a small stone cross that marked the summit of the pass, there was a wide patch of bare earth that formed a car park for walkers in the summer. My bike was parked up against the low stone wall separating this from the rough ground beyond. Gut's was beside it and he stood resting against the wall, behind me and a little way off to my right. In my hand I had a military walkie talkie that had come out of Dazza's supplies.

'Why're you trusting Wibble?' Gut asked as we waited, 'he was Dazza's guy after all and you had him jumped and smacked up? Dont'cha think he'll bear a grudge?'

'Nah Gut,' I said without looking round, 'Wibble's OK, he'll come round, you'll see.' I wasn't going to tell Gut this but Wibble was probably the one guy I reckoned I could count on trusting the most. You can't trust your friends who think you owe them, as much as your former enemies, who know you don't, and who know they have to work harder for you to make up for it.

The three riders rumbled up the final rise and crested the top of the hill, rolling onto the uneven surface and coming to a halt opposite us.

The one in front was short and wiry. The two behind were obviously along as his bodyguards. They were hulking, large, and I would guess, armed to the teeth.

It hadn't taken long for the call to come. And as we were going to have to do it sometime, I thought sooner rather than later.

I stood and waited as they kicked out their side stands and settled their bikes at rest as they killed the engines.

Polly pulled the lid off his short silver hair and perched it on the end of his bars.

Then, taking off his gloves, he dismounted and stepped towards me with his hand outstretched. His guys remained behind. Having slowly scanned the horizon and our surroundings, they slouched back against the seats of their bikes, watching us warily, jackets unzipped and thick arms folded across their chests.

Shoulder holsters, I assumed.

Well there was no point in fucking about I'd decided.

'Hi, I've got something for you,' I said cheerfully.

'Oh really? What's that then?'

I picked up an object draped across the dry stone wall and handed Dazza's cut off to Polly.

He took it and held it up at arms' length to inspect the bloody mess.

'And there's more where that came from,' I added.

'What, cuts or blood?'

'Both.'

'Unhuh,' he seemed to consider his options for a moment, 'Well colours are always club property so we'd better collect those in hadn't we?'

He let his arm holding the cut off fall to his side. I knew without him saying anything he had seen that the 'President' title was missing from the front of Dazza's colours and he had clocked that it was now sewn onto my chest of my colours.

'Well,' he said after a moment, 'Just out of interest, what's to stop us taking you out right now over this?'

I shrugged and lifted my hand with the walkie talkie, 'That my guys on the hills with the rifles will take you out as well?'

He seemed to consider this and looked slowly to either side. It was a waste of time. Although I thought I knew where Popeye lay hiding, even I didn't have a hope of seeing him. I had considered that he might think I was bluffing, but I didn't think so. He would know that I wouldn't be so stupid as to come to a meet like this without back-up.

'OK, fair enough,' he grinned, 'So I guess the question is, do we have a problem?'

'I don't know. Do we have a problem?'

'Not necessarily, I guess. Not if we don't want to.'

I considered this. 'Don't suppose we do really.'

'Well that's good news,' he seemed quite cheerful.

'But before we go much further it seems to me that you're missing something,' he continued reaching into his pocket and pulling out a knife.

There was a tense urgent crackling question from the walkie talkie.

Polly caught the sound. Behind him, feeling the change in atmosphere his guys suddenly stiffened upright, hands reaching under their jackets. As if sensing this even though his back was to them, Polly held up his hand and there was a moment of stillness. For a moment it seemed as though everyone was holding their breath. His guys froze, hands not moving further under their jackets, but not moving them away either.

I lifted the walkie talkie to my mouth and pressed the send switch 'It's OK,' I ordered into it, 'it's all under control.'

Polly and I exchanged looks. I nodded to him and he flicked the blade open. 'It's OK guys,' he said over his shoulder, without actually turning round and with an exhale I saw their hands slide back out from under their jackets as they settled back carefully against their bikes.

Lifting up Dazza's cut off, with a few strokes Polly had hacked The Bonesman patch from where it had been sewn on and held it out to me.

'It seems to me that you are entitled to one of these now.'

I took the proffered badge and holding it between my thumb and forefinger looked at it for what seemed an age. Thinking I guess about how Dazza had earned it in the first place.

'Yeah, I guess so,' I said eventually, letting my arm fall to my side and gazing back impassively at Polly.

'What's up?' he asked.

'Just a bit surprised I guess.'

'Surprised, what about?'

'Just the attitude. I think I'd assumed you'd have more of an issue with the situation than you seem to have.'

Polly clicked his knife shut again and slipped it back into his pocket. He held Dazza's cut off out behind him and one of his guards stepped forward to take it from him without a word, before retreating back to his bike. Polly shrugged as though the answer were obvious, which of course it was really.

'Well it is what it is, ain't it? You guys are the new reality aren't you? It's just survival of the fittest and all that. Why, what were you expecting me to do? Break down in tears for the dear departed?'

'No, I guess not.'

'Nah. You and me, we have business to discuss, and anyway, at least you didn't put any holes in the colours,' he grinned, 'you'd get fined for that.'

'Look I know what you're thinking,' he continued conversationally, 'about The Duckies and all?'

'It's just it makes sense. Peace with The Rebels works. If you think about it, this way we make a cut on their sales, we each stay on our own patch, no bust ups to get the cops interested, and we all just quietly get on with making some serious dosh. It's perfect, a great little scheme. The only potential problem was the ambition of the guy running it.'

'I'm not an ambitious guy,' I said, 'I have what I want here.'

'That'd be good for us, agreed Polly, 'So now we have someone running what's a sweet deal for everyone and we don't have to worry about where you're going to be trying to take it next. That works for me.

'Don't get me wrong. Dazza was good, he was smart, he was a good operator, but he also had his drawbacks. Some people thought he was getting too ambitious, and that's something that you have to watch carefully. And he was becoming too high profile, too violent. Fucking up with The Rebels like that with your mate. It ended up that I had to speak to their main guy. He denied it was them that did it of course, but I told him that whatever, it stopped there anyway which he was OK with. Trouble is bad for business, we both know that. When there's trouble it stops people earning so no one on either side wants a war or too much heat. It just gets in the way.

'So down to business then. You have the stuff?'

'Yes.'

'And Dazza's connections?'

'Yes.'

'So the route is safe and still works?'

'Yes.'

'And our money? Is that safe?'

Right, I thought, as Polly confirmed my suspicions. Even with his local dealing network and own international connections, I had always assumed Dazza wouldn't have been able to fund and arrange this sized operation on his own. He would have had to have partners, people with access to serious cash to put up the seed money and the contacts and credibility in The Brethren's international network to help him make the right connections to get this thing set up.

And Polly had been that partner.

'It's all still where I put it for Dazza.' It did no harm in reminding him that I was the key to him accessing the cash that Dazza had been dealing in.

'OK, so we have the outlets. So do we have a deal?'

'Same deal as you had with Dazza?'

'Same deal, same terms.'

'Business?'

'Just business.'

So it looked as though I was going to get a new silent partner as well.

'OK, but on one condition.'

'Yes? What's that?' he asked.

'All the other Legion guys are in. No question about striker status. I'm talking about a straight patch over, full membership for all.'

He considered it and then nodded.

'OK, I can wear that. We've seen what you can do. You're obviously guys who need to be treated with respect. But I've got one condition as well.'

'What's that?'

'This is a one-time offer. They take it now or they leave it and that's it. Finito.'

That was fine by me. 'OK, that's fair enough.'

'Now, do we have a deal?' he asked.

'Yes we have a deal,' I told him, and we spread our arms and embraced in a backslapping hug.

'Well, congratulations on making P,' he said as we broke apart again, 'it means you've stepped up. I have to say I always thought it might be you. So how's it feel?'

'Pretty good, but a big responsibility.'

'Yeah, you've got that right. That's the mistake guys make who just want it for the tab. It's not just strutting your stuff, about being up front at runs, about having people kick back up to you. It's more than that.'

I listened.

'It means the guys'll be looking up to you, looking to you to look out for 'em, to make the tough decisions. You've gotta be ready to lead. Are you ready for that?'

'Yeah, I think so.'

'Yeah well, I guess you are,' he said, 'Mind some advice? P to P? I've been doing this a while now.'

'Sure, shoot.'

'As a P you're an officer. I know you've been Road Captain and all but this is a step up again.

'As P you're the top of the tree. The shit stops with you, when it comes down to it, comes to a decision there's no one else to turn to; the guys, the club, are all relying on you to do the right thing, whatever it is. Which is an honour and also sometimes I have to tell you a complete pain in the arse. But I guess you've found that out yourself already?

'As Brethren we're the top club. You know it, I know it, everyone around knows it. We run the show in our territory so first thing you need to do is keep on top, keep all the other clubs in line, don't stand for any crap. But hey you know this already, otherwise you wouldn't be standing here today like this anyway.

'So all you gotta do is keep your guys tight, keep the club strong and secure and keep focused on your reputation. Your rep is what works for you. It's what people know about you and what they know is what makes them act. Shit, your reputation is all you have so guard it tight. You can't be everywhere at once making sure every shitbird that's working the ground is doing it right, paying respect and kicking up, but shit, your reputation can be everywhere, breathing down everybody's neck and working for you twenty-four seven.'

'So that's the secret?' Perhaps he knew more than I had given him credit for, I thought. After all you didn't get to be The Freemen P without having something about you.

'Yeah. Make it your business to manage your rep and your rep will manage your business for you.'

'Thanks, that makes loads of sense.'

'No problem,' he was obviously starting to think about getting going again, 'Well now you're P we'd better get you to meet some more of the guys.'

'Yeah, that'd be good.'

'OK, leave it with me, I'll get some meetings set up. You need to meet the other Ps.'

'Just so as I know, anyone I'm likely to have a problem with?'

'Problem?'

'This shit?'

He smiled, 'Nah. I don't think so. Remember mate, it's reputation, reputation, reputation. That's what matters.'

'And delivery.'

'And delivery of course, but then you've shown you can deliver and what d'ya think your reputation's like after what you guys have pulled off here? No, I wouldn't worry too much on that score if I was you.'

So Dazza wasn't going to be sorely missed it seemed.

After that he was ready to be off. We exchanged some details about how we would make contact going forwards, as we walked back to where his bike was. We shook hands and he and his guys pulled their lids back on and remounted their bikes.

With a whirr of starter motors the bikes burst into the familiar roar of starting Harley engines before dropping back down into the burbling crobba crobba of idle as Polly turned to face me again.

'Look after yourselves guys. This is your territory now, so good luck with it. Just make sure you make it work for you, and all of us.'

And with that there was a clunk as he mashed the box down into first gear, his engine rose into a snarl and he was back off down the road the way he had come, his two guys slotting in behind for the long run back down south.

Gut stepped forward to stand beside me as I stood and watched as the patches disappeared into the distance.

So much for loyalty to your brothers I thought.

What a disloyal, treacherous shit Polly was. There was only one thing Polly was ever interested in, and that was what was in it for Polly. Not that there was anything wrong with that. It's an attitude that any leader needed. But his problem with it was his ego. He was so sure of himself that he wasn't subtle about it at all. And worse, it only ever went in one direction. Anyone working for Polly was ultimately disposable as far as he was concerned. Loyalty as far as Polly went was a one way street, and that, I decided, was likely to be his downfall.

Of course to a degree Polly was right. Dazza's private enterprise and the way he had been running it just for himself, and Polly of course, was bad for business.

If something was club business, it should be club business, after all everyone who was wearing the colours was taking the risk on this trade whether they knew about it or not. If it went down, everyone in the colours would suffer the fallout and the heat. Of course you had to keep things tight to ensure security, but at the same time you had to ensure everyone enjoyed some of the rewards. If you didn't, it would ultimately lead to bad blood and trouble within the club between the haves and the have nots. It stood to reason. If everyone is earning off a deal, it's in everyone's interests to keep it sweet. Cut people out and what's in it for them to ensure you succeed?

And what's more it just made sense of who we are. Polly and Dazza had forgotten what the club is about.

That was an error I would not make.

Gut was obviously feeling some of the same things too. As he stood there beside me he asked, without I think, ever really expecting an answer, 'Did we just save him a job?'

Or did we just save him his job? I wondered to myself.

With the power and cash that Dazza would have had from his route, with his own private army of Butcher's boys, with the guns he'd had in from the Ruskis, with even The Rebels becoming dependent on his stuff, what would Dazza have wanted next? How ambitious had Dazza been? How long would he have been prepared to continue to take orders from the existing Freemen leadership, seeing as he hadn't even actually been let in yet?

'*The unarmed man is never safe from armed servants,*' I said quietly to myself.

'What was that?' asked Gut.

'Nothing.'

It was a delicate balance climbing the greasy pole. Dazza had to show himself good enough to be useful to those above him. But like any organisation, there was always the problem that if you showed yourself to be too good, at what point did you become a threat to the position of those above you?

No, all things considered, I guessed that Polly wasn't too upset that Dazza was gone. And as someone only new into The Brethren's network this year he wouldn't see me as anywhere near as much of a threat.

Yet.

'Just some old shit. Don't worry about it.'

*

It was the type of riding I always enjoyed. It was very Zen somehow. The speeding solitude, with just the sound of the wind, and the mix of unthinking instinct, and fierce full mind and body concentration required on the here and now of the riding freed my mind to wander, it gave me time to think.

Tonight was no different.

As I rode I reflected on where I had got to and what I had achieved.

I had had my revenge on Dazza, but more than that. Of course sometimes in business you have takeovers. And sometimes, just sometimes, you also have reverse takeovers.

I also had his badge, his charter, his network, his business.

And in bringing back in The Legion I had a charter filled with guys who were now loyal to me.

Sweet.

Now all I had to do was keep it.

I had watched Dazza carefully over the years and over the last few months particularly. I could learn a lot from Dazza I knew. But both from his achievements and his mistakes.

And so building on his successes I had a plan.

I had become President through my own efforts and skill.

It hadn't been by luck.

Dazza had been powerful and good. He had had strong and ruthless guys working for him, he had had the forces, the cash, the weapons to be strong and he had had a hold on lots of people that mattered through his business network.

And I wasn't handed success by anyone else for their own reasons who could just as easily take it all away again.

No, I had seen when there had been an opportunity, and I had taken it. And I'd done so by raising and leading a group of guys who I had made loyal to me.

What I had achieved with difficulty I thought I should be able to hold with ease.

The old Legion club, at least the ex-Reivers, ex-Fellmen and ex-Devil's Henchmen would be loyal to me. They were the democrats, the guys that I had successful appealed to in the name of our traditional freedoms, which I had restored to them.

The rest of the charter, Butcher's boys from Wearside and the remaining members of the original Brethren charter would be no problem either I knew. They had each been used to working under the direction of a single controller whom I had now replaced. Not only were they used to taking orders, Dazza and Butcher had each ensured that no one had been allowed to rise within who might pose any kind of a threat to their own authority, so there were no obvious internal challengers for the others to unite around as an alternative to our reverse takeover.

But it seemed obvious that the best way to make a real success and to ensure my position remained secure, I needed to make keeping me in charge in the best interests of everyone who could possibly be a threat to me.

Make my health and security the cornerstone of everyone's self-interest and I'd be safe for life.

Never try and make people do what they don't want to, that's a mug's game. No it's always far better to make what you want, be what they want to do. Then you're just going with the flow.

And that meant firstly keeping the money flowing. I would ensure that profits were shared sufficiently widely so that everyone was earning enough to be content and to be reliant on my operation. But I knew that in itself wouldn't be enough. People are never content forever with what they have, there would always be someone who decides they want more.

So I also needed to make myself irreplaceable. That way, any move against me would be seen as a threat to the others' livelihoods. Then they would help to police each other, as a threat to me would be a threat to their own interests, and if anyone did try something on I could rely on the others for support.

I would split the roles, so not only could no one see the jigsaw's whole picture, but I would make sure that no one who could be a threat would be in a position to find all the pieces with which to try and put it together.

The only people who could be a threat to me were other club members. No outsider could hope to try to take over.

So I would move a lot more of the 'doing' to outsiders. That way the people who knew how their little bit of the scheme worked could never be in a position to try to take over. At the same time I would mainly use the club members to enforce security and obedience amongst the outsiders. Given our reputation that shouldn't be hard.

By splitting these jobs between the guys it would make it difficult, if not impossible, for them to work out how the whole system worked as they wouldn't be actually doing anything. They wouldn't see the accounts, or the gear, they wouldn't handle the traffic or the cash. They would just have to put muscle on someone when I told them to, and wait for the cash to roll through.

It would also distance all of us on the inside from direct contact and involvement in anything that the cops could catch. And even if they did bust someone working on the outside, you'd have to be pretty fucking stupid to even consider ratting out a member of The Brethren as your contact. Life would be nasty, brutish and short for anyone who did.

And we would make sure that everyone involved knew it. You can work on the basis that people like you, but that's risky and if you rely on that alone you are leaving yourself open to trouble. Like I said, if you have to choose, it's better to be feared than liked.

But I'd also make sure that we didn't take steps against anyone involved in the network capriciously. When we acted I would always made sure that there was an obvious and compelling reason for it that everyone involved would know about. It's not a question of being soft. Christ no one would accuse us of that. But it was important to avoid being hated or to have people think that they might get done over on some trumped up pretext. Either of these could make people forget their fear sufficiently to risk the consequences to work against us or betray us.

Niccolo would be my guide in everything I would do.

Well, unlike Polly I had actually read Machiavelli, many, many times.

Should work a treat.

After all, it had done so this far.

*

It was gone eleven when, bike locked up around the side, I walked in through the back door and parked my lid on the table.

'How did it go? What's up? Can you tell me?'

Sharon was an old school old lady. She knew that club business was club business and that sometimes I couldn't tell her everything.

I hadn't yet decided how much I would tell her. But I had to say something.

'Nothing much.'

AFTERWORD

I first met Martin 'Damage' Robertson in 1999, just after he had become President of The Freemen and therefore in practice the national leader of The Brethren's UK charters at the age of thirty-six.

At the time, I was researching an article on bikers for the national newspaper on which I was working. Like many outlaw bikers he was wary of journalists as a profession and so it took quite a while and an introduction through mutual contacts before he would agree to firstly a meeting, and then subsequently to being interviewed. Given his and The Brethren's fearsome reputation, I was nervous about our initial encounter, but I soon found that whilst guarded and reserved in some ways, he was very personable to talk to, and within limits, and only to the degree that he obviously felt it within his and the club's interests to do so, he was prepared to talk to me.

As a journalist I naturally sought to stay in touch and I spoke to him on a number of occasions over the next few years.

In 2003 based on the evidence of Michael 'Fat Mick' Cooper who had become a police informer, Robertson, together with Matthew 'Gut' Gordon, who had taken over as president of the north-east charter, were convicted of conspiracy to murder Simon 'Pretty Polly' Pollio who disappeared in 1998, believed strangled, and whose body has never been found.

Gordon received a much reduced sentence for turning Queen's evidence and in a subsequent trial Robertson was also found guilty in a separate trial of the execution style murders of Darren 'Dazza' Henderson, Sam 'Doggie' Collier, Mike 'Spud' Williams, Richard 'Scottie' Green and Clive 'Bagpuss' Armitage on the night of Wednesday 14 September 1994. Their bodies have never been found but are widely believed to have been dumped at sea.

Robertson received life sentences for these offences with a recommendation that he serve a minimum tariff of thirty years.

Such was Robertson's reputation and position within the club that police sources widely believe that despite his incarceration, he continued to be The Brethren's de facto leader, directing operations from within prison.

Gordon was found hanged in his cell in 2004. The verdict was suicide, although inevitably there remains speculation that he was murdered, with the finger of suspicion pointed at Robertson for directing this. Other rumours suggest that members of a Rebels' support club were responsible.

It is believed that Cooper was provided with a new identity under witness protection arrangements, and his whereabouts are unknown at the present time.

I spoke to Robertson once while he was in prison after his conviction but he didn't have much to say.

Then in early 2008, Robertson asked me to visit him in the Long Lartin maximum security prison in Worcestershire as soon as I could. There then followed a swift series of meetings at his request over the following three months during which I interviewed him at length and collected the information that makes up this book. During these sessions he seemed to want to be completely open with me and to answer all my questions about the events he wanted to discuss. In fact looking back through my notes and the transcripts of our conversations, it is striking that other than on one solitary occasion, I do not remember any question that he did not answer.

During one of the last of our meetings I asked him whether there was ever anything he had done about which he felt guilty and it seems to me to be worthwhile including here what he had to say verbatim.

MR   *For what I've done? [Pause] No.*

IP   *Would you do anything for the club?*

MR   *Yes.*

IP   *Anything at all?*

MR   *Sure, yes.*

IP   *Why?*

MR   *It's about commitment, total commitment, it's about being part of the elite. The Angels have got it, they showed that at Laughlin[14].*

---

[14] *The River Run at Laughlin Nevada is the largest bike rally in the Western USA. It's held in April and attracts up to 100,000 bikers from across the country, mostly normal types, but as it's such a public event the patch clubs always show up as well and 'put on a show', most notably the Hells Angels who dominate the US South West.*

Having originated in California, the Hells Angels have had a running feud with The Mongols since the late 70s after The Mongols adopted a 'California' bottom rocker without the

IP   *What about the drugs?*

MR   *What about them? [Shrugs]*

We sold whizz, coke, E, acid, basically anything that people wanted to buy and enjoy. We dealt in stuff that was fun and basically wouldn't kill them so what's the problem?

IP   *You made enough money out of it.*

MR   *Yeah we did. So what?*

Just think, next time one of your mates has a snort at a party or your bird drops a tab at a club, someone's had to source it for you, someone like me.

This coke and shit doesn't smuggle itself in y'know? It takes a bit of good old entrepreneurial risk-taking and effort on somebody's part so's you can get off your face.

There's demand, we take the risk and supply, and we get the rewards. Ain't that how it's supposed to work?

Anyway, big tobacco sells stuff that kills you and if you've got a pension I bet you own some of it.

[Laughs]

So who's got the problem to be guilty about now?

IP   *OK, so you got me.*

MR   *Yeah. Bang to rights. [Pause]*

Angel's permission. Over the years this war had rumbled on in a low key way involving shootings, stabbings and car bombs. Tension had been growing again between the two in the late 90s as The Mongols membership in the South West grew much faster than that of the Hells Angels.

In 2002 both clubs were at the River Run when a group of Hells Angels from San Francisco found themselves in the bar of the Harrah's casino where a much larger group of Mongols had assembled. Hearing the news, members of other Angel charters rapidly gathered and rode to the casino where they entered, and although knowing they were still outnumbered, immediately launched an all out attack on the Mongols on the floor of the casino in full view of the security staff and surveillance equipment. One Mongol and three Hells Angels were killed in the ensuing fight.

Under the ferocity of the assault some Mongols were seen to flee the scene or to take off their colours to escape detection. But despite the odds, and their own level of casualties, the Hells Angels remain proud to say that, as Martin had put it to me earlier in the same interview when we had been discussing it, 'No Angel ran and no Angel hid their colours. Every Angel knew that in a fight to the death like that [with a rival gang], they could rely on each other totally, they would each die for each other.'

217

You know people like to think they're so clean. But really they're all dirty in some way or other. I suppose part of the difference is just that we don't try and pretend otherwise.

IP   *So you're telling me you're just more honest about it?*

MR   *[Laughs] Yeah, I guess so. No bullshit from us.*

IP   *So you've never felt guilty?*

MR   *No. I did what I needed to do. It was all [pause] necessary. So no, I don't feel guilty.*

IP   *What... [Interrupted]*

MR   *But if you ask me whether there are things I regret then there are a few.*

IP   *Like what?*

MR   *Well I regret being in here for a start.*

IP   *What, getting caught or being in jail?*

MR   *[Pause] Bit of both I guess. It's tough on Sharon and my girl so I'm sorry for them about that.*

IP   *But not for yourself?*

MR   *No.*

It's my life. I make my choices. I don't complain about the outcomes.

Anyway, it's my own fault I should have done something about that wanker Fat Mick years ago. I knew he was a weak link and he knew that I knew, so he hated me for it.

So I knew that he was a threat that I should have destroyed.

IP   *Why didn't you?*

MR   *Well I didn't actually have anything on him so I didn't want to act against him.*

IP   *Why not? Doesn't sound like you?*

MR   *Because the last thing I wanted to do was unsettle everyone else. If I'd taken him out just because I didn't feel comfortable then I risked inducing paranoia in everyone else. If I'd offed Fat Mick just because I didn't like or trust him then everybody would've started to feel nervous, everybody would've felt at risk and then everybody would've become a threat.*

IP   *OK.*

MR   *And then there's the fear thing.*

218

IP   *Fear?*

MR   *Yeah. Even though he hated me, Fat Mick was still too scared of me to do anything and that was the hold I had over him. The only problem would be if he fell into the hands of someone who scared him more.*

IP   *Like who?*

MR   *Well the plod, I guess, the way it turned out, but it could have been anyone else who got a hold over him. If it comes to a choice between fear of me and fear of the system and the time if you get caught, some guys are always going to go the wrong way.*

        That was the one thing I could never quite work out how to deal with. It wasn't something that old Nick covered in The P[15] so there was no help there. And in the end that's what got me.

IP   *So do you feel responsible for being in here, for bringing this on Sharon and Lucy?*

MR   *[Pause – shakes head, does not answer]*

IP   *So what about the violence? The deaths?*

MR   *Like I said, no, I did what needed to be done.*

IP   *So you don't regret any of the killings?*

MR   *Listen, the guys I knocked off, they were all in the game you know? They all knew what they were into, what the risks were. No civilians. They were all guys that would have done it to me if it had suited them, so no, I don't regret any of them.*

IP   *Did you hate Dazza?*

MR   *Hate Dazza? No.*

IP   *But he had killed your friends.*

MR   *Yes he had. And I resented that. But really it was business. I didn't have to like it, but I could understand why he'd done it.*

---

[15] Martin's somewhat ironic nickname for 'The Prince' which possibly rather justifies Bertrand Russell's famous description of it as 'a handbook for gangsters.'

From speaking to Sharon I understand that the version he read was the Penguin classics George Bull translation of 1961 which I have therefore consulted (together with a more recent translation by Tim Parks), although in practice Martin did not tend to quote it word for word but to paraphrase the bits that were of interest to him.

	I could respect it.
IP	*And Polly?*
MR	*He was different. I was glad he got done.*
IP	*Why?*
MR	*He was just a cunt.*
IP	*So you don't regret any of the deaths?*
MR	*Well there is one.*
IP	*Which?*
MR	*The dog, Wolf. [Pause]*
	He was great. I really liked him y'know?[Shakes his head]
	I remember him looking up at me as I aimed.
	Pulling the trigger. That was the hardest thing to do.
	I still regret that I guess.
IP	*But that's it?*
MR	*Yeah, I guess that's it.*

*

Martin 'Damage' Robertson was found stabbed to death on 17 July 2008. He had just celebrated his 45th birthday in jail and left behind his wife Sharon and their daughter Lucy, aged seven, a pretty little girl that I met once on a prison visit, dressed in a black and red stripped T shirt with the words '*My Daddy's a Menace*' across the front.

Despite his reputation and the acts that he confirmed to me he had taken part in during our meetings and discussions, I have to say that right from the outset I came to respect him as a person and to a degree I think he wrote his own epitaph in the excerpt quoted above, *No bullshit from us.* While I will never now know why he decided to speak in 2008 as he gave no clue that anything was up, in many ways I guess this book is his last will and testament.

But if it is, one question has to be, so is it true? It's a question I have had to face as I have edited these pages for publication. And on balance I think it is, but that equally it's not a complete truth.

It's striking, for example, that not only did he really only want to talk about the crimes for which he had already been convicted, on looking back through my notes, the only people he ever mentioned in connection with any crime, from Adrian 'Gyppo' Leverton and Peter

'Tiny' Gresham or William 'Billy Whizz' White, through to Darren 'Dazza' Henderson were all dead (even Stuart 'Popeye' Shaw who died of a heart attack while running an 'Iron Man' marathon in South Africa in 2005). So nothing that he ever said to me ever implicated anyone living in any crime other potentially than Steve 'Wibble' Nelson.

Even though I now think that he had only asked to see me, and was only speaking to me because he must have discovered that others were moving against him, and he would have known who they were and how that was going to end, he never once spoke about it. Instead in the end he kept to the code of silence that he believed in, never once implying that anything was wrong.

*

He was buried in August 2008 in Enderdale.

It was a full dress, full turnout Brethren funeral. Amongst a large but restrained police presence every Brethren member in the country that was not inside or in hospital made it, and charters from around the world sent representatives to pay their respects, many anonymous behind their scarves and skull printed bandannas. So, together with contingents from other friendly clubs, on the Saturday morning of the funeral the village was completely overrun with parked bikes, the small central market square filled with serried ranks of The Brethren's parked up Harleys, guarded as always by the strikers working their way towards their colours, and leaving only a thin driveway for the flower decked hearse.

After the service the huge convoy of bikes roared off through the village, a thunderous torrent of noise tearing up through the country lanes and out across the moors to the clubhouse where the surrounding field had become an impromptu tented camp, to kick off a party and wake that lasted until dawn the next day.

At around about midnight Police reported that the revellers blocked off the road below the clubhouse for an impromptu set of races. Petrol was poured over the bikes' back wheels and set on fire as the riders gunned the engine, front brakes locked on and span the back wheels in a roar of flame, exhaust noise and choking tyre smoke. It's an old drag racing technique used to get the tyre good and hot and sticky for maximum grip, to launch away from the line when the

Christmas tree lights turn and you dump the clutch and the brakes and hang on for dear life against the savage gut wrenching acceleration of a big bike at full power. But of course for show, the more petrol that's used, the more spectacular it is and local witnesses reported the sight of the flaming back wheels spinning crazily into the darkness.

At some point during the night, police sources later learnt that The Freemen met to elect a new President. Based on the northern powerbase that Martin had established within The Brethren in the UK and the apparent control of the main organised element of drugs trafficking carried out by some of the club's key members, Martin was then succeeded as leader of The Brethren in the UK by Steve 'Wibble' Nelson.

*

No one has ever been charged in connection with Martin's death.

The police say that no one has been prepared to cooperate with their enquiries.

I think that's the way he would have wanted it.

> *When men live without a common power to keep them all in awe, they are in that condition called war, and such a war is of everyman against everyman.*
>
> *For ... the nature of war consists not [only] in actual fighting; but in the known disposition thereto during all the time there is no assurance to the contrary.*

Leviathan, Thomas Hobbes (modernised spelling)

Iain Parke, London, 2009

Author's note: fiction and respect

All characters, events and in particular the clubs named in this book are fictional and any resemblance to actual places, events, clubs or persons, living or dead, is purely coincidental. None of the views expressed are those of the author.

I have had to ascribe certain territories and names to my fictional club charters, for which I apologise to both the 1%ers in those areas and any clubs with similar names.

While I'm a biker, I'm not, and never have been, a member of any 1%er club. To the extent that over the years I have met and talked to 1%er club members, I have found them to be intelligent guys who have lived by the motto which is repeated by the central character in this book, 'if you show respect, you will be treated with respect.'

So I hope that any 1%er who reads this book will feel that, while this is obviously a work of crime fiction which therefore has to involve some crime, it treats them and the lifestyle seriously and with respect.

Also by Iain Parke from bad-press.co.uk

The Liquidator

'Don't take this as your safari reading.'

Dangerous things happen in Africa.

People disappear.

Everybody knows that.

As an ex-pat outsider, Paul thinks he is safe, even from the secret police, whatever happens as the country holds its first multi party election with a genocidal diamond fuelled civil war raging just across the border.

But when he finds himself trapped holding a deadly secret while the country implodes around him, what will he be prepared to do to protect him and those close to him?

A dark contemporary political thriller set in East Africa.

ISBN 978-0-9561615-5-0

Also available on Kindle

Heavy Duty Attitude

Book Two of The Brethren Trilogy

Iain had written a book about The Brethren MC and how powerful they could be.

He knew it was a dangerous thing to have done, whether they liked it or not, and one that had taken him part way into their world.

And now it was his turn.

Now a new President, with big boots to fill, was going to make him an offer he was going to find difficult to refuse, and once in the outlaw biker's world, would he ever be able to get out again?

And as an outsider on the inside, with serious trouble looming, who, if anyone, can he trust?

ISBN 978-0-9561615-3-6

Also available on Kindle

Coming in late 2012
Heavy Duty Trouble

Book Three of The Brethren Trilogy

Support Your Local Small Press

For small presses, getting exposure in the market place in competition with the publishing big boys is one of the key challenges; but it is also one where you as a reader can help us enormously by spreading the word.

So, if you have enjoyed this book please help us to promote Iain Parke and bad-press.co.uk, as well as other small presses' books by for example:

- Recommending the book to your friends;
- Posting a review on Amazon or other book websites;
- Reviewing it on your blog;
- Tweeting about the book and giving a link to our website at bad-press.co.uk;
- Linking to Iain Parke's facebook page and Linkedin profile; or
- Anything else that you think of.

Many thanks for your help – much appreciated.

The bad-press.co.uk team and Iain Parke.

13863875R00128

Printed in Great Britain
by Amazon.co.uk, Ltd.,
Marston Gate.